A Story of Survival

Dane Greene

ISBN: 978-0-578-66181-0

Contents

v

DEDICATION

Thank you to my mother, my first reader, and source of
encouragement, Lorene Greene

Thank you to my final editor and source of joy, Liz Greene

Thank you to my cover designer who made my books world
come to life, Veronica Steffen

And a final thank you to anyone I didn't name here but who
supported me along the way

Chapter 1: Aaron

March 13th

The screeching sirens of my reliable alarm clock ring. In reaction, I roll over and hit the snooze button. Even after a year of working morning shifts, I still hate waking up this early. When I look at the clock, I see that it's thirty minutes past the time I usually wake up.

"Crap, I'm going to be late. If I leave in the next five minutes and speed, I can make it to work on time."

I jump out of bed, pull on my lumber yard uniform, and grab my keys and wallet before running out the door. My car's engine roars to life and I speed through my dark and quiet town. Lucky for me, it seems the police officers are in bed, sleeping with the rest of town.

Once I reach the outskirts, I relax. Work is a straight shot from here. Even though I'm speeding, I still have a half-hour commute, so I set my cruise control and wait.

My mind starts to wander to what I'll do at work today, and my stomach growls. In my rush to get out the door, I realize I've forgotten to eat breakfast and didn't pack a lunch. Sighing to myself, I say, "Guess I'll have to settle for fast food on my break."

As the drive progresses, the uncluttered view of the flat countryside relaxes me. As the barren fields pass me by, I wonder when they'll show signs of the recently planted crops. It's mid-spring, and the weather has been unseasonably warm.

A white dot is at the edge of my vision, and when I focus on it, I realize that it's a minivan several miles in front of me and in my lane. The van grows larger, and it's clearly traveling much slower than I am.

As I come closer to the minivan, it becomes apparent that I'll need to pass it. Once I make sure there are no other cars in the oncoming lane, I change lanes and start to pass the van, but my steering wheel locks up and I freeze.

Several moments pass before I realize I don't hear the steady rhythmic drone of my engine. Instinctively, I fumble for the ignition key, but before I can get a hold of it, a sickening impact hits me.

My body screams as I'm jerked around in my seat. A loud, unending roar forces its way into my ears, like a thunderous chorus screeching nonsensical metallic words.

I pray for it to end when my car slams to a stop and my head hits something hard.

"Am I going to die? I don't want to die this way. I want to live." My consciousness fades while I grasp the severity of the situation. Trying to force myself to stay alert, I find my body betraying me. Everything fades and darkness overcomes my consciousness.

When my eyes open, I'm immediately blinded by the sun. Drawing in a long, slow breath, I smell cooking asphalt and burnt rubber. Listening for sirens, I'm greeted only with silence.

Looking through what remains of my passenger side door, I see the remnants of a tree. In a rush, the memory of everything that's happened floods back. It's then that I realize this tree is what stopped me. I suppose I should be grateful that I'm alive and that my car landed right-side up.

I go to unbuckle my seat belt and notice some dry blood on my hand. Thinking that I'm more injured than I realize, I check over my body. Luckily, I find everything mostly intact. That's when I first feel the signs of a sunburnt face.

Other pains accompany my sunburn, but most of them seem mild enough to ignore. Suddenly, my stomach growls, breaking the silence surrounding me. My best guess is that it's around late morning. I look through my car windshield, squinting up at the east-facing sun, and I realize that sunburns take longer than a couple of hours. My stomach growls again, and the clues start to form. Signs point to it having been at least a full twenty-four hours.

As if on cue, I notice a smell and realize I must have soiled myself in my sleep. With newfound motivation, I climb out of my car and do the best I can to clean myself up. It only takes a few minutes, but by the end, I find myself exhausted and short of breath.

A powerful thirst comes over me, and I realize that my first priority should be finding some water. I search the remains of my car and am lucky enough to find a half-full water bottle wedged under the passenger seat.

I fight back the urge to drink the water all at once and instead sip it slowly. After I'm done with it, I decide to try walking back home. I'm not sure how emergency vehicles missed my car, but staying here without food or water any longer wouldn't be wise.

As I walk along the highway, I see nothing except a white van about a half-mile south of me. Remembering that it was the car I hit, I decide to investigate. Hopefully whoever was driving it fared better than I did.

As I walk toward the car, I'm surprised by the eerie silence around me. For miles around, I see nothing moving. It's late enough in the day that I should see some other cars, and I'm beginning to suspect I'll have to walk all the way back to town. Luckily, it's a clear sunny day and it isn't too hot yet. After the half bottle of water, I feel much better, and as I move, I find much of my body's stiffness working itself out.

While I'm walking, something in my pocket rubs my leg, and I realize that it's my cell phone, so I dig it out of my pocket to call 911. Luckily, the screen is completely intact, but when I hit the unlock button, nothing happens. So I try every trick in the book to turn it on, but after a few minutes I decide the phone is dead or broken. "Crap," I mumble.

With the dream of speedy salvation through my cell phone dead, I continue walking toward the minivan. If I'm lucky, the occupants survived and left some water behind. If I'm walking home, I'll need water and I don't think the half bottle I had will get me far.

When I reach the van, I find its door ajar. Not wanting to look inside yet, I search around the car. From the looks of things, I must have pushed the car off the road before going out of control. A flood of relief hits me that no one died from the car accident.

There is no one nearby, so I search the inside of the car. I find a treasure trove of small snack packages and water bottles. Aside from the plentiful snacks and water, I find some baseball uniforms and gear. I take as many water bottles and snacks as my bag can carry, and as an afterthought, I grab a baseball bat as well.

Even though I doubt I'll need the baseball bat, something compels me to take it. After I check through the contents of the van once more, making sure I didn't miss anything, I decide to take a minute to eat. Taking advantage of the shade in the van, I sit down in one of the abandoned seats. After resting a minute, I eat some fruit snacks and drink a bottle of water. Once I start eating, I realize how ravenous I am and devour half of my supplies, only forcing myself to stop because I might need them later.

Refreshed by the food and drink, I start my walk to town. At first the walk is painful, but my muscles and bones get used to the motion. The task of walking gives me a newfound purpose, and I start to enjoy it. After what feels like a few miles, this enjoyment starts to fade, so I take a break under a nearby tree. After a few minutes of rest, some water, and food, I continue my journey.

After what feels like several more miles, I spot another car on the road. When I look inside the abandoned car, I find it empty and free of any visible damage. Checking the doors, I find them unlocked. I try to start the car, hoping for the best, but nothing happens.

Thinking the car battery doesn't have enough charge to start the car, I decide to pop the hood and take a look. Since I have no way to charge the battery, I break off the antenna and drop it on top of the negative and positive terminals. My experiment is a success and I'm sprayed by a brief shower of sparks.

The battery should have enough charge to at least turn on the lights. For some reason, it won't. Not knowing what else to do, I spend a few minutes checking out the different engine parts under the hood. Everything is in pristine condition, and when I take a closer look at the car, I don't see a dent or scratch on it.

"I wish I had more time to try to get this running," I say to myself. However, sundown is approaching, and I want to get home before night descends.

Before continuing my walk, I search the car and pocket a lighter I find. There's nothing else of use to me, so I go. Mile after mile slips by as the sun beats down on me, and the dread of not seeing any other moving car or person weighs down on me. As I get closer to town, I pass dozens of cars, all of them in the same condition. After the first few, I don't even bother stopping to check; I know they are all dead.

Fear fills me. Right now, the thing I want most is to find my family and make sure they're okay. There appears to be no power to anything, anywhere. I feel as though, somehow, I might be the last human in existence.

My hopes lift when I find a manual water pump outside a barn on the very edge of town.

No longer worrying about running into anyone, I strip and bathe myself and my clothes. Though the water is cold, the feeling of being clean again gives me comfort. After washing myself and my clothes, I redress, struggling to put on my damp clothes.

Knowing I'm not far from home, I finish off the last of my food and water, then leave the makeshift sling bag by the water pump. Though I debate leaving my baseball bat there as well, I'm once again compelled to take it.

Everywhere I go, abandoned cars litter the road. This, combined with the silence, worries me. Seeing no signs of any people, I'm unsettled when I can't detect the hum of technology. Strange how I never realized, until now, how much noise I heard on a daily basis. The silence is almost unbearable.

An idea enters my mind, and I realize what might be going on. Before I can finish my thought, I notice the silhouette of a person moving in the distance.

A sigh of relief courses through me, and for a brief second, I consider running up to them. But for some reason, caution and common sense tell me that I should approach carefully.

Seeing a white wooden fence in front of a nearby house, I move behind it. I look through the space between the boards and manage to estimate that I'm about ten feet from four men.

Three of them have their backs to me, but the fourth is facing my direction. The man has a humble stature and neat brown hair. He's wearing glasses, and I realize that he's a friend of mine. My relief is so strong that I start to walk toward the nearby fence door, only stopping myself when I hear someone speak.

"Shit, Jason, I told you yesterday: no one leaves their houses. The feds are gone, and I own this street. You get protection, and all you need to do is pay my tax. You already paid me yesterday, so unless you're here to thank me, why the hell are you outside?"

Hearing this confirms I must have been unconscious for more than a day. There's no way things could get this bad in a few hours, even if all power has gone out, like I'm beginning to suspect.

Knowing I'm in the worst part of town right now, I'm not surprised by these thugs' actions. Hopefully idiots like these guys aren't trying to rule neighborhoods everywhere. Not wanting to make things worse for Jason, I decide to stay hidden and watch for now. Jason is a smart guy, and I'm confident he'll make these thugs see reason—or, at the very least, not harm him.

As I look through the crack between the boards, I see Jason start talking.

"I told you yesterday, there are kids who will go to the mission center. They need me there to help them, especially now."

As I watch, the man in the center reaches to his side and draws out a large hunting knife from its sheath. Shock rushes through me, and fear of what could happen to Jason overtakes me. I realize that, if I'm going to act, I'd better do it soon. There's no way I'll stand by and watch my friend get gutted. Even if this is only a scare tactic, this guy is going too far, and I know I have to help my friend.

Trying to remember my martial arts training, I pull out the dead cell phone in my pocket. Throwing open the gate of the fence, I scream as loud as I can and run toward the group. All four men are startled, and the thug on the right starts turning toward me. I throw my phone at him, hitting him square in the nose with accuracy that can only happen in a crisis. The man stumbles back and is open.

Ignoring the man, I go for the thugs' leader, the one with the knife. Swinging the baseball bat at the man's arm, I feel a sickening impact as the bat hits his right elbow. A metal ringing sounds as the knife hits the ground. Immediately, I swing in the opposite direction and bring the bat around with all my might. The bat slams into the dazed leader's arm and throws him to the ground. As this happens, my grip on the bat slips, and it falls with the man.

The man I hit with my phone has recovered, and the other thug is now facing me as well. Not wanting to fight two men at once, I yell out to Jason.

"Jason, help!" A look of recognition hits him, and he charges the man on my right. His fist hits the man on the side of the head, and he falls unconscious before he has the chance to react. The third man hesitates, and I take the opportunity.

My friend and occasional sparring partner and I slip into our martial arts stances.

"If you want to go, now is your chance. You can yield and take your friends out of here." The man looks like he's about to agree when the still-conscious leader shouts out.

"If you don't shoot these assholes, I'll kill you and your whole fucking family." Hearing the word "shoot," I realize it's possible the man has a gun, so I react before he does. Jumping the distance between us, I automatically throw a combo I've practiced. Jab, cross, left hook, right elbow, and uppercut. Teeth cut into my hands and elbow, but I don't feel them. The man falls to the ground, along with several of his teeth. He doesn't move. He must be unconscious.

The leader screams in anger, but he can't move well enough to be a threat. This is why I'm a little surprised when Jason walks over and kicks him in the head. The man's screams stop.

Jason looks shaken as he walks toward me. Everything that happened catches up to me, and I fall to my knees. My breath comes in gasps, and I try to force my shaking body to calm. Jason sits down next to me and waits for me to calm. After I've steadied my breathing, I check to make sure the three men are still alive and find that they have pulses. Relieved, I go back to Jason.

Even in the present circumstances, the relief of finding another person is overwhelming. Even better, I'm lucky that the first person I run into is someone I know well. Perhaps I can finally get some answers about what's going on.

"Nice to see you, man," Jason chimes. "You look like hell. I didn't recognize you at first. Where have you been?"

"My car crashed on the way to work. I'm not sure how long I was out. Mind catching me up on everything?" Jason looks a little surprised, but he catches me up on everything.

The first thing I learn is that I was unconscious for three days. The chaos in the town makes more sense and confirms my suspicions. Jason also says that all power has been gone since my car first crashed. He shows me that even his digital watch doesn't work. He also tells me the light bulbs exploded, and anything with circuits is dead.

"The only thing that could cause this is an electromagnetic pulse, otherwise known as an EMP blast," Jason says.

I'd hoped this wasn't the case, but after what he's told me, I know it must be true.

Jason continues. "An EMP is a pulse of electrons that overloads all circuits and electronic wires. Basically, anything that uses circuit boards or wires receives a powerful electric surge. This surge burns them out. It may be possible to repair mechanically driven things. Everything that runs on microchips will be useless, though. Luckily, batteries still have a charge, so rebuilding some things might be possible."

Jason proceeds to tell me about the mission center as we walk. He tells me that, with the help of others, he plans to try and get the pumps in the water towers running again. His only concern is that he can't think of a way to provide a permanent power supply. His comments remind me of the construction zones I passed earlier. Since he might need them, I tell him there might be some solar panels in some of the devices there. Jason becomes excited and tells me I should join him at the community center, but I have to refuse.

Although helping our community sounds like a great idea, I still need to make sure my family is alright. Jason understands, and we go our separate ways. He wishes me luck, and I do the same.

On my way home, I'm careful to stay off the streets and out of plain sight. Even though I doubt I'll run into more trouble, I want to be sure. The town is silent, and if I didn't know any better, I'd presume all the houses were empty.

I don't blame people for hiding, but they'll have to come out of their houses at some point. After three days with no power or electricity, people are surely running out of food and water. Sooner or later, people will have to look for more supplies.

When I reach my neighborhood, I'm so excited that I run toward my house. Taking a second to catch my breath, I do a quick visual survey. Everything seems okay, so I knock on my front door.

Waiting with my breath held, I hope it'll be one of my family members who answers. While waiting, I pray they're still here and that they're all healthy and alive.

The seconds stretch into minutes as I wait. Right before I start checking the windows, the door bursts open. My excitement turns to fear as I stare down the barrel of a shotgun. Instinctively, I freeze.

"I told you, you come back and I'll kill you." I stay perfectly still. My terror melts into joy when I recognize that gruff voice. The voice who threatened me belongs to my father.

"Dad, it's me, Aaron. Lower the gun." My father looks at me, and I see relief wash over his face. He lowers the gun, and tears come to his eyes as he hugs me.

"We thought you were dead, Aaron. I'm so glad to see you." Our embrace ends, and my father looks around. "It's not safe out here. Stuff has gone south. Come inside and you can tell us about what happened to you."

My father leads me inside to safety, locking and dead-bolting the door behind us. He leads the way and I follow him around the corner of the entry, through the hall, and toward the bathroom.

While we're walking, I notice my father has a slight limp, which tells me he's in pain. It's hard to tell how bad his injury is. Whatever happened to him, it scared him more than he's willing to admit or show.

Before I have any more time to think, we arrive at the main bathroom. This is the only windowless room in the house that's large enough for my whole family. It's secure, and I approve of my dad's choice of it as a safe room. As my dad opens the door, the first thing I notice is the smell of my mother's favorite candle, lilac and jasmine. The second thing I notice is my mother, illuminated in the candle's flame, standing a few feet from me. Tears come to my eyes as I hug her. Before our embrace breaks, two more sets of slender arms curl around me. The next few minutes are spent crying and embracing my two sisters and mother.

As if on cue, the tears release tension I didn't realize I was carrying. Relief washes over me. As I tell my family about what happened, my body relaxes. Smiling and laughing, I tell my story, glad to be alive and grateful my family is alive as well. After I'm done telling my story, my mother and sisters tell me about what happened to them during the last three days.

During the first night without power, my father was injured in a brutal attack. He believes it was a robbery gone wrong. After the attack, my family moved into the bathroom to be safe. After we all tell our stories, I turn to my dad. "So, Dad, what do you think is going on?"

He looks at me for a while before speaking. "There's been a nationwide and possibly even a worldwide EMP strike." His simple statement confirms what Jason and I already suspected. There's been an EMP strike, and until this moment, I didn't consider how far it spread.

A nationwide EMP would be possible if many key targets were struck simultaneously. America has adversaries capable of creating a synchronized strike. Filled with wonder, I ponder how my dad can be so sure the EMP isn't contained to our little town in Illinois. On the same note, I also wonder what makes him think it might be a worldwide strike.

"You're probably right," I say, "but how can you be so sure that it was a national EMP?"

My dad pauses, and I can tell he's struggling to tell me. For a few seconds, I think he's going to keep the information to himself, but then he speaks. "Well, no aid has come, so I know it isn't a local problem. If it was contained to Illinois, we would have seen emergency response teams already. Besides, I haven't seen a single plane in the sky since the power went out."

The lack of planes flying overhead is enough evidence for me to believe he may be right.

"Hopefully," my dad continues, "the power only went out in America, but every day that passes makes it harder to believe that it was only us. America has enough allies that we should've received some form of aid already—unless there's something preventing others from helping us. I have to presume the nation, and the world, has lost power and gone dark."

My father's words hit me hard. It's not difficult to understand why he hesitated to tell me. The idea that mankind could've receded back into the dark ages is terrifying. When I search his worn, bearded face for a trace of hope, I find none. In the end, I have to settle for the comforting scent of lilac and jasmine—that and the lingering warmth of my family's embrace.

Chapter 2: Jason

March 16th

Aaron walks away from me and I'm glad he showed up. The last thing I expected when I left the house this morning was that I would run into him. I also didn't expect to get into a fight, but I'm glad Aaron was there. When I look at the three men on the ground, I decide they deserve the state they're in. They'll live, so I have no problem leaving them where they are.

Everything that's happened catches up to me, and I realize that it's a miracle I'm even outside. Ever since the power went out, my parents have done their best to keep me inside. It's not like I don't understand their concern, but I'm eighteen and I should be able to make my own decisions. Sadly, I can't tell them about what happened. If they knew I was in a fight, I'd never be able to leave the house again—not as long as they're alive, anyway. Sure, I love my parents, but sometimes they can be overprotective and overbearing.

Now that I've collected myself, I start to walk toward the mission center. As I step over the bodies of the men, I notice the knife on the ground and pick it up. It's beyond me why someone would pull out a knife for something so petty. I'm lucky that Aaron came when he did; he might have saved my life.

Fear is something I understand. Everyone has been afraid these past few days. Why would someone try to erase their own fear by dominating and hurting others? Using a knife is too far-fetched for me. It's much easier to be peaceful.

Even now, I regret hurting the men. True, they deserved it, but I've never enjoyed hurting others. I fear that, with the power gone, this might not be the last time I'll have to hurt someone to help others. So much has changed in three short days.

As I walk along the abandoned streets full of dead cars, I notice the trash and debris. To me, it looks like it's been months, not days, since the power went out. Strange how quickly things crumble when not maintained.

I was in the mission center when the power first went out. The center is a childcare facility. It has an indoor gym, a few small offices, and a nice outdoor playground. Families rely on the center as a place for their children to stay after school while parents work. It doesn't cost anything, unlike a traditional daycare.

The kids panicked at the loss of power. Everyone figured it was a blackout, so we moved the children outside to the center of the playground. The gym doesn't have enough windows for good natural lighting, so the playground seemed like a great place to occupy the kids while we waited for the power to return.

Fortunately, the mission center is state-run, so it's required to have emergency supplies. The food rations came in handy as the minutes turned to hours and we waited for the power to return.

When the power first went out, I found a few flashlights in the emergency supplies. Unfortunately, none of them worked. Over the next few hours, I tried to find any electronic devices that worked. That was when I discovered everything electrical was dead. Clocks, watches, phones, and even light bulbs were fried.

As I checked electrical devices, I remembered a book I read a couple of years back about EMPs. I explained the concept to the other leaders. A couple of us had seen television shows about EMP bursts, and it was the best explanation we had at the moment.

There are several ways an EMP blast can happen, but they all have similar results. Electronics are overloaded by electrons released from gamma rays. As the rays pass through the atmosphere, they create a barrage of electrons. These electrons are what damage electronics. Every light bulb had a burnt-out filament, which endorsed the idea. It makes me wonder how badly circuit boards and other heavily wired electronics must be damaged.

Electricity is still possible since lead-acid batteries can be recharged or remade. But they'll only be able to power things without microchips or circuitry. Even if we made or found lead-acid batteries, there would be no way to charge them. My thoughts are interrupted when a radar sign unit draws my attention. This unit would usually tell people how fast they're driving and alert them if they were speeding.

The radar unit has been here for about a year, to help slow cars down in the area. The reason it catches my eye this time is because of what's on top of it. The sight reminds me of what Aaron mentioned about solar panels on devices along the highway. This makes me realize that there are dozens of devices like these speed traps that use them. If we gather all the panels in and near town, we should be able to create a small-scale power generator.

I walk over to the machine, then climb my way to the top, making sure to be careful. The solar panels on top look to be in good condition. Sure, I don't know much about solar technology, but I do know they don't have circuits in the panels themselves. Though there might be some damage to the wires that connect the solar cells, it may be possible to get them working again. If I can repair them, then I should be able to use them to charge lead-acid as well as other batteries.

Thinking about the radar units gives me hope that it might be possible to recover from this EMP blast. It will take years and possibly even decades to rebuild technology, but it should be possible. Climbing off the radar unit, I continue my walk along the deserted roads.

When I enter the mission center, I'm greeted by the subdued noise of children. The atmosphere of the place is full of fear and indecision. Through that, the innocent mirth of the children is palpable. The center, once full of only kids, now has some adults as well. Surely they're here because they're afraid. Even so, I'm a little surprised that people are here, though with no other course of action, I would do the same in their place.

As I look around, I can't find the director. Knowing he has a large family, I can't fault him for not coming. He asked me to keep this group together and to create some order. Pretty tall orders from a man who didn't come today, though I'm sure we can achieve this if we work on a communal project together. The solar project I have in mind will be the perfect thing to do this.

The mission center has always tried to focus on the community. The project I have in mind is much larger in scale than anything we've done before. Since the power went out, we've had water, but I don't know for how long. Thus far, it's come from the water towers, but without power to refill the towers, I figure we have less than a week of clean water left.

With the panels from the radar unit, I have an idea of how to fill the towers. To complete this plan, though, I'll need the help of the parents who came here today. With them helping me, fixing the imminent water shortage might be possible.

I look around for other staff members, hoping they can support me and strengthen the argument I'm about to make. My search is futile; there are no other staff members. While looking around, I notice everyone's eyes are on me. Most of these parents have met me before. They know I work here, and right now, I imagine my position overshadows my age. Preparing myself, I ready a speech, thanking all the speech classes I took in high school.

Eyes follow me as I walk into the center of the crowd. Everyone's looking toward me.

"Hello, everyone. I know it must have been hard to come here today, and I'm sure each of you faced some sort of challenge. I want to personally thank you all for taking risks to be here today. We are dealing with some hard times. If we don't band together as a community, I'm afraid we will split apart and fight among ourselves. Today, on my way here, I was stopped by some people who thought they owned my street. If this can happen three short days after the loss of power, what will it be like next week, when we run out of water? Our community must band together to prevent the loss of structure and the ability to coexist."

When I look around, I see looks of understanding among several of the people watching me. Many of them might have faced similar circumstances to be here. I hope I've captured these people's desire to do something.

"I know that this mission center is usually a place for the community to serve its members. Today, we need to broaden our community service. We need to send a message to those who want to exploit our fear. We need to tell them that we refuse to be their slaves. No longer will we let fear control us. We here at the center need to go out and help our neighbors by fixing our community. We need to show people that there's no reason to hide or be afraid. If we can rally others in this town, together we can rebuild our community. If we stand united, there's no force that can stop us."

These people look back at me, and I know my speech has had an impact. The faces around me show determination. Every single person here decided to take the risk to come here today. Their determination shows that they already want to make a change, and now I have a way to give it to them. Strength is visible in this group, and I know it will follow me.

I tell the crowd about my plans to use solar panels to power the pumps to the water towers throughout town. Several members step forward to offer their input. Many of the members have not only ideas, but also specifics on how to do what needs to be done.

A week ago, these people would be seen as working class or poor. These plumbers, electricians, and handymen are more valuable now. In my view, they're better than any professor, surgeon, actress, or CEO. Strange how, less than a week ago, society looked down upon the skill of working with your hands. Now, I imagine these people are desperately needed everywhere.

The specifics of the plan come together. To put in place the project, we'll need more than the dozen people here. With that many, we could get the water tower project done in a few days, but my goals go past our current project. That's why I want to create a sense of community with this project and set a basis for future ones. If we could recruit every person in the town, I'd be happy.

To that effect, the first stage of our plan is recruitment. My hope is that our group can convince others to join us. If we get enough help, I know we can get the pumps working before the water runs out in the towers.

We need to start by gathering the solar panels throughout town, taking them from nearby speed traps, construction equipment, and various other sources. With the solar panels in one place, we'll work on networking them together so we can power our makeshift water pumps and charge our batteries.

The pumps will draw water from the aquifer under our town, supplying our water towers. It'll take quite a bit of manpower to put everything in place, but once it's set up, it'll run itself. Or at least that's what I'm told by some of the people here. Most of the details are a bit beyond my understanding.

By the time we finish planning, it's dusk. When I get home, I fall asleep, exhausted. The next morning, my parents ask me what's going on. I lie to them, telling them nothing has changed at the mission center and that I'm helping watch kids. They know I'm dedicated to those kids, so they believe my story and I'm allowed to go back.

Knowing they'd try to stop me if I told the truth, I push down my guilt. Under different circumstances, I wouldn't lie, but I fear that if I don't show up today, the plan will collapse.

No one stops me on my way to the center today, and when I get there, I'm shocked. There are at least a hundred people here, if not more. Among the multitude are some of the old staff and, from what I can tell, people of all previous classes. My dreams and hopes of creating a community are prospering and I'm encouraged and ready to move forward.

Before the day is through, we manage to set up a working pump at one of the four water towers. By the next day, word has spread and our numbers triple. Representatives of the center become nominated and elected to go recruit others. The mission center becomes the town's temporary relief center. Several groups form to cover every need: trash duty, farming, construction, repair, scavenging, policing, and even medical.

I lose my place as the leader of the movement, as it starts gaining its own momentum. This doesn't bother me, since I'm glad to see the danger of isolation fade. Soon, the town starts to rebuild itself into a place that can survive without power.

Instead, I become the new head of the mission center as it once again becomes a place for children to stay while their parents work. The center transforms into a place for children to play, learn, and be watched over. The main difference now is that the kids are from every part of town, not only the parts that used to be poor.

Time moves rapidly while I'm busy leading the mission center. Weeks pass, feeling like days. The only time I allow myself a break is when Aaron stops by to visit. His visits remind me of when we used to hang out on the weekends. Aaron's visits provide a nice relief from the stress of my new job and responsibilities.

During one of Aaron's visits, he tells me about the revival of the police force. He tells me how he joined. The police help form the backbone of our growing town. They work to keep order and protect us from any malicious outsiders.

The police also detain people for trial by our justice system. The new justice system mimics our old one, but punishments are usually quick and severe. Without jails to hold criminals, the police have resorted to immediate sentencing. Forced labor, community service, whipping, banishment, and executions are the only punishments now.

I agree with most points in the system. It's proved far more effective than the one we had before. The only aspect I find hard to cope with is the executions. Although they're rare, they don't sit right with me. I never believed in the death penalty before the power went out, but I understand why it has to be done. The people sentenced to death are on destructive paths. They would only terrorize others if banished. Some people won't learn, but I'm not sure death is the best option. No man should play God.

The fear of dictatorship also worries me. Our town is currently running without solid leadership or a solid political system. The death penalty under the wrong leader could create a violent dictatorship. A dictatorship would threaten the cooperation and prosperity we currently enjoy. Without any power to change anything at the moment, though, I'm forced to put my worries to the side.

Weeks turn into months, and a democratic system emerges, staving off my fears of a dictatorship. So much else changes in this time as well. There's still no power on the grid, but it's possible to live in relative comfort. Since we live in the Midwest, there's enough corn and pigs available to make it through a few winters.

We were also lucky that the power went out right after crops were planted. This ensures we will have abundant food in a few months.

My primary concern is after winter. Sure, there's plenty of arable land, but it's been a long time since people farmed by hand. Many fields have already been left to themselves. Without the large combines and other modern farming machines, the land is too much to manage.

My other concern is the lack of an economy. Right now, our town is doing well, sharing what we have, but I doubt that will last forever. Eventually, an economy will arise, and I'm worried about what will replace the dollar.

My thoughts return to the present when I hear someone hollering outside my office. Yelling is nothing unusual at the Mission

Center. The kids are always pretty loud when they're on the play equipment. Wanting a break, I decide to investigate who's making the ruckus.

The sense of community and the kids are why I enjoy working here. I love the children and the way they've adapted. Of course, they miss power like the rest of us, but they don't show it as much. They're happy to enjoy life, and I find their outlook invigorating.

Unfortunately, because of the number of children and staff here, I rarely interact with the kids on a one-on-one basis. The daily tasks and organization of staff keep me too busy. If I could, I would gladly step down from the responsibility. Even when I tried to pass the mantle, those around me pushed me to keep it.

As I go outside, I see the children playing on the equipment. Smiling, I sit on a nearby bench, happy to take a break and watch the children play. After I watch for a few minutes, my tensions fade away.

When I'm about to get up, I notice one of the children sitting next to me. At first, I'm startled since I didn't see her get there, but I decide to say hello.

"Well hello, why aren't you playing with the others?"

The girl looks at me and smiles sweetly. "My mom sent me with cookies. She told me to share with the adults."

Without another word, the girl hops off the bench and pulls a backpack off and rummages inside it. After a second, she pulls out a metal container and opens it.

"Only take one, though, okay?"

I look at the girl; she can't be older than seven or eight. She has a big smile as I reach into the container and take a cookie. She closes the container and watches me. Realizing she's waiting for me to take a bite, I do so. The cookie is oatmeal and chocolate and I'm surprised at how good it is. Amazed, I ask myself how this girl's mother managed to make these.

"These are very good. Be sure to thank your mom, okay, sweetheart?"

The little girl gives me a toothy grin, then nods before putting the container back into her bag and running off.

As I finish my cookie, I savor each bite, doubting I'll ever have anything like this again. The thought that this might be the last cookie I ever eat is a sobering one. Things like oats and chocolate won't last much longer, and when they run out, I'm afraid that food will become much more basic and bland.

Lost in my thoughts, I walk to my office and sit in my chair, letting myself daydream about things that will change in the coming months. I'm stunned when my door crashes open. All I can do is stare blankly at it. In the doorway, a man stands, holding one of my workers hostage. He has a knife held against her throat. His right arm dangles against his side.

"There you are, Jason. How have you been? I myself have been lying in a bed, trying not to die. Thanks to you cocksuckers, I lost the use of my right arm! You fucked me up! Now it's your turn, you piece of shit!"

That's when I remember him as the man who tried to pull a knife on me. The bones in his right arm must have been broken and never reset.

"You're going to tell me where the man who did this to me is. Then no one but you will die. Shit, I'll even make your death quick."

His words come out erratically, and I can tell he's in a frantic state of mind.

Holding up my hands, I stand. "Alright, I can take you to Aaron, but only on one condition: you let the woman you're holding go and take me hostage instead. Don't worry: I'm unarmed, and you have a knife. I won't resist." The man looks at me, and I can tell he's thinking about my proposal. Fear fills me since I'm not sure he'll accept it.

"Fine!" He shoves the woman away from him. That was the last thing I expected him to do. Until this point, I was planning on going with him. But now that he's left himself exposed, my plan changes. Reaching behind my back, I pull a gun from my holster.

At first, I argued about having a gun in my possession, but now I'm glad to have one. My only wish now is that I'd learned how to use it. Luckily, I know enough to click the safety off and chamber a round. The man looks betrayed and furious as I aim the gun at him. He starts to move toward me as I squeeze the trigger. The gun cracks and forces me to blink. As I look to my target, I find him on his knees and holding his stomach in a grimace of pain. He falls to the floor face-first, and somehow, I know he is dead.

For a brief second, everything seems alright—that's until I hear a strange choking sound coming from right outside my office. Wanting to know what it is, I scramble around the man who's bleeding out on the floor. The woman he held hostage earlier is screaming in the corner. Ignoring her, I open the door to the office. The door hits something, and I have to squeeze my way through it. When I look to see what was blocking the door, I see a little girl lying on the ground, blood pouring from her neck. In her arms is a tin of oatmeal and chocolate cookies.

The bullet—my bullet—must have hit her. Dropping the gun, I go to her side to try and stop the bleeding. Her eyes look at me and I can see she is confused and in pain. The blood is flowing too fast and I can't stop it. Tears fall from my eyes as I watch the life fade from hers.

"This was done by me." How could I think I could save others by stopping the man? I was wrong.

"Carla… who…? What happened?" Looking up, I see who I presume is the girl's mother. She sees my hands against the girl's neck, blood covering the floor and a gun by my side. Her screams of agony hurt me more than any words ever could.

Wanting to explain, I try to stand up. Before I can, the woman shoves me. Losing my balance, I collapse to the ground.

"You bastard! You killed my baby. You killed her."

The woman screams as she kicks me in the stomach. Her anger is blameless. She's right—I did this. Once again, I try to get up, but I feel a sharp kick to my throat. When I try to speak, I can't. Others are inside as well now, drawn by the sound of my gun. "He killed my daughter!" the woman screams.

When I try to say something, I only wheeze. For the last time, I try to stand, but an unseen foot strikes me down. What were a few weak kicks a second ago turn into a frenzied mob attack. Someone kicks me in the head, and my vision starts to fade. The last thing I see is my blood-covered hands. My only thought is whether the blood is the girl's or mine.

Chapter 3: Aaron

May 10th

"Put your hands up or I'll shoot!" My voice echoes off the walls of the narrow alley as I shout at the man. He's about ten feet in front of me, and all I can see is his back and arms. In front of the man is a pile of people who are ripped apart. My stomach churns, and I have to force myself not to throw up. The man turns, and I see his face twisted in a sick smile. Blood drips from his lips and chin. His blood-red eyes burn into me with an inhuman rage.

"We're coming for you, Aaron." As the man speaks, bits of flesh fall from his mouth. I lose control of my stomach and throw up. Before I recover, my legs are swept out from under me, and I land hard on my back. I try to sit up, but before I can, something heavy slams into my chest. As my eyes focus, I see a grotesque creature of a man bent over me, his knee digging into my chest. Two pale hands wrap around my neck.

"Why run, Aaron? There is no escaping me." My vision starts to fade. I'm dying. I make one final attempt and throw myself forward. The man strangling me vanishes as I jerk up. My movement halts, ending in a sharp pain in my head.

My hand moves toward my head, but it hits something flat above me. As my vision clears, I realize I was dreaming and that I rammed my head into the ceiling. Before I can think about the dream or the pain in my head, I'm startled to hear someone speak to me.

"Hey, Aaron, are you alright? You scared the crap out of me." I turn and look down to see my friend Jason standing at the side of my loft bed.

"Jason, what are you doing here?"

"Man, you must have hit your head harder than I thought. Don't you remember? We stayed the night here."

Jason's remarks remind me that he and my friend Luke stayed at my house last night. "Yeah, I remember. You, Luke, and I were supposed to hang out today. Sorry about startling you. I just had a nightmare."

Jason's face grows somber, and he nods. "It's okay. I understand."

I still have no idea what happened to Jason after the power went out two months ago. My department at the police station didn't handle it. The officers who did take care of it decided it was best to keep the details private. All I could find out was that a few people died.

It took about two months for Jason's physical injuries to heal after whatever happened. The same can't be said for his mental state. He seems to be withholding something, and I can tell that his psyche is still pretty banged up. Part of the reason I wanted to hang out today was to cheer him up. I was hoping that if we hung out like we used to, he would recover a little.

"Wait a second, Jason. Where's Luke? Did he leave already?"

Jason looks at me, and I'm surprised to see him smile. "Oh, him? He's still asleep."

I laugh and move to get out of my loft bed. Sure enough, I find my friend Luke sleeping on the futon under my loft. "I know better than try to wake him up," I say. "He won't get up until he's ready. Tell you what: I'm going to shower. You can go after. If Luke still hasn't woken up by then, I suppose we'll throw him into the shower to wake him."

Jason smiles for the second time, and I'm glad to see him do so. "Sounds like a plan. Only problem is, now I hope he doesn't wake up."

Chuckling, I grab a change of clothes and make my way into the bathroom. Our area of town still has water thanks to Jason's quick thinking and leadership when the power first went out. The only downside is that, without power, all the water is cold, even in the middle of the afternoon. When our solar water heater is absorbing the sun, the water comes out mildly warm.

I know from experience that it's too early for warm water. After preparing myself, I turn the shower on and shudder as the cold water sprays onto my back. I scrub myself down with homemade soap, washing my body and hair and trying to be fast.

Even after six months of cold showers, I still find the experience awful. Luke better wake up before it's his turn. I can't think of a worse way to wake up than getting hit by a freezing blast of water. When I'm done with my shower, I head to my room to find Luke wide awake. I leave Jason and Luke to shower and head into the kitchen to make some breakfast.

Most of the morning is spent inside my house. Without electricity, we entertain ourselves with a few board games. After a while, we find ourselves itching to move around. Around what I would guess to be three in the afternoon, we decide to go to the park not far from my house. We mess around in attempts at parkour—running, jumping, and climbing around the equipment. We would all parkour like this before the power outage, but since then, we've gotten much better at it.

The lack of power has forced everyone to do more physical labor. These everyday tasks have sculpted my body, and I'm in better shape now than I've ever been.

I finished a difficult parkour trick involving jumping a large gap and rolling to a stop. Excited by my success, I jump up and look to my friends for praise. I find their focus locked onto something else out of my field of sight. I turn toward whatever they're watching, and I see a man walking down the street and staring at us.

The man picks up his pace and starts running toward us. As he gets closer, I notice that his skin is unnaturally pale. Glancing behind me, I see that both Jason and Luke are as tense as I am. The pale skin of the man reminds me of my dream. Shivers crawl up my spine as I decide to go to the highest point of the playground. My friends follow me. I can only hope that we'll be safe up here.

Things have been peaceful for the past few months, but part of being in a powerless world is being ready for things to go wrong. Of course, there are still some thugs that disturb the peace on occasion. Anyone willing to go outside understands that and is usually prepared to deal with them. The man gets to the playground and steps onto the wood chips. I put my hand on the gun in my holster in case he tries to attack. The man comes to a stop and stares at us with murderous intent.

"Run! Run for your lives. They're coming." The man is hysterical, and I start to think we'll have to scare him off. My hand draws the pistol from its holster. The man stares at my gun and looks angry, but I can tell he won't come closer.

"Why don't you take a breather and tell me what's going on?" I say.

Tears spring into the man's eyes and he crouches into a ball, covering his face in the fetal position. The sudden change from murderous rage to helpless catches me off guard. "They're coming. You must run! They attacked me! They are so pale! Their eyes burn like fire! Dark blood running red! Their teeth seared into my flesh! I'm dirty, unclean!"

The man rises and starts moving toward us. I aim my gun at him and flip the safety off. He stops and falls to his knees, laughing. This man is clearly schizophrenic. The medication to treat these disorders is long gone, and I can only pity the man. Not wanting to shoot him, I decide to holster my pistol and approach him, making sure to do so slowly.

As I get closer to him, he jerks his head toward me. For the first time, I have a clear look into his eyes. A web of spidery red veins weaves all over his irises, giving the illusion of blood-red eyes. His pupils are far too large for the sunny day, and I begin to think he's tripping on something.

His eyes remind me of the creature in my dream. A pressure pushes onto my chest, almost like an invisible knee pinned against me. A sense of foreboding enters me, and I'm sure that I'm about to be attacked. Before my premonition can come true, I see a tree branch swinging toward the man from the corner of my eye.

The branch hits the man hard, and he falls. When I get closer, it looks like the man is unconscious, though his eyes remain wide open in a look of fear. Jason stands beside me, still holding the branch. Somehow, I know that he saved me from a horrible fate. Pushing the foolish feelings aside, I tell myself to be rational. Memories of my dream attempt to haunt me, but I push them away.

Checking the man's pulse, I find him alive. Unsure of what to do, I pat him down but find no weapons. The man appears to have nothing on him but his clothes. Luke, Jason, and I talk about what to do. We decide to leave him here. He'll likely wake up and be on his way. Though he might be crazy, there's no reason to try to do anything, and killing him would be wrong.

With the fun of the playground spoiled, we decide to go back to my house. When we arrive, I warn my parents about what we saw. They share my concern but agree that leaving the man was for the best.

Jason, Luke, and I don't let it dampen our spirits, and we decide to get on with the day. After some discussion on what to do next, we settle on playing a card game in my room. After a frustrating round of squinting at the cards in the dim dusk lighting, we decide to put the cards away. It's in the middle of doing so that we freeze when something slams into my window.

"What the hell was that?" Luke says, speaking the thought we all have.

When I look toward the window, I see the pale outline of a man. Focusing on his face, I notice that it's the same man we saw at the park earlier today.

"How the hell did he find us?" Jason mutters in shock.

My mind is racing, trying to understand what's going on, when the man throws his face into my window again. I pull my gun out of the holster and aim it at him for the second time today.

"Leave now, or I'll shoot." The man shows no signs of understanding me, and he slams his head into the glass again. I've never shot a person before, and I'm debating if I'll have to when I hear a scream coming from the other room. When I look away, I hear glass shatter, and pieces of it hit me in the back. It's only a matter of time before the man comes through. Not wanting to shoot him, I back out of my room. Jason and Luke are following behind me. I get a final look at the man struggling to climb through the window. He's oblivious to the remaining shards of glass cutting into him.

"Get into the bathroom. I'm going to get the others." Without waiting for confirmation, I head toward my older sister's room, where the earlier screams must have come from. Running into Sarah's room, I'm greeted with a sight like the one in my room. Four sets of hands are reaching through my sister's windows, grasping for a hold to pull themselves through.

"Go to the bathroom, Sarah. Now!" Sarah looks panicked, but she does what I tell her and runs past me and toward our bathroom. I follow behind her, shutting the bedroom door as I do so. Once I'm out of the room, I'm startled to see Melany, my younger sister, in the hallway.

"Aaron, what's going on? I heard screaming."

"I'm not sure, Melany, but for now, go into the bathroom with Luke and Jason." Melany nods and runs to safety. I follow behind her, walking backward to make sure no one attacks from behind. When we arrive at the bathroom, I glimpse everyone inside. They're all clearly worried, but I can tell they aren't frantic. Jason, unlike the others, seems collected and calm. Realizing they are weaponless, I give Jason my gun.

"Those are my sisters. Protect them with your life. And, Jason, don't open the door for anyone other than me or my parents."

Before Jason can respond, I hear gunfire coming from my parents' room. Without another thought, I run into their room. When I get there, I'm greeted by a terrible sight. One of the attackers has managed to force his way into my parents' room. He has cuts along his body, and blood drips from them and onto the carpet. His shoulder has a large wound, mangled by what I presume is a bullet. Despite this, the man seems unfazed. He rushes toward my parents, and a sense of dread overtakes me.

My instincts kick in and I run to intercept their attacker. I manage to run between the crazed man and my parents. He seems uncaring and charges me as if I was his original target. Before he can reach me, I swing my right fist into the side of his jaw. The blow connects and the force of it snaps his head back.

38

I know from experience that a blow like that should knock out or disorient someone. Knowing this, I let my guard down. With an unnatural suddenness, the pale man starts swinging his head at me. His jaw agape, he appears to be moving to bite me, and I know by some primal instinct that I'm in trouble.

I pull my hands up in defense as the pale man's face races toward mine. Before he collides with me, I hear a gun fire and feel something warm splatter onto my arms. I look down and see the man lying on the floor. Only a fragmented mess of skull and gore remains of what was once his head.

My stomach turns and threatens to dislodge its contents. I know I don't have time for that, though, so I force my nausea down. I look to my father. He looks as shocked as me, and I can tell that he's struggling with what he did. "The girls are in the bathroom. We should regroup in the garage."

My father nods in agreement, regaining his composure. Together, my parents and I leave the room. We make our way to the bathroom, and once there, my mother knocks on the door.

The door swings open, and I see Jason holding the gun up at us, ready to fire. My mother jumps and lets out a quiet yelp. Jason's face is calm, and he lowers the gun.

"What's going on?" Jason asks as if nothing happened.

"We're moving to the garage to regroup and figure out what's going on." Jason nods. Before we leave the bathroom, I grab a towel and clean the blood off my arms and face.

"Alright, Jason, I'll take front and you can take the back. Whatever's going on, these people won't stop unless they are dead. Don't hold back if they attack. One more thing: they don't seem to stop from wounds, so shoot to kill."

Taking the lead, I stay a few feet ahead of everyone else. As we make our way through the house, I hear doors closing at the end of our little group. I assume it's Jason's idea and commend him on it. The doors should delay any pursuers and let us know when they're coming. Everything is quiet in the home, and I don't know where the attackers are. Did they even make their way outside? We don't run into anyone and make it to the garage unscathed.

"Whatever's going on," Luke whispers from behind me, "I don't think this garage will be a good place to stay for very long."

"How are we supposed to stay safe from these Palemen?" I ask. And for the first time, our attackers get a name.

My mind drifts to other thoughts. These things are so like science fiction zombies. The Palemen attacking us don't seem like healthy humans. They have no self-preservation instincts and don't show any signs of understanding us. It's hard to believe it, but how can I deny what I've seen?

Whatever's affecting these people has turned them mindless. I don't know how the infection spreads, but it's safe to assume it isn't airborne. The man at the park comes up in my memory, and I recall how he said that he was bitten. Whatever changed these people, I bet it spreads through bites or blood.

Thinking back, I try to remember if any of the blood from the Paleman my father shot entered my eyes or mouth. Remembering the spray of blood, I know that, chances are, it did.

We reach the garage and look around. It's clear of any Palemen, and other than old unusable tools, the only thing inside is a motorcycle with a sidecar that my father managed to get working.

My thoughts halt when I see everyone looking at me. They look as if they're expecting me to come up with an answer. My focus shifts to figuring out a way to get everyone safe. If I'm infected, I'll know soon enough, but right now, I need to get everyone to safety.

While I ponder different plans, I'm hit by an epiphany. The Palemen don't think; they broke through the windows, cutting themselves on the glass. They didn't even try to avoid our attacks. They didn't listen to reason or respond to warnings. Furthermore, they seem to attack senselessly. So the safest place I can think of would be a place someone couldn't reach without using reason or problem-solving skills.

Somewhere you could only reach with a ladder.

"Hold on. I know where to go. Do you guys remember that decrepit building we worked on earlier this summer? Before the power outage?"

Jason nods and answers me. "Yes, I remember, but why are you mentioning it?"

"It's high up on a second story, and we can defend it pretty well. I doubt my house is the only one under attack. Think about it. These things are mindless. If we went there, we could remove the stairs and be safe on the second floor. I doubt they're good climbers. Besides, can you think of anywhere better?"

Jason looks at me, and I can see that he's thinking my plan through. "No, it seems like a pretty good place to be right now." Everyone else nods in agreement with the plan.

"Alright then," I say. "Let's grab food, supplies, and anything else you can think of. Let's go under the assumption that we'll be there for an extended amount of time."

Everyone agrees, and we get to work gathering food from the nearby kitchen, packing it into duffel bags that my dad keeps in the garage. Even better, we find that my dad packed several months' worth of food and supplies into our crawlspace. With everything we grab, we should be pretty well supplied for a month or two.

When we finish gathering supplies, we let the dogs in from the back yard. Since the back yard has a fence, it's free of any Palemen. I'm not sure how useful the dogs will be, but I'm still glad we aren't going to abandon them.

We load everything into the motorcycle and sidecar. The fact that we have a mechanical motorcycle is amazing, and I know my father went to a lot of work to build it. I've never been more thankful or proud of him than at this moment. The motorcycle has a two-person cab, so altogether, it has a four-person capacity.

Looking at my father, I see his gaze is on the motorcycle. We both understand who will take the bike. "I'll see you there," I say to my father, knowing he understands what I mean. "Plus, I'm sure Jason and

Luke want to get their own families anyway, so why don't I help them with that?"

My father nods and helps my crying mother and sisters onto the bike and cab. I can't blame them for crying; everything is moving so fast. If I'd let myself, I'm sure I'd be crying right now as well. Taking a long look at them, I pray that it isn't my last. The bike starts, and I take that as a signal to open the garage door. I pull a latch, and a few suspended sandbags fall slowly as the garage door opens.

Jason readies the gun I gave him. As the garage opens, a scene from some hellish horror greets us. Palemen are stumbling through the streets. From where we are, I can see several corpses littering the streets. Smoke billows from some distant, unknown fire. Right outside the garage are two Palemen. Luckily, neither is blocking the motorcycle's path.

To Jason's credit, he doesn't hesitate. He opens fire, and one of the Palemen drops to the ground, lifeless. My father, seeing a clear path, accelerates out of the garage. One of the dogs rushes the other Paleman shortly after. Looking past the driveway, I can see several more Palemen coming toward us. They ignore the motorcycle, which is making a clean escape.

"Aaron, we have to go now. If we stay any longer, we'll be trapped." Jason's voice pushes me into action, and I nod at him. Together, Jason, Luke, and I start running. We run along my drive and onto the street. Before long, several Palemen are chasing us. Their movements are clumsy and erratic, so it's easy to stay ahead of them. The fear of death keeps me from slowing, and it's only when we hit a patch of grass and the Palemen stop pursuing us that I slow down and stop. The others follow suit, and we watch as the Palemen seem to have lost us.

Luke starts to say something, and like a radar, the Palemen home in on us. Once again, we run, but learning from experience, we lose them by going into another patch of grass. Jason and Luke look at me, both not making a sound. I motion for them to follow, and we make it a safe distance from our pursuers. Only when I can look around and not see any Palemen within a few hundred yards do I dare whisper to them.

"Weird, it seems like they only react to sound. Maybe they are blind or something."

"If that's the case, it wouldn't surprise me if that gunshot earlier attracted a bunch to your house." I nod at Jason's remark. He comments about how few guns we have. I know my dad has a pistol, but we forgot the shotgun at home. I suppose there's no retrieving it now. I do have a good idea of where to get some more guns, though.

"Why don't we head down to the police station so we can arm ourselves?"

Both Jason and Luke agree with my idea, so we take a detour to the police station. On our way, we see total chaos. Screaming people run in the streets, and Palemen are everywhere. Gunfire pops and fires blaze through the town. We do our best to stay silent and hidden from everyone, and somehow we make it to the police station.

We go into the police station and find several dead bodies inside. One look at the bodies on the floor tells me these Palemen aren't immortal. The floors are littered with not only dead Palemen, but also several officers I recognize. Grief threatens to overtake me, but I force myself to maintain my composure. We cannot afford a breakdown now. I shut my emotions off, knowing they'll only get in the way. Looking at the dead, I see that they haven't transformed into Palemen. Whatever is creating these monsters doesn't appear to happen after death, like in the movies.

As we walk through the station, I lose hope of finding survivors. We push past the dead, brutalized bodies. I hear someone throwing up along the way, but I don't look to see who it is. When we arrive at the station's armory, I notice some movement against the far wall. At first, thinking it might be a Paleman, I prepare myself. On second look, I see that he isn't turned—or at least not all the way. His skin is pale and his eyes are tinged with red. Something about the way he looks at me tells me that he's still in control.

He's bleeding from several wounds. The bodies of his fellow officers and those of Palemen surround him. It's obvious that a large fight took place here and that he is the only survivor. The man sees us and tries to raise his arm. It's only then that I notice a gun in his hand.

"Don't come any closer or I'll shoot." I look at the man and feel sympathy for him. I don't recognize him as an officer, but that isn't surprising. There are plenty of officers I've never met; I was only on the force for a few months, after all.

"Calm down. I'm an officer, like you. I was off duty today. Could you tell me what happened here?" The man relaxes, and I approach him. When I look closer, I can see several bite marks on his arms.

"Those things—they came in and attacked us. I'm the only one that survived."

The man sobs and spits up some blood. He's clearly in deep physical and emotional pain. After a few seconds, he continues.

"Some of the other officers were out on patrol this morning in the fields a few miles outside of town. They were bitten by something. Of course, we patched them up when they got back."

The man's breaths come in gasps as he fights off whatever is attacking him. He seems to become more frantic, and bloody spittle collects at the corners of his mouth.

"They declined into a mad state and started attacking us a few hours later. It's like I've seen in the movies: they are vicious and act as though they aren't alive. We got things under control, but that's when the rest of them arrived."

The man starts laughing and screams something unintelligible and full of anger. It seems as though the man is slipping, and Jason looks ready to shoot him. I motion for Jason to give me the gun, and when he does, I see a weight lift from him. As I walk toward the man, I realize that my suspicion of transferal through bite is accurate. I also realize that the dead officers didn't change. These aren't supernatural living dead. This realization is somehow comforting. It's reassuring to know that what we are facing is as mortal as we are.

"I don't have much more time. Please, kill me now, before I turn into one of them. I beg you: at least let me die with my sanity."

I look at the man, knowing that he is right. I ready myself to shoot him. I hesitate. I've never taken a human life. Even though this man is asking me to kill him, I'm not sure it's the right thing to do.

The man's gaze is starting to fade, and I realize I have to decide now. Without another thought, I steady my aim and turn off the safety. The man smiles at me and mouths "thank you."

I hear the bang. I want to blink and look away, but I don't. The bullet hits its mark, and the man's head splatters against the back wall. All the emotion I've been holding back floods me, and I fall to the ground, weeping. It isn't until Jason puts a hand on my shoulder that I'm able to put myself back together and stand up.

"There are some guns in that locker, and the rifles are in the one next to it," I say, directing Jason and Luke to the lockers. They collect all the guns and bullets they find. After taking another moment to collect myself, I go through the building, gathering guns from the dead police officers. They no longer need them, and we could use them to protect our families. That's what I tell myself to make it feel okay.

After we have all the guns and ammo we can find, we load them into police-marked duffel bags and head out the back door. It won't be long before more Palemen arrive, attracted by the sound of the gunfire. Fortunately, we find two bicycles in the back of the station. "Well, it looks like I'm walking," I say to the others.

"You guys get to your families and get them to come to the rendezvous site, where my family should be now. We'll need a ladder and food. Jason, you bring the ladder, and both of you bring food. I have to presume my family is safe, so I'm going to go check on one of my friends and try to get his family to join us. I know plenty of people are dying right now, but I wouldn't feel right letting a friend face this horde on his own." Both Jason and Luke nod. Before they go, I grab another pistol and some ammo, which I put in my pockets. I also take a hatchet and combat knife from the supplies.

After I do this, they ride off without saying another word. I hope they remain safe, and I know the weapons will go a long way to help. With them gone, I start walking toward Brian's house. The walk is slow. I try to shut out the death and screams for help as I sneak my way through town. Part of me wants to help, but I know that every minute I delay is another chance for Brian and his family to die.

Chapter 4: Brian

May 10th

My eyes open and the dreams I was having fade into forgotten memories. As I roll over, a part of me wishes I could go back to sleep. A sigh of frustration escapes my lips as I turn over to look out my bedroom window. Through the window, I see the sundial I set up for this exact purpose. The sundial tells me it's around 5:30 in the morning. Though I'm a little frustrated that I'll be the only one up this early, I do enjoy the solitude. As I roll out of bed, I grab the set of clothes I laid out the night before. The pile is missing socks, so I walk over to my dresser to grab them.

I pull open my sock drawer and panic when I see a gun. It takes me a second, but I remember that it should be there. The gun scares me, but I know it's a good idea to have it. My parents and sister still have no idea that it's here. Three months ago, Aaron gave it to me, and I've kept it a secret since.

My parents haven't been able to cope with what's happened. If they knew I had a gun, they'd try to take it away from me and give it to a police officer. In their minds, they think nothing has changed in the world since the power went out. I don't understand how they can still believe that the power will come back on in only a few days.

My parents' refusal to face reality has confined my sister and me to our house. They've refused to let anyone come over, except for

Aaron, and that's only because he's a police officer. Aaron is the only connection to the outside world that my sister and I have.

Pulling myself out of my thoughts, I take another glance at the sundial and see that it's now seven. There are chores that need to be done, so I finish getting dressed and leave my room.

The first chore is lighting the fire for breakfast and coffee. I get to work gathering wood and starting the fire on our makeshift woodstove. It's a shame that the food we'll be eating wasn't earned. My parents' refusal to go outside has prevented us from helping our community recover. Every day, the moral burden of being a societal leach grows heavier.

We're lucky to be in a community that's willing to help all its members. It would have been better for me and my family to have been thrown out of the town. If we were, my parents would face reality—or at least I hope they would.

When the fire is almost ready, I hear someone walking through the house. Looking toward the origin of the noise, I see that my sister, Alexis, has woken up.

"Morning. Are Mom and Dad up yet?" she asks.

Having not seen either of my parents, I shake my head. "Not yet."

My sister nods, and I know she isn't surprised. Alexis comes closer to the fire and grabs a cup of still-cold instant coffee.

"I wish Mom and Dad would finally figure out that we aren't getting power back," she says. "We need to move on and do something useful. Being confined to this house is driving me crazy. It's pointless to cower in the house and wait for things to get back to normal. Power is gone, and it isn't coming back. I don't know how much longer I can take care of Mom and Dad."

As my sister rants at me, I watch her. I know she isn't looking for input; she never does, or at least she doesn't expect it from me. It isn't that I don't agree with her—I do. Short of abandoning my parents, I don't see anything else we can do. Alexis and I could manage on our own, but I can't leave my parents the way they are. Without us, their lives would fall apart, leaving them to fall even deeper into their depression.

Alexis's string of complaints comes to a halt when someone opens the basement door. My parents live downstairs, so I figure it's them getting up. When I turn to look, I see my mother. She enters the kitchen with her head down. She looks like a defeated dog, sad and hopeless. Anger flares in me for a second before I remind myself that she isn't acting like this to hurt me. My mother is defeated. She may never find the courage to admit that to herself, but I wish she would. If she did, we could all move on with our lives.

I can feel Alexis's anger from across the room, and it's directed toward my mother. Unlike me, Alexis tends to wear her emotions on her sleeve. I'm not the same, since I figure all emotions do is get in the way of things—something I believed even before the world went to shit.

My mother starts cooking silently, and Alexis leaves the kitchen in a huff. She moves into the living room, and I follow her. Staying in the same room as my silent mother is too uncomfortable. As I walk into the living room, I see Alexis reading, and I decide that reading sounds nice. Choosing one of my favorite fiction books, I find myself lost in its pages. My immersion is shattered when my mom calls us to breakfast.

As I set the book down, my escape from reality broken, a pang of regret goes through me. My sister and I make our way to the kitchen. When I enter, I see the table set up and my father sitting at the head. Alexis and I sit down, and my mother joins us a second later. Throughout the meal, no one speaks.

After everyone finishes breakfast, my mother finally breaks the silence.

"Your father and I are going to be doing some renovating in the basement. Could you and Alexis please organize and document our food and supplies?"

Hearing Alexis sigh, I cut her off before she can complain. "Yes, we will get to it after dishes." My sister shoots me a poisonous stare as she stands up and walks out the door. Alexis and I have been doing dishes outside lately. We told our parents it was less messy to do it by the outside faucet. The truth is, we were desperate for fresh air and some small sliver of freedom.

My mom has asked us to organize the food and supplies three separate times this week, so I understand my sister's frustration with the pointless task. It's nice to have something to do, but doing the same thing almost every day is absurd.

My parents stare at me as I gather dishes, and I'm glad when I finally walk outside and away from their gazes. Once outside, I find

Alexis with dish water ready to go. We clean the dishes, and she vents her frustration and anger to me. Normally, I don't mind her venting; I understand her need to express her frustration. Today, though, I wish she would be quiet so I could enjoy the sun and air.

After we finish cleaning all the dishes, we go inside to start organizing our supplies. Neither of us are in the mood to work fast, so we finish our job very slowly.

The first few times we organized supplies, it took us an hour. We've done it so often now, though, that we get distracted. That's why I'm not all that surprised when I check a sundial and find that it's around 7:00 p.m. Wanting to finish for the day, I complete the rest of our list. After I do, Alexis suggests we go to my room and play a game. Part of me wants to continue reading the book from earlier, but I figure I should spend time with Alexis. We both walk to my room, and I pull out a card game. We manage to set it up but stop playing when we hear a loud slam.

"What was that!?" Alexis hisses with a frenzied voice. Signaling her to be quiet, I motion that I'm going to check it out. During his last visit, Aaron told me about some house raids that happened not too long ago. Since my house is in the middle of town, I never thought it would be a target. Making my way to the front door, I prepare myself for the worst.

When I reach the door, I freeze at the horrific sight of what's in front of me. The front door of my home lies broken, smashed inward and resting only on the bottom hinge. In the doorway are several people with pale skin and blood-red eyes. Most of the creatures are bleeding from tears or gashes on their arms, necks, and faces. Instincts kick in, and I run back to my room and slam the door shut.

"Alexis, help me block the door!" Alexis looks at me, and I can tell she's both confused and scared. Dragging my desk toward the door, I'm joined by Alexis. As we slide the desk in place, something starts slamming against the door. I'm pretty sure the door will hold for a little while, and I think we're safe until I hear the shattering of glass behind me.

How could I not think of the window? My head turns toward the noise as I ask myself this. When I've turned around, I see a horrific figure trying to climb through the window. His hands rest on shards of glass, and as he tries to pull himself through, his skin ruptures. Blood trickles from his hands and onto my floor. He doesn't even take notice.

Everything slows down as I realize that these things aren't human anymore. Doubt fills my mind, but something in my gut tells me I'm right. Whatever these things are, their only goal seems to be attacking us.

Out of the corner of my eye, I see a wooden chair. Having no better weapon and not wanting to be a victim, I grab the chair. I run forward and swing it at the pale creature coming through my window. The chair slams into the man, and the recoil from the impact splinters the chair apart. Still needing a weapon, I grab one of the pieces and try using it to attack the man.

My fear of hurting another living being vanishes. An instinct to protect myself and my sister overtakes it. Over and over I hit the man until he lies still in a bruised, bleeding, and broken mess.

Closing my eyes, I prepare myself to fight the men outside my room. As I turn around, I hear the door open. Stunned, I ask myself if Alexis has somehow found the gun hidden in my drawer and is planning to fight. Then I realize my own stupidity.

Why was I ready to fight these things with a chair leg when I had a gun in my drawer the whole time? No time to get it now. I have to face whatever's coming into my room.

When I look through the door, instead of seeing a pale horror, I see Aaron. He's standing in the doorway, holding a hatchet in one hand and a combat knife in the other. At his feet are three dead creatures. His clothes and face are covered in blood. A reassuring sight at this moment.

As I'm looking at Aaron, my sister runs over and hugs him. Taken aback, I remain frozen, confused about what's going on. Surrounded by the three dead creatures, my sister and Aaron stand in the doorway. How can they stand there like nothing happened?

This man is strong, and I need to be like him. No more hiding, no more pretending. If the world changes, the only way to survive is to change with it.

"Hey, Aaron. Thanks," I manage to mutter.

Whatever is going on, Aaron wouldn't be here without a plan. Before I can process much more, I remember that my parents are downstairs.

"Let's go get my parents. They're downstairs."

Aaron looks at me and replies, "Alright. After we get them, I know of somewhere safe we can go. Also, stay quiet. The Palemen react to sound."

Aaron's description of the creatures as "Palemen" tells me that these things are everywhere. It also tells me that he doesn't see them as human. A weight I didn't realize I was carrying falls off my shoulders. I'm not a murderer; the thing I bludgeoned to death wasn't a human. True, I suspected that it wasn't human, but having someone reassure me makes me feel better.

A sigh escapes me, and I grab my gun before following Aaron and my sister. We walk through the house in a line, Aaron leading and me guarding the back. Just when I was starting to hope that all the Palemen left, we make it to the basement stairs, and my hopes are dashed.

The stairwell to the basement is full of the Palemen. Their bodies wriggle against each other as they try to break through my parents' door. There's no counting the number in the wriggling mass. Even by my best estimates, I would have to say there are twenty or more.

The sight of the squirming pale bodies mesmerizes me and fills me with dread. The bodies move in an almost symbiotic fashion, like they're communicating with each other. They've joined as a single working organism, one helping the other. As I watch, I try to understand them. I don't come out of the trance until I feel a tap on my shoulder.

When I turn, I see Aaron and my sister signaling for me to come outside. Naturally, I follow them. Once we're outside and out of earshot of the Palemen horde, Aaron says, "You two get on the roof. And stay silent. I'm going to create a diversion to lead the Palemen away. The Palemen aren't agile, so I can lose them if I run."

Aaron's plan is solid. I nod and grab Alexis's hand and walk to the nearby air-conditioner. As I help Alexis get to the roof, Aaron goes back inside. Once Alexis is up, I pull my gun out and speak to her. "Watch Aaron. From up there, you should be able to see his path. I'm going to stay down here and take care of any Palemen that stay behind after his diversion."

Alexis looks like she's about to argue, but before she can, several loud cracks of gunfire silence her. My gaze moves to the front door, and I see Aaron running, followed by a horde of Palemen.

Not wanting to attract attention, I remain still and silent until the Palemen and Aaron are out of sight. Once I'm sure it's safe to move, I make my way into my house, ready for the worst. Luckily, Aaron's diversion worked well. Three Palemen are all that remain on the basement stairs.

From my vantage point, it's easy to see that all three sustained wounds from Aaron's attack. The cold steel of the pistol in my hands is comforting, even though I know I can't use it, if what Aaron said about the Palemen's reactions to sound is true. Shooting these three would only draw in more. If I'm going to kill them, it will have to be silent.

As I start to plan, I look at my three adversaries. Two of the three Palemen are on the ground. They lie at the bottom of the stairs, one with a leg wound and the other with a stomach wound. The one with the stomach wound lies on top of the one with the leg wound.

The third Paleman stands facing the basement door. He's a few steps up, but when I watch him, I see that his right side is limp and unresponsive. Trying my hardest to be quiet, I sneak toward the standing Paleman. Fortunately, he's several feet away from the other two. Once I'm behind him, I swing the butt of my pistol into his temple as hard as I can. The impact of the blow shakes my arm, and the Paleman falls to the floor. Not wanting to risk a surprise attack, I examine the now unconscious Paleman.

As I do, I hear moans from the other two. When I look at them, though, I see that they're unable to move toward me, so I choose to ignore them for now.

Moving my hand over the unconscious Paleman's mouth, I find it breathing. Whatever happened to make these things the way they are, they're still alive. When I check for a pulse, I find one. So I sit down next to the creature and think for a minute. Strangulation would be the easiest way to terminate these creatures without making noise. Since I've never strangled anyone before, it takes me a little while to find the unconscious creature's windpipe.

The act of strangling something should affect me, but it doesn't. I feel nothing as the creature struggles and stops moving. I check the creature's pulse to make sure it's dead. After confirming it is, I move on to the other two and dispatch them in the same manner. A sense of calm envelopes me now that I know these creatures are mortal.

With the creatures dead, my focus shifts to my parents. I go to open their door and I find it unlocked. The fact that the Palemen couldn't think to turn a doorknob tells me they've lost their problem-solving abilities. It also tells me my parents are idiots. Who wouldn't lock a door when there's a home invasion?

When the door swings open, the first thing I see is my parents cowering in the corner, waiting for their deaths. Any respect I had left for them vanishes. Fear I can understand, but cowardice to this extent is pathetic. Finally, I understand that they've given up. They gave up shortly after the power went out. Ever since then, they've waited for someone to save them or for death. There's no way I can respect someone who's cowered for that long.

Even though I still love my parents, I now know that I don't want to be trapped under their fear anymore. If they'll go, I'll take them to safety, but that will be the end of my responsibility to them. Never again will I stay still and rely on others to help. I'll leave this house tonight, with or without my parents.

"You're safe. It's time to get up and get out of here." As I'm saying this, my parents look up at me, standing. Without waiting, I turn around and start walking up the stairs, avoiding the bodies of the dead creatures. Before I reach the top, someone puts a hand on my back.

"Brian, why do you have a gun? Give the gun to your father. Brian, did you kill these people?"

My mother's questions shock me. Do they not see these creatures for what they are? My anger and disappointment in them silence me. My parents should be comforting me right now, not the other way around. My thoughts are interrupted when I hear a cough. I move my body and throw my arm and head toward the source of the noise. I ready my trigger finger but stop myself when I see the noise is Aaron, not a Paleman.

"Are we a bit trigger-happy there?" Aaron asks as I attempt to calm down and catch my breath. I lower the gun and close my eyes for a second, reminding myself that everyone's safe and that this could've gone much worse. Aaron's plan worked well, and we need to leave before something can go wrong.

Only now do I realize how I can convince my parents to leave the house. They see Aaron as an authority figure, and there's a good chance that they'll listen to him if he tells them to leave.

"Hey, Aaron, what's going on?"

"Well, something horrible has happened and I was in the neighborhood, so I wanted to make sure you guys were okay. Now that I know you're safe, I can head back home. My family and a few others set up a secure place. You guys should come with me. It's much safer there. I'll go tell Alexis that it's okay to come inside. Your family can make a decision after she gets here. Keep in mind that the noise will lead more here, so one way or the other, you need to hurry."

"Thank you, Aaron."

Aaron turns around and walks out the door. Once I lose sight of him, I turn around and walk to the downstairs couch. I sit down, but my parents remain standing. A tense silence fills the room until Alexis joins us. She doesn't even make it to the couch before my mother starts.

"I don't care what Aaron said. We're going to stay here. It would be foolish to go out into a riot."

All I can do is stare at my mother in shock. She looks angry, like she's made up her mind. Behind my mom, my father nods, agreeing with her. *I'm done with both of you*, I want to say. Looking at Alexis, I know she feels the same. Before I can tell them my thoughts, though, my mom continues.

"Brian, I want you to give the gun to your father. He'll get rid of it, and we'll wait for the authorities to help us."

There's no question in my mind anymore: I'm leaving, and if they follow, so be it.

"Mom, the gun is mine, and I'm leaving. If you want to come with Alexis and me, you can."

My mother's face changes from one of anger to one of betrayal. But I don't feel sad; her decision no longer has any bearing on me. If I don't leave now, I know I'll die. Deep down, it hurts me that my mother feels betrayed, but I know what I have to do. I just hope that my readiness to leave convinces Mom to come along.

Without another word, I stand and start walking to the stairs. Alexis looks at me in disbelief. Usually, she's the one to face my parents, so I understand her shock. She snaps out of it, though. Alexis quickly turns around, walks up the stairs, and goes out the door. Following behind her, I leave the basement and my broken parents. Once out my front door, I see Aaron smiling at me. I'm about to speak when I hear some voices behind me.

"How do we know that we'll be safe?"

The voice makes me turn around, and when I do, I see my mother. Their decision to come shocks me, but as I lock eyes with her, I can see that she's angry. Not wanting to fight with her, I turn around.

"Sorry, but I can't promise you safety," Aaron says. "What's going on right now is very dangerous. You have a chance of getting hurt or dying if you come with me. If you stay here, though, I promise that you'll die. Where we're going is large enough for several families. Once it's secured, it'll be the safest place in town. We don't have time for this, though; we need to get there soon. Grab any supplies you can carry and come with me."

Aaron's suggestion makes me realize that we'll need food and other supplies to stay safe for any amount of time. For once, I'm thankful that my mother forced us to count supplies almost every day. Because she did, packing away all our clothes, food, and medical supplies takes mere minutes. From now on, I'll always keep a close eye on supplies.

After we pack, we leave the house and follow Aaron through town to a large abandoned building. Several times, Alexis stifles my mother's cries. The city burns and Palemen walk all around. The only reason my parents make it through is their cowardice. Their willingness to follow when scared amazes me. When we make it to our destination, I get a good look at the building we're going to stay in.

From the look of things, it has two floors. The first floor consists of a glass-walled shop, empty of anything. Inside the store, I see a set of stairs but notice that they aren't long enough to reach the second floor. The stairs must lead to some kind of storage space.

From what I can tell, the second floor is an apartment. The only way up to the second floor is through a doorway to the side of the storefront. Something tells me the second floor is where we'll be staying.

We open the door, and sure enough, wooden stairs lead to an upstairs apartment. The space is large enough that I know we'll be comfortable with one or two families. It isn't long before Aaron's friend Jason approaches me. He explains the plans to break apart the stairs. That way, the only way to reach the second floor is by using a ladder. The plan seems like a good one since the apartment is so high up. You'd have to be a skilled and agile climber to make it up here without a ladder or stairs.

After hearing about the plan, I'm anxious to help. It feels good to focus my mind on something other than what's going on. It takes several days to destroy the stairs. While I work, idle talk catches me up on everything that's happened.

Every day that passes confirms that my choice was the right one. The chaos I see outside through the upstairs windows tells me that if we had stayed in our home, we would have died.

My mother and father carve out a place to hide in the apartment, and I haven't spoken to them since we arrived. They're still angry with me, I imagine, but I don't care. Even if they hate me, so be it. They're alive, and so am I. Even better, I'm finally free of their constrictive grasp and free to make my own choices.

Chapter 5: Sophia

March 13th

My eyes open, and all I see is white. As I survey my surroundings, I realize I'm strapped to a hospital bed. Trying to remember how I got here, I find that I don't remember anything. I have no memories of who I am or where I am. Other than basic skills like math and English, I don't remember anything. The straps of the hospital bed panic me. Scared, I question what's going on. My arms strain as I try to pull free of my confinement.

As I kick and struggle, I hear a loud snap. When I look down, I see my arm bent in a way that isn't natural. My arm rages with pain, and I start to scream. My body becomes still as I try to move as little as possible. Each movement sends fresh waves of pain through me. My vision starts to fade. At first, I fight it, but it overtakes me.

When my eyes open again, I find myself in the same room. My first reaction is to look down to my arm, knowing it's broken. When I look down, I find myself strapped to the same bed. There's a cast on my arm now and an I.V. line on my finger. When I see movement out of the corner of my eye, I focus on it. A man stands above me, holding what looks like a recording device.

"Patient S is hooked into a morphine pump. She is the first of the infected to show signs of pain or any reaction to her environment. She, unlike our other subjects, has a regular heartbeat and organ function. Whatever suppresses the other subjects' metabolisms hasn't

64

affected her. The subject seems to be unique in her immune response to the disease. There are some physical signs present, as well as the melanin deficiency common to her illness."

My mouth opens as I gasp for air, and I try to speak to the man. When I try to say something, all that comes out is air. A cold sensation runs up my arm, and I realize that it's morphine coming through the I.V. in my finger.

My consciousness starts fading, and I fall asleep. My dreams are dark and full of anger. In them, I find myself killing others, ripping them apart. Anger courses through me. Hate and fury blur my senses. My dreamworld is as red and warm as blood.

There are others here with me. We move together with a common purpose. They feel the same things as me; nothing drives us but our anger and need to survive. When my eyes open again, I find myself still full of rage. Sweat beads off every inch of my body, and I have to force myself to calm down. The memory of my recently broken arm helps calm me. If I struggle, I know I'll only break something else.

After I've calmed myself, I glance around the room. The lights are off, so it's hard to see. My room is devoid of any windows or clocks, so I have no way of telling what time it is. My only sign of the time is the lights. Something flashes, and I'm blinded for several seconds. As my eyes adjust to the bright lights coming on in the room, a man stands above me. Once again, he holds a recording device.

"The specimens have shown some ability to form basic coordinated groups. We are still unsure of how this communication occurs. It might be some pheromone or chemical released by them. On that note, tonight, a unique reaction occurred. Patient Sophia started to scream in her sleep. This isn't all that uncommon, and it has been observed in several of the other patients as well. After Sophia started screaming, the other patients frenzied. Every single one of them struggled to break free, as if to answer her call."

My ears strain as I try to hear every word. To my dismay, the cold sensation of morphine puts me back to sleep. Even though I fight the drug's influences, I soon find myself in the land of dreams again. This time, my dreams are no longer filled with rage and death.

There's only drifting and floating in nothingness. There's no telling how long I'm asleep. It could be minutes, days, years, or lifetimes. Inside of the rift, I find peace and calm. Accepting what's happening to me, I decide I never want to leave this state.

My wishes don't matter, though, and I find myself pulled back to consciousness. The sensation of waking up feels like falling, and I gasp as my eyes open. Now awake, I realize I'm in the hospital room.

When I look around, I see the room is full of men in lab coats. One of the last times I was awake, I remember one of them saying that I showed unique resistance to symptoms. If I had to bet, I would say they are here to examine me more closely. This time, I'm determined to communicate with them. One of the men comes forward.

"Sophia, do you know where you are?" His hands prod my eyes roughly as he flashes a bright light into them. Tears build, and I try to blink them away. When I try to tell him to stop, I discover I'm unable to talk.

"She is like the others. She might show some improvement, but there is no chance she overcame the disease. I'm sorry, Charles, but you were wrong about her." The man lets go of my eyelids and walks out of the room. Every other person leaves the room except for one man. He comes over to me, and I recognize him as the same person I saw the last two times I woke up. Something tells me that he's Charles.

"I'm sorry this has happened to you," he says. "For a second, I believed that you were different. I guess I was wrong, though." As the man says this, he looks at me. Looking him in the eyes, I nod my head no. The man looks astonished and speaks again. "Sophia, do you understand me?"

I nod my head yes.

"My God!"

The man turns around and runs out of the room, screaming for the others to come back. While he gathers them, I try to speak, only accomplishing grunts, but after a few tries, my mouth starts obeying my commands. A few half-formed words slip out. My mouth and throat are so dry that even the few words I manage feel like sandpaper. Several men start coming into the room, and most of them look annoyed. Wanting to wait until they are all here, I remain silent. Charles is the last man into the room, and after he closes the door behind him, I mutter, "Water. Please, water."

The energy of the room shifts. Before, there was an air of tedious annoyance. Now, when I look around, I see disbelief—and even fear. Charles is the first to react. "Yes, right away. We can get you some water."

The man calls for some water, and it arrives only minutes later. Charles helps me drink it, lowering the glass to my lips. The drink moistens my mouth and throat, and I'm reinvigorated. After a few sips, Charles looks at me with curiosity and asks, "Sophia, do you know where you are?"

The water has made me feel much better, and without thinking, I say, "No, I don't know where I am, who I am, or where I'm from. All I remember is this room. And you." There's a silence, and I look around the room. I realize that all the men here are doctors or other lab technicians. Most of them appear very uncomfortable. No one makes a move for a few seconds. They must be too shocked to speak.

Once again, Charles is the one to break the silence. "Well, you're Sophia, and you're in a private hospital because you have been infected with a rare disease. So far, you're the only patient we've had that has shown any recovery. To be honest, we have no idea why. All our research so far indicates that you should not have recovered."

As I stare at the silent room, I question why they all seem startled and scared. These men are doctors; I'm sure they've seen surprising results before. Their reaction to my recovery seems way over the top. Something in my gut tells me that whatever I was infected with is incurable. If that were the case, my miraculous recovery would be beyond their understanding. Foolish doctors. Do they not remember that many diseases were once thought untreatable?

Shifting in my bed, I feel the restraints tightly constricting me. "Can you let me out of this bed?" I ask. "Or at least loosen these straps? I think I have a few bed sores, and the straps are chaffing me."

Charles looks at me with a mix of sincerity and regret. "Well, Sophia, like I said earlier, you were infected with a very serious disease. The disease makes people very violent. I'm sorry, but for your safety, and our own, I have to keep you restrained."

Disappointment threatens to overwhelm me. Refusing to let it, I remind myself I would do the same in his place. Pushing my disappointment aside, I decide to ask a few more questions. "What has infected me, and how did I get it?"

"You were infected through bacterial exposure induced by four puncture wounds sustained to the upper right quadrant of your torso. The bacteria converged on the brain stem, resulting in the total loss of motor and autonomic functions. We aren't sure why you were able to fight the infection. Every other case of this disease has led to a conscious catatonic state."

Charles's explanation is thorough, at least in medical terms. The answer is probably all I'll receive, so I put further questions about the infection aside for now. The only question I have is how I was able to understand what the doctor said. Before I can ask my captors, someone speaks from behind Charles.

"For God's sake, Charles, she might have been a med student before, but she has amnesia. Try to explain it in simpler terms."

The man's comment isn't necessary, but it answers my silent question. Even though I'm suffering from amnesia, I remember my medical training. Before I have the chance to explain this to them, Charles speaks.

"Right, I'm sorry. You were bitten in the side and infected with bacteria. Those bacteria took over the functions in your brain. We have no idea why you were able to take them back."

Charles's new explanation upsets me a little, and I'm flustered as I say, "Thank you, Doctor, but I understood you the first time. Apparently, I remember my training but not my name. It almost goes without saying, but I'm presuming the bacteria are immune to antibiotics."

As I say this, I see Charles's face express a look of embarrassment. He nods, and I continue. "Since I've never heard of a bacterium that does this, I'm guessing that it's a new variety—or that it's a weaponized strain. Considering I'm in an underground hospital, chances of the second option being true are much greater. Can you please tell me what the hell happened?"

Charles looks at me in shock. "Well, you're right. The bacterium is a weaponized strain. We received the strain from a government agent. It was recovered from an enemy country. Intelligence told us that what was recovered was everything. In case we were wrong, we were ordered to make preparations to combat it. Unfortunately, there was an accident with the sample. About a hundred people were infected and quarantined because of the incident. We learned that the disease was not transmittable through the air. What we also discovered is that the bacterium forms a parasitic bond with the brain stem." Someone taps Charles on the shoulder and hands him a paper. He looks at me, astonished.

"Sorry to change the topic," he continues, "but I was handed a report from your last brain scan. Your brain regenerated the majority of the damage done by the infection. That alone is astonishing, but because you fought off the disease, you now have antibodies built up against it. There is a good chance you would survive the event of reinfection. Do you know what that means? You could be the key to our cure."

Men all around start moving. They all shuffle out of the room in a hurry.

As I stare at the now-empty room, I'm confused about what's going on. Even with those results, the man shouldn't have acted like that. Something doesn't add up, and I'm sure they're withholding information. A few anxious minutes pass before Charles bursts through the doorway and comes over to my bed.

"I'm sorry. What I told you wasn't completely true. Intelligence knows there's more of the weaponized bacterium. They are confident that it could be used on us any day now. We have received orders to operate on you immediately. We need to extract some brain tissue to create an inoculation. I realize that this might be scary, but think of the lives it could save. You won't be harmed, I swear. We have one of the best brain surgeons in the world here."

"Wait a second. Don't I get a say in all this?"

Charles looks at me, and I see a tear in the corner of his eye. "The orders are to extract the tissue immediately. The state you're in after infection has been proclaimed legally dead. You don't have the rights to say no because you're no longer a living member of the United States of America."

Shock and disgust move through me. As I look at Charles, he mouths that he is sorry.

I nod in anger, but I force myself to calm down. Screw the government; I would have consented to surgery, no matter how risky. With an inoculation, far fewer people will die from the disease. Who could live with themselves if they put their life over countless others?

"It's fine, Charles. I want you to do the surgery." Charles smiles as he looks at me. He must have known me before I was infected. As I'm thinking this, Charles pulls out a syringe. He fills it and pumps it into my I.V. My vision starts to fade, but not before I see and feel Charles move his head down to kiss my forehead.

"I promise I'll explain everything after the surgery, sweetheart." Shock moves through me as my world turns black. For a second, I think I've passed out, until I hear Charles say, "What the hell? Where's the auxiliary power? Why are there no lights?"

By the time Charles finishes speaking, I'm fighting to keep my eyes open. My consciousness fades as I lose the pointless battle.

When my eyes open, the first thing I notice is that my restraints are gone. The second thing I notice is the all-encompassing dark and silence. There are no monitors, no lights, nothing. When I look around, I see nothing, but somehow, I sense that I'm still in the same room as before. As I sit up, something pulls at my finger. Remembering the I.V. line, I pull it out.

"No need for that anymore," I say as I swing my body around and stand on the floor. The linoleum is cold against my feet, but I'm glad to be standing again. Trying to think about what I should do, I decide to try looking around outside my room. The first steps are scary, but after a minute, I find myself walking through the hallways of the complex with ease. Each footstep I take echoes off the walls, and I realize after a while that I'm using them to situate myself in the dark. That, combined with some uncanny knowledge of the building's layout, guides me to my unknown destination. I only stop when I find myself in front of a door.

Feeling around the wall, I find a plaque with an engraved name: "Charles Emeret." It's then that I realize why I came here. Judging by the way he acted, I guess that Charles was my boyfriend, husband, or father. Intuition tells me that it's the latter. My hand moves to the knob, and I turn it to try and open the door. The door is wedged closed, and I strain to move it. Something gives, and I manage to slide the door and the desk behind it enough to get through. Before I can do much else, I hear a familiar voice say, "Come to finish me off, have you? Very well. Get to it. I don't ever want to be like you."

Doing my best to point my head toward the source of the noise, I say, "Charles? It's me, Sophia. What happened?"

"Honey, is that you? I'm so glad you're alright. You went to sleep right before the EMP blast. Whoever had the weaponized bacteria must be behind the EMP. I'm afraid for the world. I wish I could explain everything to you, but I can't. Someone infected me, and

I've injected myself with a lethal dose of potassium chloride. Before I die, take this."

As Charles says this, he lifts his hand, which is holding something. Going to him, I take what feels like a three-ring binder.

"Honey, your mother and I loved you, and I'm sorry that you had to go through what you did. I know you can't remember me, but I hope somewhere deep down you still love me after you learn the truth." Charles's words slur near the end, and I can tell that the injection is working. The realization that this man is my father is shocking, but without any memories of him, it's hard to feel anything. Still, no one deserves to die alone, so I do my best to hold him in his last moments.

"I love you, Dad. I promise I'll see you again." The words sound hollow coming from me, but the way he holds me tells me they meant something to him. Charles holds me as he takes his final breaths. Then I set his body down and grab the binder he gave me. There will be time to grieve and question later. For now, I need to focus on getting out of this bunker.

As I walk through the hallways, I avoid the lifeless bodies scattered throughout them. Whenever I hear the patter of footsteps, I hide, knowing there are likely some infected down here. Before long, I make it to the emergency stairs unmolested.

The stairs are much clearer than the hallways, and I climb up to the surface. Once I'm outside, my eyes adjust to the light of the moon. When I look around, I see a barbed-wire fence surrounding the compound I've emerged from. While I'm looking around, I notice a sign nearby: "CDC Headquarters, Atlanta Georgia."

There's no one in sight, and everywhere I look is dark. No artificial light emanates from anywhere. Remembering my way around the city, I'm confident I can escape it before dawn. Without another thought, I start walking. The only thing I stop for is to loot clothes, a backpack, and other supplies from some empty stores. The walk through the city is a silent and empty one.

Once I'm a few miles from the city, I lie down under a tree and rest. What I first intended to be a rest turns into sleep.

When my eyes open, they react to the bright noon sun. It takes a few seconds for my eyes to adjust, but when they do, I look around. From what I can tell, I'm at a random tree along some road. All I remember after escaping the city is walking, without plan or purpose, in one direction. Remembering the map I took from a gas station, I pull off my backpack and open it.

Digging around the bag, I stop when I see a three-ringed binder. My hand grabs it, and I immediately pull it out. As I open it, a thirst for answers overwhelms me. My eyes scan the pages; most of what I read only confirms what I know. I only learn anything once I get past the medical files and onto the last pages, which are personal.

My name is Sophia Emeret, and I was doing observation at the local hospital. Unfortunately, that was the site of the outbreak—and also the place I was infected. My family, except my father, was visiting that day and was murdered. The suspicion is that I fell victim to the disease and killed them.

The impact of the words hit me, and I feel like I should be devastated. For some reason, I feel nothing, even though I know these things are true. Without memories of them, it feels like I'm reading a story.

"I'm sorry, Charles. You were so kind to me, and I've let you down."

The book falls out of my hand, and I sigh and look to the sky. Staring at the noontime sky calms me, and I watch clouds for a while before looking back down. The three-ring binder lies next to me, and I go to pick it up and put it away when something catches my eye. When I pull the binder closer, I see the last page. There is a hand-scrawled note. The writing is sloppy and barely readable.

"Dear, Sophia. Go to Chicago. The weaponized bacterium originates there."

Spatters of blood cover the rest of the writing and make it unreadable. Part of me is glad I can't read the rest of the note. Chicago is a direction I can move toward. As wrong as it makes me feel, I'm better off without family or grief to tie me down.

My first few days of travel are difficult, but I adapt to the efforts. The skills I had before the infection come back to me. My other memories don't. As I travel, I run into plenty of people, and I learn to offer my medical skills in exchange for food. The first few times I try to warn people about the disease, but I learn to avoid the subject. I never stay anywhere for long. Instead, I stay on the move. A few months pass, but I reach the city of Chicago.

Throughout my journey, I don't run into any of the infected. For the first time, on the edge of this city, I face an infected. A man stands pale and foreboding. Even from this distance, somehow, I know what he is. My spine tingles at the feeling of pure hated directed at me. Without another word, the man screams and starts moving toward me. His jagged movements are rough as he stumbles forward. My limbs freeze, and I stare as the man approaches.

My body finally snaps to action when his fingers rip across my face. Throwing up my hands, I push him as hard as I can. As his body flies back and slams into the ground, pain assaults me and blood gets into my eyes. As I scream, some primal sense awakens in me and I can feel the echoes of my wail bouncing off the surrounding landscape. Despite the blood in my eyes, I can see, or rather feel, where he is. Something snaps inside me, and the pain fades. With no sight, the world becomes an echoed red image in my mind, and I run to the man on the ground and slam my foot into his head once, twice, three times. Eventually, I lose count. The head caves in, and instead of revulsion, I feel joy.

My joy fades when my leg slips on the gore, and I fall back. I fail to catch myself and roughly hit my head against the ground. The only thought in my mind is that I want more.

Chapter 6: Aaron

Sunlight burns my eyes as I open them. Even though I know it's morning, I find myself wanting a few more minutes to sleep. I try to roll over but stop when something cold and hard pushes into my side. Curious, I open my eyes and take a closer look. Seeing a black handle, I realize it belongs to a gun. My first instinct is to panic, but then I remember where I am. The dreams I was having a few minutes before fade, and reality sets in. With a sigh, I get up, knowing I won't be able to sleep anymore.

As I leave my family's room, I do a quick headcount to see who's still asleep. That's when I notice that my dad is missing. He volunteers for patrol duty often, so I'm not worried. His dedication to patrol shouldn't surprise me, since he has always focused on his work. He means well by it—he always has. In some ways, I guess he has always been doing it to protect us. Now, his dedication is just more obvious.

Since it's still too early to try to do any work, I decide I'll go talk to him. It'll be nice to figure out what he's thinking. My father is easy to find. A basic perimeter sweep brings me to him. He's perched on the now-destroyed stairs, the only entry into our new home. As I approach him, my dad speaks to me without turning around.

"Hey, Aaron. Up already?"

Memories of my parents saying they have eyes in the backs of their heads come back to me, and I smile. "Hey, Dad. I was up, so I figured I'd talk to you about what we need to do now that the top floor is secure."

"Well, I was thinking of doing some renovations. We've managed to get along well these past few days. As things calm down, tempers and personalities will clash if we're all in the same small space. My walk around the perimeter gave me a couple of ideas of things to do that will expand our living space. The most important thing is building a way into our sister apartment, which shares the stairway with us. I checked it out earlier this morning, and it's as secure as this one. There's also office space in the store below our space here, and it's raised high enough to be safe. If we remove the stairs and put a hole in the floor up here, it should give us a little extra space."

"Sounds like you have your plan pretty figured out. How long would it take you to get those spaces ready?"

He looks at me. "Well, it depends on how much help I have, but if we don't run into any trouble securing the areas, it'll only take one day. Making them livable after that will take much longer. What are you planning to do today?"

"Well, I was looking at our supplies, and we need more. I was planning on recruiting some people to come with me to the supermarket. We would raid what food and supplies we could there." Telling my father my plan is risky, especially since it involves leaving our sanctuary. My hope is that he's grown to trust my judgment these past few days. Looking at him, I see some apprehension in his expression. He looks at me, and I find it hard to read him.

"Suppose we'll both have a busy day today," he says. "Why don't you start waking everyone up. There's a lot of work to do, and we're losing daylight. Make sure to ask if anyone wants to help me. If anyone volunteers, send them here. I'll stay put. Oh, and be safe out there, okay?"

Smiling, I nod. "Yeah, of course I'll be safe, Dad."

Following my father's advice, I go through the apartment and wake everyone up, starting with my family. It only takes a few minutes for everyone to gather in the room closest to the stairs. This room has become our unofficial meeting room, and whenever we gather together, it's in here. Once we're all gathered and everyone has their attention on me, I begin speaking.

"Hello, I want to thank everyone for their strength these past few days. We've all pulled together and created a place where we don't have to fear attack. If you're like me, you're starting to feel a little constrained by our current living conditions. My father has a plan to expand our space three times over. He'd appreciate any help he could get. Aside from our living conditions, there's also the matter of food. We currently have enough supplies to last a few months. It'd be best to scavenge the supermarket for anything edible before others get the same idea. My plan is to go myself, but anyone willing to brave it with me is welcome company. Anyone who's interested in either task, come talk to me and I'll fill you in on the details."

As I look around the room, I expect to see excitement and some apprehension. When I see that many of the faces looking at me are filled with annoyance, I'm shocked. All the adults, aside from my mother and Jason's grandfather, look at me with reluctance and flat out disrespect. They still see me as a child.

"What do you or your father know about anything?" Jason's grandmother says. "Why would we risk ourselves when there's no need? You say we don't have enough food, but how can I be sure that you're not trying to trick us into doing your dangerous work? As far as helping your father goes, my family already has a place to live. Why would we go through the effort of helping you make a home for yourself?"

As I stare at Jason's grandmother, I'm filled with anger. How could she be so foolish and blind? She's lucky she ended up with my family; most people would have thrown her out into the streets to die. Before I reply to her, Jason's grandfather cuts in.

"Honey, you're being very disrespectful. If it wasn't for this kid and his family, we wouldn't be alive. We owe it to them to help. We're all in this together, and being selfish is dumb."

Jason's grandmother throws him a venomous look, but she backs down. Jason and his grandfather have always been the only sensible members of that family. Without them, it would have been too risky to invite Jason's family here. Calming myself down, I reply. "Thank you. Before we start our work, I want to see if anyone else has ideas about what needs to be done around here."

Silence is my answer, and as I survey the room, I start to conclude that no one has anything to say. That's until my mother stands and walks forward. "I can think of one thing that might be useful. We don't know enough about the disease that drives Palemen. For all we know, it could be curable or we could be immune. It would be wise to capture and examine someone who's become infected to learn more."

My mother's idea is a very good one. Having a solid understanding about how the disease transfers and functions is invaluable. Palemen are incurable monsters to me; I never thought to learn more about them or the disease they carry. Now I start to doubt my presumptions. It's quite possible that this disease will die out or that there will be a way to combat it without the use of violence. The one thing I'm unsure of is how she plans to study the Palemen.

"You're right that knowing more would be helpful, but what are you planning?" I ask.

"Well, it might seem crazy, but I need to get someone who's been affected by the disease. They also need to be alive, since it's the most efficient way of collecting information. Also, I need someone to help me get supplies for the examination. If anyone's interested in helping me, talk to me after we're done here."

After my mom finishes, she sits back down. Scanning the room, I see that, aside from my mother, the adults have looks of disgust on their faces. Why is it possible that my friends and I can see what needs to be done, but our parents can't? Age may beget wisdom, but it also degrades critical thinking, I decide. No one else speaks, so I prepare to close the meeting. Before I can say anything, Jason speaks up.

"I'll do anything if it helps us against the Palemen. Let me know what you need, Stephanie."

"Thank you, Jason," I say. "Unless someone else has some input, I say we get our days started. If you want to talk to me, I'll be packing supplies for my supermarket trip."

Smiling, I walk away, glad there was no heavy opposition in the meeting. Next, I get to work, starting with a list of supplies I'll need. It isn't long before I'm joined by my sister Melany. She tells me she's going to join me.

"Melany, I appreciate the help, but are Mom and Dad okay with you going?"

Melany smiles and answers me. "Yeah, Mom said I'd be safe with you, and I want to get out of here. I haven't contributed to our home yet, and I want to. Besides, if I go with you to get supplies, I can decide what to bring back."

Smiling, I pat my sister on the head; I know she has no reason to lie to me, so I trust that my parents gave her the okay. She isn't wrong. If she comes, she'll be able to grab any books or supplies to keep her entertained for the next few months. Food will be our primary target, but without entertainment, we'll go crazy with boredom before we starve.

Not long after Melany starts helping me, Brian joins us. There's no reason to ask him about his motives. If he's here, that's enough for me. With three sets of hands, we finish the packing and are on our way.

We walk a few miles, and after checking to see that there are no Palemen around, I stop my sister and friend. They look at me, confused.

"Sorry to stop you guys, but I wanted to fill you in on the plan. As you know, we're heading to raid the old supermarket. It should still have supplies since it was converted to a trade market after the power went out. If things go well, I was hoping we could also stop by some other places. My old martial arts gym is close to the supermarket. My hope is that it's still supplied with melee weapons. Some are for show, but the majority are authentic—and sharp. While we're out, I also wanted to check up on Luke. I'm sure he's fine, but it'd be nice to confirm it."

Brian looks at me and gives me a quick nod. He's okay with both stops. Melany also remains silent, which is normal for her. Convincing them was easier than I anticipated.

After finishing our preparations, we leave the apartment and start walking toward the supermarket. The walk is uneventful. We avoid the Palemen we run into, and unlike a few days ago, there are no fires or people screaming. All that remains of the chaos is the bodies of the dead littering the streets.

When we reach the supermarket, I see the shopping carts all over the parking lot. It's then that I realize we don't have a way to bring the supplies back home. My face flushes with embarrassment, and I stare at Brian and Melany. Out of nowhere, Brian speaks up.

"Um… how about kid-carriers?" Brian halfway mutters his sentence, and I look at him, confused. After an awkward second, he clarifies. "I figured it out on the way over. Why don't we use kid-carriers that you attach to bikes? I'm willing to bet that there are some bikes and carriers here. They might be our best bet for moving supplies. Also, on a different note, pet foods are edible, and people wouldn't have thought to grab them. So if you want, we can grab all the pet food. We might find we need it to ration our supplies. We don't know how long we'll be stuck in the apartment." Brian avoids making eye contact with me as he's speaking. Both of his ideas are brilliant.

"Brian, you're a genius. Let's get to work." We start working on the task at hand and gather supplies. Brian was right about people leaving behind the bikes and dog food. With the bikes and carriers, we manage to make several trips to the apartments in only a few hours. We clear the store out of anything useful, and we find ourselves with plenty of time to go to my martial arts gym.

We decide to leave the bikes in the storefront under our apartment. They work well for carrying large amounts of supplies, but their maneuverability is rather poor. We all agree that walking to the martial arts gym will be safer.

As we walk to the gym, the sun shines down on me. Even under these circumstances, I find myself enjoying the exposure to the outside. The apartment is safe, but the windows are small, and not much light comes in. If I'm going to be inside the apartment for the next few months or years, I'll definitely have to find a way to the roof.

The sun also helps us spot any groups of Palemen, so staying a safe distance is easy. Only when I notice a group of two Palemen on their knees do I become curious and want to risk getting closer. Before now, I've only seen Palemen milling about. From where we are, I can't see what they're doing.

"Hey, do you see that?" I whisper while pointing. Brian and Melany look toward the Paleman, and I can see that their curiosity is piqued as well.

"You want to check it out? It looks like they're digging or something," Brian replies, and I nod. We move toward the Palemen. As we approach, I see what they are doing, and my stomach churns. Beneath the Palemen lies a body. The Palemen above it have ripped open the stomach and are busy chewing on the man's intestines. It all makes sense: the Palemen are still living, so of course they have to eat. Before I turn away in disgust, some movement catches my eye.

Behind the Palemen, hidden in some bushes, is a little girl. She's waving but not making a sound. Seeing the danger she's in, I immediately decide that these two Palemen have to die. Not wanting to draw in more Palemen, I pull out my hatchet and combat knife. I signal Brian and Melany to stay put, but Brian shakes his head and pulls out a homemade garrote wire. With his help, we should be able to take them out at the same time.

The Palemen are easy prey, since they're kneeling. By the time they notice me and Brian, we're only a few feet away. My hatchet lodges into the first Paleman's head before he can respond. Brian pins the second Paleman to the ground with his boot, then wraps the wire around his neck. I watch the two struggle, ready to interfere if Brian loses control. He doesn't, and after a moment, the Paleman stops moving, and Brian steps off the creature.

"Aaron, behind you," Brian says, pointing. I turn around to see that the Paleman I used my hatchet on is still alive. It must not have made it all the way through his skull. He's crawling toward me, but I'm not afraid. As I move to the Paleman's side, intending to finish him off, I hear him let out a moan. Dismissing it as a dying creature's sound, I ignore it until the man moves toward me. Startled, I jump back. My curiosity demands I examine this further, but I realize that the hiding child must be terrified.

Taking a quick peek at the girl, I see that she's still hiding in the bush, and I also see that she has her eyes covered. Wanting to help her, I decide to finish off the Paleman. My knife slams into his neck, and the Paleman's life spills onto the ground. After I'm sure he's dead, I pull my weapons from the creature and clean them on the ground.

With the creature gone, I walk over to the girl, joined by the others.

"Hey there. I'm sorry if we scared you, but it's safe to come out now if you want." As I say this, I look at the little girl, and I see that she's frightened. How can I blame her for being scared? She can't be older than ten or eleven. For a second, I think she's going to refuse to come out, but then she gets out and comes toward me. She starts crying, and before I can react, she runs and wraps her arms around me. Not knowing what else to do, I pick her up and hold her in my arms, letting her cry into my shoulder.

"It's okay. It's all going to be okay now. You're safe. I'm going to look after you now, so don't worry."

The girl cries in my arms for a while, and I hold her until she calms down. After I set her down, I decide to try and find out what happened to her.

"So, kiddo, how did you end up here? Did you get separated from your family?"

The girl immediately tears up, and I think she might start crying again. She calms herself down, though, and answers me. "I don't have a family. I'm an orphan, and ever since the power went out, I've been on my own."

My jaw drops at her words. How could she have managed to survive all this time on her own, without someone figuring out she was alone? Now that I know this girl has no family, there's only one choice. If she agrees, she'll come with us to the apartment.

"Tell you what: come with me. I'll look after you, if you want, and take you back to the apartments that my family and a few others live in. There's plenty of food, and it's safe from the Palemen." The girl looks at us. Realizing that she doesn't know our names, I say, "By the way, I'm Aaron, and this is my sister, Melany, and friend, Brian."

The girl looks at us, appearing a little distrustful. After a few seconds, she nods. "Okay, I'll come with you, but you have to promise you won't leave me behind if we get into trouble."

Smiling, I reply to her. "I would rather die than leave you behind."

She smiles back. "Okay, I believe you. My name is Evelyn." Her 180-degree turn from distrust to trust amuses me, and I chuckle. She's still a child, and though I'm sure she doesn't trust us, I know she's ready to.

"Alright then, Evelyn, we're out here because we're doing a mission for the people we live with. Is it okay if you come with us? If you do come with us, you'll have to be quiet and stick close to us. If you would rather be safe, we can take you straight back to the apartments."

Evelyn shakes her head fervently. "No. I'm coming with you."

Smiling, I nod, and without another word, we start moving. After a few minutes of walking, Evelyn comes up to me and grabs my hand. We walk hand-in-hand until we reach the gym.

The front of the gym has glass walls, which are intact. Scouting inside, I see that there is one Paleman loitering about. Remembering the moans from the dying Palemen earlier, I decide to try out my theory. Telling the others to stay put, I make my way into the gym.

Avoiding the Paleman inside, I make my way to the display case, where a pair of Dao swords hangs. These swords always caught my eye when I trained here in the past. Now I can own them. I open the case, pull out the swords, and test their edges. Finding them razor-sharp, I smile with satisfaction. They're well balanced and deadly. I'll enjoy owning these weapons.

Turning around, I see that the Paleman inside the gym has noticed me. My experience earlier led me to think that Palemen might use their moans like sonar. To test this theory, I run to the Paleman and move around him, silently stopping behind him. After a second, the Paleman lets out a moan, then quickly turns to face me.

So I was right. Smiling, I prepare to strike the Paleman down. When I look into the eyes of the creature, I ready my sword. Stopping myself right before the blades impact, I realize I recognize this Paleman.

"Luke?" Though the eyes are red and the skin is pale, there's no mistaking it. The Paleman standing in front of me is my friend Luke. Luke lunges at me, and I'm forced to jump back. My brain tells me he's past saving, but my body won't listen. There's no helping him, but how can I kill him now in cold blood?

Tears come to my eyes as the realization hits me. As my vision starts to blur, Luke charges me. If I don't kill him now, I'll be at a disadvantage and I'll be scratched—or worse. My sword arm readies, and I swing the blade. It goes through Luke's neck as I step to the side. His body and head fall to the floor.

Tears start falling from my eyes, and I want to fall with them. If Luke was here, there's a good chance his family came with him. His father was an active member of this gym, so coming here to stay safe would make sense.

Trying to think through the grief, I realize the best place to hide would be the bathroom. My body feels heavy as I move through the gym. As I open the door, I'm not sure what I'm expecting. What I find causes my swords to clatter to the ground. My stomach churns, and I fall to my knees and vomit. Scattered around the bathroom is the gore of Luke's family. Their bodies are torn to shreds, but for some reason, their faces remained untouched. Their expressions are full of pain and sadness. The cold, dead eyes haunt me.

Retching, I crawl away from the bathroom.

Is this my future? Will I kill everyone I love while they cower in some bathroom or shower, waiting while they cling to their humanity and their lives? Is that what this world has come to?

My thoughts spin out of control, and I collapse onto the floor. Someone's arms wrap around me, and I think it's Luke here to drag me into death with the rest of his family. When I try to fight him off, I find that I'm too weak.

With great effort, I manage to turn over and see the face of my attacker. Instead of seeing the cold, red eyes of Luke, I see soft, green eyes. They are sad but also full of hope. As my vision clears of tears, I recognize the person hugging me as Evelyn.

One life saved, one life condemned. This world is cruel and dark, but hope isn't gone.

Chapter 7: Stephanie

My mind wanders as I stare at the empty street below our apartment. A Paleman breaks my concentration when he stumbles into my view. As I watch the creature wander, I think back to the first time I observed one.

It may have only been a few days, but it feels like it's been much longer. My life has regained stability since the infection broke out. Despite that, I still mourn the days when I was a nurse practitioner and my life had a purpose. Now I'm not sure what to do. If we're going to be trapped inside this apartment until we starve to death, I'd rather not have made it here. Survival is not enough for me.

My worries once again make me wonder how this disease functions. Aside from the obvious symptoms like the loss of melanin production, blindness, hypersalivation, and insanity, we know nothing about this disease. Nothing in my medical training was anything like this.

Whatever this disease is, I'm certain that it's a weaponized virus or bacteria. It's the only thing that makes sense. This disease could've originated in nature, but it seems too refined for that to be the case.

As I watch the Paleman walk around a corner and out of sight, I decide that it's time to go to sleep. My desire is to learn more about this disease so I can know for sure if there's a way to cure it or not. Without an infected patient to examine, though, there's very little I can do. That's why I resolve to go to bed tonight and face the problem of learning more about the disease tomorrow.

On the way to the cot my husband built for us, I run across Brian. He nods but refrains from saying anything to me. Part of me still sees Aaron and his friends as children. After hearing everything they've done and been through, I know that's not true. Aaron and his friends have done more to preserve our lives than me, my husband, or the other parents.

They are so young, but somehow, they're the ones who've taken on the burden of surviving. Part of me rejects their willingness to take responsibility. It should be the job of a parent to protect the child, not the other way around. Yet I know it's too late to change anything.

Seven months ago, Aaron was an adolescent, and I could dictate when he had to be home. Now forced to grow up, he and his friends are responsible for the lives of three families. He's growing up too fast, and I wish I had some way to remove the stress from him.

As I walk through the dark rooms of the apartment building, I'm careful to be silent. It takes a few minutes of weaving around the sleeping bodies, but I reach the cot my husband and I share. I find it empty, but I'm not surprised. My husband has always had his obsessions, and now, patrolling our home is one of them.

While I'm glad he's found something helpful to do, I wish he was around to talk more. I suppose I could always go and find him.

Marcus almost never sleeps anymore, and I miss him lying next to me. Even though I long for him to be by my side, I understand why he isn't. Ever since the power first went out and he sustained his hip injury, he's had a hard time sleeping. He's always been a strong man who didn't balk at pain.

Even now, I'm the only one who knows about his hip. In all honesty, he's lucky to be as functional as he is. It might be painful, but he can still walk. He'll never run again without surgery to correct his hip, but it should remain stable if he's careful with it.

Thoughts blaze through my mind as I lie on my back and try to fall asleep. My consciousness drifts and I dream of my life before the power went out.

When my eyes open in the morning, my dreams fade, and I forget them like they are a distant memory. I turn to see what disturbed my sleep, and I see my son Aaron sitting next to my cot. He looks like he's about to try waking me up.

Willing my grogginess away, I sit up. "Good morning, Aaron. Did you need something?"

Aaron jumps, startled, but recovers. "Morning, Mom. And yes, I do need something." My son starts talking and catches me up on everything. His plan to gather everyone together and ask for help is good. As we wake up, my daughters and I talk about what needs to be done to help us survive in the apartments.

Thinking back to last night, I remember my desire to learn more about the creatures. Aaron and I decide that meeting will be a good opportunity to speak about it, so I try to imagine the best things to say.

My mind is so busy during the gathering that I don't hear much of what's said. When the chance to bring forward anything else comes up, I take it. As I speak, I look at everyone. I'm not surprised to see horror and shock in many of the adults' faces. The younger members of our group surprise me when I see curiosity—and even desire to help—in their faces.

When the gathering ends, I look around for someone to come forward and help me. Jason said he would help, but he hasn't come over to me yet.

As everyone starts to leave the gathering room, I start to lose hope, thinking that Jason's family has prevented him from helping. Before I decide to leave, Jason walks up to me, followed shortly by Alexis.

Relief floods me when Jason fulfills his promise to help and I realize that his parents aren't preventing him from keeping his word. With his and Alexis's help, I should be able to move my study forward significantly. My best-case scenario would be learning what causes the disease today. I'd also like to learn how to avoid and cure it. As the two volunteers walk toward me, I contemplate the ramifications of any discoveries for our small community.

"Hey, sorry to make you wait. I had to, um, talk to my family. Anyway, what can I do to help you learn more about the Palemen?"

Before answering, I look at Alexis to see if she has anything to say. After I see that she's going to remain silent, I think about what the best thing for them to do is. To study a Paleman, I'll need one, so my choice is easy.

"Well," I say, "all I need from you two is a live Paleman. Without one, I can't study what causes their symptoms. If you're willing to capture one, I'd be very grateful. Also, if you wanted to continue helping me after it's captured, I'd appreciate it. The work might be more difficult, and I can't promise that you won't be exposed to the disease. Also, since it involves blood and tissue samples, it might be a little gory. So if you don't think you can handle it, then I understand."

Jason looks at me, and I can see pain in his eyes. He may hate this disease, but I don't think he wants to see anything or anyone suffer more than he has to. "I'd be glad to help capture one for you, but I don't think I can help you past that."

I nod and tell him I understand. After the formalities, Jason tells me his plan to capture one of the infected, and I agree with it. With his task assigned, Jason leaves to fulfill it.

Alexis surprises me by staying behind. Before I can ask her what she wants, she speaks. "I understand that you need a patient to examine, but Jason can take care of it himself. What I want is to help you in another way. Having only one person treat wounds is foolish. My hope is to learn from you, and I want to start today."

Alexis is speaking to me so frankly it catches me off guard. She's not wrong. Having two people who can take care of our group's medical needs would be smart. Seeing no reason not to train her, I decide that I will.

"Okay, I'll teach you what I know. You need to understand, though, that it won't be easy. It took me years to learn what I know as a nurse. The best approach would be to teach you how to deal with trauma and wounds, then move to other fields if possible. If I'm going to train you, we'll need some supplies. The supplies I need to examine our patient and the supplies to train you should be in the same place."

Alexis looks at me, and I can tell that she's glad I agreed.

Smiling, I continue. "You'll need to come with me to the high school. There, they should have some equipment in one of the labs. Since you went to the school, I figured you could lead me to the right lab. Also, while we're there, we can pick up some books to train you in anatomy. I want to leave as soon as possible, so why don't you gather whatever you need for the trip and meet me by the door?"

Alexis nods, turns, and leaves to gather her things. Not wanting to make her wait, I start gathering things for the trip, too. I'm so busy that when my daughter Melany taps my shoulder, it startles me.

"Hey, Mom. Sorry to interrupt, but I wanted to ask you if it's okay if I go with Aaron to the store. Dad already said it would be fine." At first I'm hesitant, but I force myself to remember that things are different now. A few months ago, I would have been upset if Melany asked to do something this dangerous. Now I realize that danger is a part of our lives.

Despite what I know, I have to let her go. Saying no would make the other families less willing to let their own children help the group. Plus, she would probably go anyway.

In the world we live in now, my daughter is an adult. Childhood is a luxury, and with our world destroyed, I don't think anyone can afford it.

"It's fine if you go," I say. "Be careful. Aaron will do his best to take care of you, but make sure you keep him from doing anything too dangerous."

My daughter smiles and laughs. It's good to see her happy, but I do worry about them getting into trouble. All I can do, though, is trust that she understands the risk of going outside.

"Mom, don't worry. I'll be able to take care of myself. I promise we'll be as safe as possible out there. We all know better than to risk ourselves unless we have to." Melany's words calm me, and I find my worry dissolving as I hug her goodbye. They'll be in the back of my mind until they return, but I trust them to stay safe.

I grab a sweater and put it into my bag, then throw the bag across my back. The bag has far more supplies than I'll need for the trip, but I'd rather be over-prepared than under-prepared.

Alexis surprises me by meeting me by my bed. I suppose she finished packing before I did. She checks to see if I'm ready, and after telling her that I am, we head out of the apartment together.

We walk through our now-empty town, and as we do, I look at the vacant windows and abandoned streets, trying to ignore the bodies. It's only been a little while, and already the town has decayed so much. Without people to maintain it, how much longer will it last?

The water towers won't hold forever, so I make a mental note to set up some rain traps on the roof this week. Silencing my mind, I focus on making it through our abandoned city.

We manage to make it to the school unmolested by any Palemen. After climbing through a broken window, Alexis takes the lead and guides me to what I presume will be the chemistry lab. As we go through the halls, I remember my own time in high school, and I feel a pang of guilt and pain. My children will never again go to school. There's no way they can have an easy, safe life anymore.

Alexis stops and points to a door. "The lab is through these doors," she whispers, "but there's a Paleman in there."

Making my way to the door, I look through the glass that's at the top. Inside the classroom, I see several microscopes and books we could use. There's also a Paleman standing by an open window. He seems to be static and almost calm. When I look at him, it's almost as if he's watching something outside in the field across from the classroom.

Since the Paleman appears still, I decide it's worth the risk of going inside. Putting my finger to my mouth, I signal Alexis to be silent, and she nods. We open the door and sneak through. Weaving my way through the lab, I head to the nearest microscope. Before leaving the apartments, I told Alexis her priority would be finding anatomy, chemistry, and, if she could, pharmacology textbooks, so she heads toward a bookcase.

When I reach the microscope, I examine it. As I look over it, I see that it's a manual microscope, not a digital one. This is what I need. I pick the tool off the table and place it into my bag. Realizing I'll also need clean slides for the microscope, I look around some more and find a small box full of them under the table.

As I slide them into the bag, I'm startled by a loud and continuous scream. The noise is disturbing, and it raises the hairs on the back of my neck. Without thinking, I look around for the source of the noise, forcing myself to stay calm. I see the Paleman at the window. He's leaning out of it and screaming in an unearthly wail. Alexis catches my eye, and I can see that it's time for us to leave.

Before I can even start to turn around, the Paleman turns toward me. His face has a sickening smile on it, and blood drips from the corner of his mouth. As I watch in horror, the previously empty field across from the school starts to fill with Palemen.

In horror, I realize that the scream the Paleman in front of me issued was a call. There's more to this disease than I understand, but I know we have to leave now. As I'm about to scream for Alexis to run, I see her darting toward the Paleman. I'm frozen with fear and unable to move.

Alexis grabs a stray beaker and throws it at the creature's face, and it shatters in his eyes. The Paleman doesn't even flinch. Unaffected, Alexis picks up a chair and swings it at the creature. The chair strikes the Paleman and knocks him back against the window.

I understand now what she's trying to do, and my muscles unfreeze as I realize that I have to help her. Running forward, I grab a chair. Together, we beat back the Paleman and try to force him over the window's edge. As I swing the chair, I see the creature's face up close.

Because of my husband's job as a pastor, I've seen dozens of dead people. Their faces always look empty, soulless. As I stare into the crazed eyes of the man in front of me, I recognize a look of death. Whatever this disease has done to its victim, there's no longer a soul in charge. Only pure madness remains, and it terrifies me.

Tears fall from my eyes as I swing desperately to kill the creature in front of me. Finally, Alexis connects, and the creature stumbles back and loses its balance. Time slows as I watch it fall. Its eyes meet mine as it hits the ground. The beast's head hits the ground last, and it cracks open.

All I can do is stand and look at the dead man. I should feel guilty for what I've done, but all I can feel is relief that it's dead. Alexis pulls me from my shock when she shakes me and screams, "We need to go, now!"

My gaze shifts to outside of the school. The formerly empty field and schoolyard now have dozens of Palemen. Alexis looks at me, and I nod, pulling myself together.

We run from the room and through the school halls. We go to the window we came through and are lucky to find it free of any immediate danger. Even when we are outside, we run, desperate to get as far away from the school as possible.

Only when we are far away and out of breath do we stop.

"What the hell was that thing?!" Alexis says between gasps of air.

Taking a minute for my breath to catch up, I think of what to tell her. "It must be a variation of the disease. Of course, it's hard to tell, but I think that it was able to call out to other infected and bring them to it. Finishing a study of these people is even more important now."

Alexis agrees with me, and we make our way to the apartment. When we arrive, we find that Jason has successfully captured a

Paleman. With his help, we tie it to a table in the basement. Since Jason managed to knock the creature unconscious, it doesn't struggle.

Once we secure the creature to my makeshift examination table, I confirm what I already know.

"The patient is unresponsive to light and has an irregular eye and skin color." Alexis stands behind me, taking notes. "Without better machinery, I can only guess that the skin and eyes are affected by a melanin deficiency. This alone suggests that the disease affects the brain stem. The medulla and other parts of the brain stem are likely the targets of the disease."

Checking the creature's pulse, I find it lower than expected. "Patient's lowered heart rate also suggest a brain stem infection." As I say this, the creature starts to wake up. Being cautious, I step back and decide to watch its response. As it wakes up, it starts to struggle. I inch forward and reexamine its vitals, finding the heart rate low. As I finish taking the vitals, I hear a loud snap, so I immediately stop what I'm doing and jump back. Looking to the source of the snap, I see that the Paleman has broken its own arm with the strain of trying to escape. The bone is exposed, and blood leaks out as he continues to struggle. If I don't stop the bleeding, he'll die in ten or twenty minutes. There's no way for me to put this creature back to sleep or end its pain. Knowing there's nothing I can do, I force the guilt and pain away and continue my examination.

"Patient shows elevated strength and loss of protective motor function, as well as a total disregard for pain. These symptoms would suggest a raised level of adrenals. They would also suggest the brain stem as the sight of infection."

"Stephanie, does it need to be alive?" Alexis's question startles me. I understand why she's asking me. Seeing this creature moving around and trying to escape, uncaring of the wound to its arm, is unnerving.

"No, not at this point, but I'll need to examine its brain, so we can't shoot it. Also, I have no anesthetics or means to kill it." Alexis nods, and without another word, she pulls out a hunting knife. I'm not sure where she got it from or what she intends to do with it. As I watch, Alexis walks up to the creature and puts the knife to its chest, right above the heart. Before I can say anything, she plunges the knife into its rib cage, and I watch as the creature bleeds out.

Alexis's willingness to kill the creature shocks me, but I'm thankful for it. Without pausing, I grab some microscope slides and get six samples of blood: two of my own blood and four of the creature's, two of which come from its arm while the other two come from its mouth.

"Alexis, while I'm examining these blood slides, please go get a slide of blood from the dog. Don't worry: I'll tell you what I find when you come back." Alexis nods and goes to do the task I asked of her. Every minute the creature is dead is another minute of decay, so I work fast. It isn't long before I make up the slides and mix some of the samples.

When I look at the first slide, I see unmixed blood from the Paleman's arm. It's then that I determine the disease is a bacterial infection. From what I can see on this slide, the bacteria in the blood is dead or inactive. To confirm this, I look at a slide that is a mix of my blood and the creature's arm blood. Sure enough, the infection isn't attacking my blood cells.

The second set of samples is the mixture of the blood from the creature's gums and our blood. Aaron told me about the bite wounds and how they transfer infections. What I see confirms this. The blood sample from the creature's mouth is rife with active bacteria. This shocks me; the infection takes over my blood in less than a minute. If you're bitten, there's nothing you could do except immediate amputation, and even that might not work.

As I finish up with these slides, Alexis comes back into the room, and I immediately take the blood sample from the dog and mix it with the infectious blood. When I study it, I find that the bacterium doesn't attack the dog's blood. That, at least, is a relief. While looking at this, I catch Alexis up on what I found, and she listens. At the end, she asks me, "Can't we cure it, then? All you need to get rid of bacteria is an antibiotic, right?"

She isn't wrong; antibiotics can help the body fight off a bacterial infection. But I'm not sure the person would be cured after the bacterium subsides.

"Well it's more complicated than that. You might be able to fight off the disease with a massive dose of antibiotics. If they do any brain damage before the infection is through, there's no fixing that. So the people who are already infected have very little chance of recovery."

Alexis looks at me, and I can tell she isn't surprised. "So what do we do now?"

"Autopsy, but first, let's allow the bacterium to die out. It shouldn't take long," I reply. As we wait, we go over the information we've learned and check over the Paleman's body several times. After we triple-check the blood in the gums to make sure the bacterium is dead, I start my autopsy.

Without proper tools, the procedure is bloody. Despite this, I do manage to extract the brain and other organs undamaged. All the organs, aside from the adrenal gland, are the proper size. The adrenal gland is swollen to about three times its normal size, which suggests a slow, continuous release of adrenals into the creatures. This would explain some of their heightened senses and the strength.

The brain is where the damage is clearest. Most of the brain remains untouched and appears normal. Only when I look at the brain stem does the damage become clear. It's black and decayed. Alexis looks at me when we see this, and I can tell that she thinks the same thing I do. There's no cure; there's no survival. If you're infected, you're dead.

Our only hope now is that these creatures die before we do.

Chapter 8: Aaron

As I wake up and see the familiar sight of the ceiling, I find myself thinking about the last two months. At first, I thought I would grow tired of living in such a small space. With my father working on making our living area nicer, it has been very bearable.

Evelyn also keeps me occupied on most days. My parents have helped me care for her, but the bulk of the responsibility has been mine. Without the distractions of a job or other old-world worries, it's much easier to raise her as my child. She even started calling me "Dad" about a month ago. Nostalgia hits me, and I realize again for the thousandth time how different things are. If we still had power, I would be working and going to college. As I'm thinking of my adopted daughter, a tear rolls down my face.

Today will be the last day I see her and my other family as well. It was a week ago today that I first noticed the shortage of food. My mother predicted that it would take three years for the infection to run its course. While the news that the Palemen had a short lifespan was good, the prospects of having to survive three years in this apartment was a hard idea to swallow.

Even if we managed to grow food on the roof, our current supplies wouldn't stretch far enough. The only way to ensure the survival of our families is if some of our members leave the safety of our apartment. I know I'm the only member of my family that can afford to leave. As a medic, my mother is too important, and my father is too injured to stand a chance of survival. Melany could come along as well, but I would rather she didn't. As for Sarah, she stands almost no chance if she left. She's too gentle. She wouldn't be able to kill a Paleman, even if her life depended on it.

Today, I'll have to convince four others to come with me. My hopes are that some adults will volunteer, but based on past experience, I'm certain this won't happen. Jason's family has proven to be resistant to any risk, and I know Jason is the only member of his family that might leave. Brian's family is no different. Even if I count on Brian coming with me, we are still one person short of what we need for the others to survive.

Sitting up, I get dressed, making sure not to wake Evelyn, who is sleeping in her bed. Once I'm dressed, I tiptoe out of my room and am startled to see Brian sitting outside. From the looks of things, he has been there for a while.

"Hey, Aaron." Not wanting to wake Evelyn, I make a sign telling him to be silent. He nods, and together we walk toward a window and climb onto the roof.

"Hey, Brian, what's up? If you needed something, you could've woken me up."

"Yeah, but you looked like you could use the sleep. Besides, I didn't mind waiting." Brian is pretty awkward, but I'm glad he decided to let me sleep. The last thing I need today is to be grumpy.

"So anyway, I wanted to talk to you about our food situation, Aaron."

"Let me stop you there," I say. "I already know what's going on and was actually on my way to tell you about it. I'm planning on leaving, and I want you to come with me."

Brian looks at me, confused for a second, and then smiles. "Well that was easy. I was actually coming to you for the same reason. My parents know that I'll be leaving, not that they cared."

Before I know what's happening, I find myself laughing. With Brian on my side, the task of convincing others suddenly becomes much easier.

"Well that's great. How about we gather the others? I'm sure we can get Jason to come with us, and then we'll only need one other."

Brian looks at me somberly, and I'm confused. Why the sudden change?

"What about Evelyn?" he asks. "I figured she would be coming along. With Jason, the four of us leaving should be enough. I get that you might be scared to bring her along, but think about how it would make her feel. She sees you as her dad. You would break her heart if you left her behind. The three of us should be more than enough to protect her, and it's not like she can't handle herself. She did take care of herself for months before the infection hit."

Brian's remarks remind me of my doubts. He isn't wrong. Leaving her behind would devastate her, but I'm not sure taking her with us would be a better option. She may be tough, but if there's a chance for her to grow up in safety, that might be the better option.

"You might be right," I say, "but I'll have to think about it. Either way, we should call a meeting to see if we can get others to join us."

Brian agrees, and we go to wake the others and gather them for a meeting. Before I wake my family, I want to find Jason to have him gather his. Luckily, it doesn't take me long to find him patrolling the perimeter of the apartments. When he sees me, he waves and says, "Hey, what's up? I saw Brian walk by a second ago. He looked all serious."

"Hey, man. We are going to hold a meeting. You mind getting your family together?" He looks at me and nods. Walking off, I'm not sure if he knows what's going on, but I'm glad he didn't ask questions. The sooner we hold this meeting, the better. After watching him for a second, I turn around and head to where my family stays. On the way through the apartments, I run across my father as he's doing his usual patrols.

"Hey, Dad. I'm on my way to wake everyone up. I've already told Jason and Brian to gather their families."

My dad nods, like he was expecting this. "I know why you're calling a gathering. Come to me after you wake everyone. I'll be by the entrance. There are some things I need to tell you before you talk to everyone." Nodding, I part ways with my father.

Waking my family is quick work. Once I've explained what we're doing, I leave them, heading for my father. I find him exactly where he said he would be. As I come up, he turns to me and says, "Hey, Aaron. I'm sorry to pull you away from your gathering, but I needed to talk to you. You must be gathering everyone to tell them about the food shortage."

At first I'm surprised, but then I remember how Brian also knew what was going on. I realize I was being foolish by letting myself think I'd be the only one who knew about our problem.

"While on patrol one night," my dad says, "I went over the supplies and I noticed the shortage. I already talked with all the adults here. I was hoping they would join me in leaving. Nothing I could do would convince a single one of them. They all had reasons, but it boiled down to lies and excuses." My father pauses to rub his eyes.

"I'm guessing you're planning on leaving," he continues, "and I'm sure you can get several people to come with you. Aaron, people need to leave, and as much as I wish it could be me and the other adults, I know that'll never happen. You have a shot at surviving all this, but I need you to promise me something. Be smart, don't get into fights you don't need to, and don't risk anything unless you have to. You'll be responsible for more lives than you know."

"Of course I'll be careful, Dad. I know I'll have to account for other people. You forget how much has changed since the outbreak. I'm not the same person."

"You're the same, Aaron. You might act different, but your behaviors are the same now as they were when you were a child. Melany wanted to come with me, so I presume she'll want to come with you."

I'd assumed that Melany would want to come with me. She's quiet, but I know that she feels the same as I do. She would want to go so that our family could have a better chance of surviving this. While I'm mulling over this, my father continues.

"Aaron, I'm sure you've thought about leaving Evelyn behind. You need to know that there's no safe way to leave her. If you do, she'll sneak out and try to find you. It'd be safer to take her with you. Besides, if you take her with you, your group will always be mindful of her. It might make the whole group be more careful. She might be one of the most important members of the group. Not because of what she brings to the table, but because of how she'll force the rest of you to act."

Two people have told me to take Evelyn now. Both my father and Brian have good arguments, and I'm forced to agree with them. Evelyn would be devastated if I left, and I know her well enough to know she would try to follow me. If she did that, she'd end up dead.

"You're right, Dad, but how could I take her? It'll be hard enough to leave as it is. The other families will try to get in the way of me taking Evelyn. How do you propose we leave?"

"There's only one way to leave, Aaron. Go to your meeting. Find out who will go with you, and when the whole thing collapses, find those who supported you and leave in the dead of night."

My father, without missing a beat, tells me all the guard duties. He lets me know where and when we could slip out without drawing attention. As he's telling me this, I hope that he's wrong, that the other families will accept what we have to do. In my heart, I know the truth. We'll have to leave like burglars, like thieves, in the night. There will be no other way to do it.

As my father finishes telling the guard schedule, I realize how much time has passed. Not wanting to be late for my own meeting, I hurry to our gathering room. There I find all the occupants of our apartment sitting silently. The tension is thick in the air, and I can feel several people's anger radiate toward me. My throat locks up, and I have to force myself to breathe slowly and appear calm.

"Thank you, everyone, for coming together." My nerves start to calm as I remember my purpose. Speaking to everyone, I explain the need for people to leave. The speech is a good one, and though no one interrupts, I can tell that my dad was right. This will collapse, and we'll have to leave in the dead of night. By the end, when I ask for volunteers, the hatred I felt earlier is almost unbearable. Jason's grandmother is its strongest source. To her side, Jason gives a slight nod, and I know that he's on my side. He'll leave with me, but not here and not openly.

Without a word, Jason's family stands up and leaves the room, Jason forced to follow. The others in the room take this as a sign that the meeting is over and start to disperse. I consider stopping them but decide against it. We already know who's leaving, and there's no point in keeping up a charade.

I spend the rest of the day gathering supplies. My family helps me. They must know what I'm doing. I may not have told them, but they know all the same. While packing, I'm interrupted twice, once by Jason while he's patrolling and once by Brian. Both ask what the plan is, and I let them know.

It's dark by the time I finish packing, so I light a candle, gather some paper and a pen, and start writing goodbye notes to my family. My hope is to see them again someday, but I still want them to have something to remember me by. There were some goodbyes today, but we had to keep everything quiet in case someone from another family was watching. At this point, I imagine that the other families think I'm the only one leaving. This is fine by me, since it'll throw them off their guard.

After I finish the last of my letters, I grab a mechanical alarm clock and set it for shortly after 4:00 a.m. Setting it under my pillow, I lie down. It seems like only seconds before I wake up to the ringing of the alarm. My arm shoots under my pillow and immediately silences it.

Rubbing my eyes, I wake myself up before getting Evelyn and Melany up. After we get ourselves ready, we head to the designated meeting spot. When we arrive, both Jason and Brian are already there. Without making a sound, the five of us start making our way out of the apartment.

Once we're outside, I take a final look back at it. Saying a silent goodbye to my family and all the people inside, I promise myself that if I survive, I'll come back someday.

As we walk away from the apartment, we talk about what to do next. We decide that we'll stop at the nearest fast food place with a tube playground and camp out on the roof.

Many of the buildings in town are abandoned, and most of the town feels the same way. Palemen still loiter around, but the carnage that littered the streets three months ago has rotted away or been devoured by birds, dogs, or Palemen. The walk to the fast food joint is silent, and if I didn't know better, I'd say it was peaceful.

As we approach the building, I see the fast food sign and am reminded of simpler times. As I think about the past, the sun breaks over the horizon.

The flash of light blinds me. Before my eyes adjust, I hear a female voice shout at my group from what sounds like the inside of the fast food building.

"You better stop walking toward me if you know what's best for you!"

Looking toward the noise, my eyes adjust to the light of the sun and I see a girl near my age step from the building. In her hand is a rusted pipe crusted with blood. While I'm trying to decide the best course of action, I hear Jason shout out.

"Dawn, it's me, Jason! What are you doing out here?" From the faint outline of her face, I can see that she's caught off guard. Dawn motions for Jason to come closer but gives a look of forewarning to the rest of us. Wanting to be prepared, I ready my weapon. Even though I trust Jason's judgment, you never know how a person has changed since you saw them last.

My focus shifts immediately when I hear a noise coming from behind me. I don't hesitate to turn around, and when I do, two Palemen enter my field of vision. I pull out my gun and aim at my targets, only stopping myself from firing when I hear, "Don't waste your bullets." The voice came from Dawn.

When someone pushes past me, I know it's her. Sure enough, I see her walk straight toward the Palemen, brandishing her rusted pipe. Dawn walks up to the first Paleman and swings her pipe into its face with as much force as she can muster. The blow is solid, and I watch as the creature's jaw snaps. Gore spills onto the pavement, and the Paleman collapses, dead or very near it. The second Paleman reacts, trying to catch Dawn. She backs up, baiting him toward her. The creature trips over the carcass of its recent comrade. As soon as it hits the ground, Dawn is on top of it, swinging her pipe down.

After a few seconds, I no longer have the stomach to watch. Turning away, I head inside the fast food place, sitting at the nearest table. It isn't long before I'm joined by the others. We sit together in awkward silence until Dawn comes storming in. She points the pipe at our group and says, "Don't move from here. I'll be right back." Dawn turns around and stomps off toward what looks like the bathroom.

As soon as she is out of earshot, I look at Jason and say, "What was that all about?"

Jason shrugs at me, and I can tell that Dawn's show of brutality startled him. "Dawn is a good person," he says. "I know she is. Dawn's always been abrasive but never violent. I mean, I can't blame her. Who knows what she has been through? We'll have to trust her to be who I think she is."

Jason's hesitation is obvious. Evelyn grabs my hand, and I can tell she's a little scared. Jason is trustworthy, and if he thinks Dawn is safe, I'll have to believe in him. If he thought we were in any danger, we wouldn't still be sitting here. To be careful, I pull out my gun and hide it under the table.

We wait in silence for a few minutes until Dawn emerges from the bathroom. She comes out much cleaner, and I notice that she left the rusty pipe behind. She walks over and takes a seat across from us.

"Okay, now what?" she says.

We all sit and look at each other, until Jason speaks up. "Well, we had a plan. We were going to stay here on the roof for the night to figure out the next step of our plan. Honestly, I never thought we'd run into anyone here, least of all one of my old friends. Look, I know it may be a lot to ask, but can we stay here for the night?"

"Okay, but only on one condition: whatever you decide your plans to be, include me in them. It's been too long since I was with others." Dawn's response shocks me, and I'm not the only one. Our whole group sits in stunned silence.

The cold steel of the gun radiates against my hand below the table. Even though I'm not quite ready to trust her, the fact that she came out unarmed is a sign of her trust for us. It would be wrong for me not to give her a chance. This is why I decide to break the silence.

"If you want to join our group, that's fine, but we have rules. One of us messes up, the rest of us could die. We can't afford to work against each other." As I say this, I move my hand from under the table and stand up. I see shock on the faces of Dawn and my friends. Before anyone reacts, I lift my arm and offer the gun to her. "I don't want to regret deciding to trust you."

Several emotions play across Dawn's face. She stands, and for a second it seems like she might attack me. Then she relaxes and takes the gun from my hand. She stares at it and I can tell she's never held a gun before.

"Okay," I say. "Before you end up shooting yourself in the foot, why don't I show you how to use that?"

"Okay." For the next several minutes, I teach her all the different parts of the gun. Jason and Brian help me. We get her familiar enough with the gun's concept that she won't panic the first time she shoots it. We can't afford to risk drawing any Palemen here or I'd have her fire a few rounds.

We decide that everyone but Evelyn and I will run to the store to pick up the camping supplies we need. While the others go to the store, I'll work on getting us access to the roof. We decide that if I need any help, I'll fire three quick gunshots.

We all start our tasks. Evelyn and I move into the tube playground and navigate our way to the highest point, which is a large clear dome. For the next several minutes, I work on scoring a hole in the Plexiglas with a knife, then kick it out.

After I clean the sides and make sure it's safe, I look at the ceiling. It's constructed from glass and steel beams. The safest way to break through it will be with my gun. It poses the risk of drawing Palemen, but I can take care of them as long as there are only a few.

After I devise my plan, I get myself back under the protection of the plastic tubes and line up my shot, hoping the glass will shatter without any of it landing on me. Holding my breath, I take my shot and watch as the ceiling shatters and falls to the ground.

With the glass gone, I make short work of setting up a rope ladder to the roof. Once done, I look at my work, proud of what I've done. From the roof, I can see what looks like my friends coming back this way.

As I'm about to turn around and head downstairs, something smashes into my back. Trying to keep my balance, I flail. Knowing that falling off the playground is going to happen either way, I do my best to fall smoothly. Falling feet-first, I manage a sloppy roll when I land. My knee is scraped, and the breath was knocked out of my lungs, but I'm otherwise unharmed. Looking around, I see one assailant. Whatever threw the trash can must be on the other side of the building. The setup of these creatures is strange; it's almost like a trap.

Pushing my worries aside, I focus on the fight ahead of me. Taking the initiative, I charge the Paleman in front of me. As I run toward it, I pull out my combat knife. The creature lurches at me, and I jump to the ground and roll into its feet, tripping him. Spinning around, I pounce on the creature, stabbing my knife into the base of its neck. Standing up, I kick the blade, and as a do, it cracks through the creature's spine.

Even if he's still alive, there will be no coming after me now. Fury overtakes me, and I see another Paleman come from around the corner. I crouch, ready for it.

It charges me and I spin around him. When he turns around in confusion, I slam my thumb into its eye and kick its feet from underneath it. Pushing down with all my weight, I force the creature's head into the ground.

The second before it hits the pavement, I hear a voice ringing in my head.

"Help me!" The man's head smashes into the ground, and I feel his life fade. The voice I heard was his—I can feel it in my being. A smile spreads across my face. For a brief second, I see a bright blue sky before a black mist ensnares me.

When I look around, I realize I'm standing. It seems like I'm dreaming, but everything seems so clear. A figure emerges in front of me, and for a moment, I believe I'm looking into a mirror. Confused, I try to speak, but before I can, the figure in front of me deforms. It looks like me, but it's feral and covered in scars.

"Hello, Aaron. So at last we meet. Allow me to introduce myself. I'm Chris."

"What is this? Where am I? Who are you?" The questions spill out of me in a jumbled mess.

"You want to know. Fine, I'll tell you. I'm the part of you that wants to survive at any cost, the part that wants to feed on the death and pain of others. There is a power in the air, and it's giving me life, giving me substance, giving me a voice. These creatures you call Palemen, I'm not them but they are me." As Chris says this, he backs up, and I see the black mist surround him. When I try to chase after him, I'm not fast enough. As I watch, he fades. Then the mist clears and a blinding light hits me. I think for a second that I'm dead, until I see a cloud above me. It's then that I realize I was unconscious.

Chapter 9: Dawn

July 6th

As I wake up, I smell plastic and sweat; these things have become my world. The days blur together and I have no idea how long I've hidden here. The only thing I know for a fact anymore is that I'm still breathing, still struggling to survive. Living is all I have now since the town succumbed to death. So many people have already died, and I see them walking the streets.

My mind drifts to the first day I came across the walking dead. After seeing a few people mauled by them, I decided that hiding would be the best thing I could do. This plastic playground I live in was the closest thing when the outbreak first hit, and it's kept me alive ever since. While I could've moved to a new place, leaving something you know is safe is hard when danger is everywhere.

Compared to those that died and those who have yet to, I suppose I live like a queen. Sometimes, though, it doesn't feel that way. These tubes are my sanctuary, but they're also my prison. My eyes start to shut as my body aches for freedom. Realizing I'm falling asleep again, I force myself to move. My body attempts to stretch, but the confines of the tubes prevent me from doing it.

As I whisper a curse, I realize it's been a long time since I heard another person's voice. My sanity is starting to wear at the corners and I've started to hear voices call out to me. Death whispers to me, welcoming me to join it. While I'm aware that it's all in my head, it worries me all the same. It's long past time I found a way out of my prison. I need to talk to people and become human once more.

Pushing my morbid thoughts behind, I move through the tubes. My brain keeps moving, thinking, and I try to ignore it. It isn't long before I make my way to the Plexiglas ball that acts as a lookout for me. The restaurant is clear, and making a food run would be safe.

I use the nearest slide to move to the ground. At one point, I would have enjoyed the slide, but now it only causes me fear. If there's something waiting at the bottom, I'll be vulnerable for a few brief seconds. That's all it would take. As I emerge from the tube, I break into a run before stopping and turning around. It may be paranoia, but I'd rather be safe than dead, at least for now.

Knowing I'm safe, for a few moments at least, I relax and stretch out all the cramps that living in a small tube will give you. The first few weeks I was hiding were different. There was almost always a few of them in the building, but lately, I rarely see them here. This must be because I'm on the outskirts of our town, but I should still see more. Not that I'm complaining.

As I make my way to the kitchen, I grab myself a few hamburger buns. They may be as hard as bricks, but at least they're still edible. All I need is a bowl and some hot water and I can make a tasteless gruel. I gather a few buns and find a bowl. As I head to the freezer, I check the stoves. They don't turn on, but I knew that they wouldn't. They've never worked, but for some reason, I can't help but try them every time I pass. There's some reason for it, but I try not to think about it.

I make my way into the old freezer and gather together my fire-making supplies. While starting a fire and cooking a makeshift meal, I busy my mind. The smoke starts to sting my eyes, and I try to ignore it. Cooking inside an old metal walk-in freezer might not be as pleasant as cooking outside, but it's a whole lot safer. Red puffy eyes and three solid walls to protect me beat the alternative.

Once I'm cooking, I sit down and try to enjoy my meal. The smoke dissipates, and I keep my eye on the door. Since it's the only point where something can come through, it's smart to keep my attention on it.

Once I finish my meal, I have the desire to clean myself off. It's been a few days since I last bathed. Being clean always boosts my morale, so I make my way to the bathroom. As I'm opening the door, I hear the smallest of noises coming from behind me, and I react.

Ducking, I manage to see my attacker. The air above me is disturbed, and I see the shadow of an arm slashing through the space I was in. Pivoting my body, I face the creature, as pale as death and with eyes full of anger and blood. I'm as scared seeing it today as I was the first time I saw one.

My fear is what fuels me; I know that, right now, I'm this creature's prey. If I don't take it out, it'll likely kill me—or worse.

Springing from my crouched position, I throw an uppercut into the creature's jaw. The blow connects, and pain shoots down my arm from the force of the impact. The creature falls to the floor, and I'm certain that it's unconscious. As I move above its body, ready to end it, hands grab me from behind.

My body is jerked and slammed into a wall. In front of me there's one of the foul creatures. His head rushes toward my neck, and I realize what's about to happen. Summoning all my strength, I hook my fingers under his jaw and pull up. Without hesitation, I sink my teeth into the soft, exposed flesh of the creature's neck.

My teeth sink in and they tear into something vital. I rip my head back and am sprayed in a shower of warm blood. The creature falls to the ground, lifeless, and I spit the flesh out of my mouth.

Without a second to stop and think, I walk over to the unconscious creature who distracted me. Grabbing a nearby rusty pipe, I ready myself. I use the pipe to snap the creature's neck. Normally, I'd pummel it to a pulp to make sure it was dead, but I already have one mess to take care of.

Safe for now, I drag the corpses outside and leave them behind the building. There are plenty of stray dogs around, and keeping them fed keeps them from trying to eat me. It's funny how they've gone feral, but I guess I'm no different.

I spend the next few hours cleaning the wall, removing all the blood from inside the building and from my clothing. While I'm in the middle of dumping my cleaning water outside, I hear something strange. When I look through the glass walls of the play area, I see something I haven't seen in a while.

In the distance, about a hundred yards out, is a group of people. They're heading toward my restaurant, and I know there will be no escaping them. Too much movement and one of them is bound to see me. There's no way to get into my tunnels unseen, so I grab my pipe and hide in the doorway they'll use.

Thinking back, I remember all that happened before I met Jason's group. Things changed so fast I even surprised myself by how fast I decided to work alongside these people. The trip to the store was so much different than anything I've done in a long time. Melany was so kind to me that we became friends immediately. Today is the first time I've actually enjoyed being alive in a very long time.

All this time, I thought it would be hard to reintegrate myself into a social group. Now I'm finding it much easier than I ever hoped. We walk alongside the road on our way back to the fast food restaurant, and thoughts swirl around in my head.

They're only interrupted when I hear someone walk up alongside me. The person next to me is Brian, and so far, he's been the only one who hasn't talked to me. I get the feeling that he's a very reserved person. As he walks beside me, I find that I enjoy his company. He's calm and quiet. I like the others, but they can put me on edge. With Brian, I feel relaxed, like he knows I'm here but he isn't pushing me to interact with him.

After a few minutes, I look at him and smile. He's pretty attractive, and I find myself blushing. I turn my face away and try to cover up my embarrassment by talking to him.

"So how do you know everyone?"

The boy looks surprised, and I smile at the look of shock on his face. I see him blush, and I realize he wasn't expecting me to talk to him. After a few seconds, he collects himself and answers me. "Aaron and Jason were my friends before all this happened. Aaron saved my life the night the outbreak happened. He saved my whole family and helped us get settled in an apartment downtown." Brian's flush fades, and his face grows more serious. "I'm not sure if anyone's told you, but the reason we left is because there wasn't enough food for everyone. My parents might not be the strongest people, but I wanted them to live through everything. Leaving was the only way I thought that would be possible." Brian speaks softly, and his mention of parents reminds me of my own.

I ran away shortly after the power went out. My father liked to drink, and when he didn't get his liquor or had too much of it, he liked to hit my mom. Without power, I knew that nothing good could happen and that it was only a matter of time until my dad hurt us.

At first, I left the house to avoid them. I didn't plan to stay away, but as the days passed, I realized the power wasn't coming back, so I decided to stay away for good.

I may not know what kind of people Brian's parents are, but I can understand wanting your parents to survive. Even now, after everything, a part of me hopes my mother is still alive. As far as my father goes, death would be too good for him.

My thoughts are interrupted when Brian speaks again. "What about you, Dawn? How do you know Jason?"

"He's an old friend. We went to grade school together. We used to spend time at his house after middle school. After we were in high school, we would still hang out every once in a while. The last time I saw him was a few days before the power went out. He's changed a lot since then. He looks sad."

As I look at Brian, he looks at me with hesitation. Before too long, I understand why. He tells me all about what happened to Jason after the power went out. He also tells me about the group and what's gone on with them since they came together. By the time the fast food restaurant is in sight, my understanding of what I'm getting involved with is much better.

These people have managed to survive. Like me, it hasn't always been pretty, but they're still alive. Knowing that this group has gone through hardships of its own makes me feel better about joining. Looking at Brian, I realize that I want to stay with him. He may not know it, but he's the heart of the group. Grabbing his hand, I walk by his side. When he looks at me in shock, I smile.

For a few moments, I'm happy, but it's all shattered when we get close enough to see the whole restaurant. My eyes go to the side of the building. It takes a moment for it to click, but I realize that the movement is a fight between two Palemen and Aaron. My body reacts before I do, moving into a full sprint. My feet hit the pavement, and I push myself to go faster. The slaps of feet echo around me, and I know the others are following my lead. While I run, I'm helpless and can only watch what's going on. At first, Aaron seems to be losing, but I see that I was wrong when he leaps onto one of the creatures and severs its spine with a dagger. Something about the way he moves scares me.

He isn't attacking with fear or acting like a trapped animal; he's acting like a predator. Right now, he's enjoying the slaughter. When

I'm about a hundred feet away, I see him take the last creature down. His movements are as graceful as they are deadly. By the time I reach Aaron, I find him on his back, staring at the sky. His expression scares me. He's smiling in an inhuman way, and there's an expression of pure fury in his eyes. Whatever's going through Aaron's mind right now, it can't be good.

Aaron's covered in blood, and I'm unsure if he has been infected. No one has ever changed in front of me, so I have no idea what it looks like. Wondering if he's starting to turn, I pull out my gun and aim it at him. Around the time I do this, the others catch up. Wanting to see them, I turn my head. Confused, they look at me, and I know it's because I'm aiming a gun at their leader.

How can his face not scare them? My own question is answered when I look back toward Aaron. The horrific face I saw seconds before is gone now, and I see that he's blinking. Whatever happened was terrifying, but I don't think it's a reason to shoot him yet. I put the gun away and say, "I thought you might be turning for a second. Sorry."

My hope is that my excuse is enough to convince the others I didn't mean any harm. Jason and Brian move forward and help Aaron stand. He tells us all what happened as he regains his strength. After Aaron recomposes himself, he shows us the work he did. We all move to the roof and set up the tents and other camping supplies that we gathered earlier.

Aaron still worries me, but from what I can see, he cares about the people he's with. During dinner, he even gives me part of his meal.

Though I want to refuse after months of eating stale bread, the food is so good I can't say no, and he knows that.

As the night winds down, watches are picked, and I end up getting paired with Brian. My stomach flutters with excitement, and I have to calm myself down.

Putting my feelings aside, I force myself to go to bed in my tent. Stretching out, I sleep comfortably for the first time in months. I sleep so well that it feels like only seconds before Melany wakes me.

"Hey, Dawn. You're up," Melany says as she stifles a yawn. I find myself better rested than I've been in a long time, and I get up, full of energy. When I remember who I'm doing my watch with, I brim with excitement. It only takes me a few minutes to find Brian.

He's sitting on the edge of the roof, watching the moon. My hand finds his when I sit next to him. He looks at me, and I smile. We sit together like that for what feels like hours. I'm content to enjoy his company, but I'm not sure why this is. Hardly any time has passed, and we've spoken very little, but I know that I want to be with Brian. I've never been this bold before, and before the power went out, I avoided having any relationships. For some reason, I'm connected to Brian, and I think it's the same for him.

We sit together, and I lay my head on his shoulder. After a few more minutes of sitting, I finally decide to break the silence.

"Brian, I saw something strange with Aaron earlier today. He had a wild look in his eyes. It sounds strange, but it was almost like he was a rabid wolf wanting to attack whatever he saw next. You seem to trust Aaron. How are you sure he won't snap and attack one of us?"

Brian sighs. "These past few months I have noticed subtle changes in Aaron. Of course, all of us have changed, but Aaron seems to be the most affected. There's something in the air. The Palemen use some kind of communication we don't understand. It's the only way to explain how they haven't wiped themselves out yet."

My head moves from Brian's shoulder, and I look at him, confused. "What does that have to do with Aaron?"

Brian looks sad as he smiles. "Sorry, I had to explain that first. Dawn, it may not seem like it, but Aaron is actually a very gentle person. Everything that's happened to him has been wearing him down. Things are starting to slip through the cracks. I think that however the Palemen communicate is affecting Aaron. I can't explain how. It's intuition. You shouldn't worry, though. I know Aaron, and I know he'd rather die than watch any of us get hurt, even you."

"Even if what you said was true, why would he care about me? He only met me a few hours ago."

"That's how Aaron is. He cares about people. He'll always protect the people he loves. Think about it: right after a disease breaks out and panic spreads, he helped his family and friends escape. After that, he came to me and my family. How many people would risk their lives to save a friend for no reason other than they thought it was the right thing to do? Dawn, the fact that Jason cares about you is reason enough for Aaron to protect you."

"Is Jason the only one who cares about me?"

Brian looks at me, and I see him hesitate for a second. "Dawn, I care about you, too. I can talk to you better than anyone else. It may seem crazy, but there's a connection between you and me. We live in a world where we could die any at moment, and I don't want to hide my feelings for you, no matter how crazy it may seem to me or anyone else."

Hearing Brian confirm my hopes lifts my heart up. He's right; death surrounds us every day, and there's no way to escape it.

It would be foolish to ignore my feelings for him. If I do, I may someday regret it. Leaning forward, I kiss Brian. At first, he hesitates, panicking. It's obvious that this is his first kiss, and that makes it all the more exciting. My arms wrap around Brian and I pull him in closer. His previous hesitation starts to fade as he wraps his arms around me.

We sit there at the edge of the roof, a world of death below, and it doesn't matter. Right now, in this moment, nothing matters but what's in front of me. No matter what happens, no matter what I have to do, it'll be worth it as long as it means I can go one more day living.

Pulling away, I breathe heavily. Brian does the same, and we stare at each other with longing. After a second, Brian looks confused.

"Is everything okay?" he asks. "Did I do something wrong?"

Smiling and laughing, I lean over and give Brian a quick peck on the cheek. "No, Brian, you were perfect. It's too much. I feel like we might've forgotten we were on watch if we kept going."

"Okay, that makes sense. Good, I'm glad I was okay." Brian smiles and is silent for a second. "So what does all this mean? To be honest, I don't have any experience with stuff like this. You're kind of my first kiss. I guess what I'm saying is, do you want to go out with me or something?"

Brian's words come out awkward and cause me to smile. When he asks me to go out with him, I feel mixed emotions. It's not that I don't want to be with Brian—I do. It's just that I'm not sure dating is something you can do in a world like this.

"Brian, please don't take this the wrong way, but things are different in the world now. You could be dead tomorrow, and so could I. We don't have time for games. I like you. Right now, I know that I want to spend more time with you. That's all that matters to me. The title is pointless." At first, I think Brian is going to be mad, but when I see him smile, I start to think otherwise.

"Yeah, I can understand what you mean. At least it makes things easier. I was going to ask you to not tell anyone anyway, and not having a title makes that easier."

Anger flares in me for a second, and I have to force myself to be calm. I don't understand why he wouldn't want me to tell anyone. "What's wrong with people knowing? Are you ashamed of me?"

"Of course not. It's like you said: we could die tomorrow. If we tell everyone, there will be people who put hope into what we have. They'll see it as normality in a crazy world, and someone could cling to it. If one of us dies, I have a feeling the other is already going to be useless. The last thing I want is something so wonderful to be the downfall of our group. One day of bad morale and we could all die."

The anger that was building dissipates as Brian talks. He stops to take a breath, then looks me in the eyes. "I could never be ashamed of being with you," he says. "It's not like I'm saying we hide anything. If someone notices, I'll be honest with them. All I'm saying is, let's not be out and in the open with what's happening." Brian looks out toward the moon, and my eyes follow. We sit there for a while, me in his arms. After a minute, he tells me our watch shift is over, and we go to wake up our replacements.

He walks me to my tent, and I go inside. He tries to say a final goodnight, but I grab his arm and lead him inside. When he tries to speak, I silence him with a kiss. At first, he resists, but it's only seconds before he's kissing me as passionately as I'm kissing him. As I lie down, I zip the tent door closed.

Even if it has no title, and even if we have to be quiet about what we're doing, I don't care. At the end of this day, all I care about is that Brian's here with me. All I care about is that I'm in his arms. Even after Brian has fallen asleep, I stare at the tent roof and think. I'm overjoyed that this group ran into me today. My sanity might have slipped entirely if I went much longer without them. My eyes close, and I roll closer to Brian, knowing I'll get the first night of peaceful sleep since all this started.

Chapter 10: Aaron

Cries and moans echo off the walls of my tent. The cries of the Palemen are as strange and inhuman today as they were three months ago.

Knowing I won't be able to sleep with all this noise, I roll over and sneak my way out of the tent. Fortunately for her, Evelyn's a heavy sleeper, and I know the Palemen won't disturb her. As I zip the tent open, a beam of sunlight shines into my eyes. The light blinds me, but I do my best to ignore it and exit the tent without disturbing Evelyn.

Once outside the tent, I stand up and let my eyes adjust to the morning light. When I look around, I see that most of my party is already up. I decide to take a quick walk around the perimeter of the roof in hopes of spotting the Palemen who woke me up. Surprisingly, I find our perimeter clear, but I figure they must have wandered off or are hiding. Remembering my close encounter yesterday, I decide that it's best to get off the edge of the roof for now.

Noticing that there's no one cooking breakfast, I decide to help myself to the task. As I cook, the other members of our party start to join me one by one. There are some conversations between my friends, but for the most part, I'm left alone with my thoughts.

My meager meal of rehydrated food finishes cooking right around the time Evelyn joins us.

Everyone digs into the food hungrily. They aren't the only ones. Once I start eating, I find myself pretty famished. After the meal is gone, I find I want more. Hoping to distract myself, I start a conversation. "Did anyone happen to grab a map while they were out yesterday?"

There's a pause before Jason answers. "I thought about grabbing one, but I didn't, mostly because I had no idea which map to grab since we haven't decided where we're going. Once we figure out where we're going, we can grab an atlas from the gas station down the block." As Jason says this, he points behind him. Looking in the direction he indicates, I see a gas station maybe three hundred yards away.

"Okay, smart call on the gas station; they should have the maps we need. So where should we go?" My question starts a conversation that lasts a few minutes. Several ideas are tossed out, from finding a cabin in the woods to staying here on the roof. None of the ideas seem like good ones until Brian speaks up.

"What about an island? Based on what we've seen, the Palemen are far too uncoordinated to manage swimming without drowning. The way I see it, as long as there's a mile of water or so between us and the shore, we should be totally safe from any Palemen. Even if there was an outbreak on the island, wiping out the Palemen population on an island wouldn't be very hard."

Brian's suggestion sparks a memory. Before the power went out, I was interested in survivalist camping, where I learned about a small island in Lake Wisconsin that might be perfect.

"Brian, you're right. An island would be perfect, and I think I know of a good one close by. It's called Garden Island, and it's in the middle of Lake Wisconsin." The other members agree that an island would be best, and we decide that we should find an atlas before we decide on anything specific. Jason stands up and says, "If an island's our goal, I'm going to grab a map real quick. Anyone willing to come with?"

Dawn stands up, and together, they grab some supplies and work on going to the gas station. The rest of us wait for them. Several of the others are talking, mostly about the island. The conversation moves around me, and I focus on watching Jason and Dawn. They don't run into any trouble, and once they're inside the gas station, I can't see what's going on.

While waiting, I take a quick look around at the other members of our group. For the most part, they're chatting away happily. The only exception is Brian. He's staring intently at what looks like the gas station, and I see a look of worry on his face. It's a little unusual, but I ignore it. At least I have a second pair of eyes watching the situation.

Knowing Brian is watching, I let myself get lost in the group's conversations. Before I know it, Jason and Dawn are back with the map. Everyone grows silent as Jason lays the atlas down. He flips through the pages and finds the one he needs.

"Okay," he says. "I found Garden Island. Looks like it's pretty big. Somewhere a bit over four thousand square feet. It also looks like it's uninhabited, though there does seem to be an old forester's cabin.

This place looks like it would work pretty well, but I do see another island here that might be better."

As Jason talks about Garden Island, I grow more excited. It sounds like the perfect place to me. Plenty of land to hunt or grow crops, and there's even a cabin to weather the winter in. Top it all off with being one-hundred percent safe from Palemen, and it sounds better than a tropical resort. His last sentence sparks my curiosity, just as I'm sure it does for everyone.

"There's a sister island that's called Beaver Island. It's much larger and populated. It has docks and an airport. The infrastructure alone is a good enough reason to go there instead. We could build a future there, not just survive."

The others are quick to agree, and I know I'm alone in my desire to go to Garden Island. Part of the draw is the lack of people. My group is trustworthy, and every person we add to it is another variable, another way for us all to die. A whole island full of people would be a problem waiting to happen.

Knowing that any disagreement I show won't only be overruled but also lower morale, I keep my concerns to myself. If the time comes, I can always bring it up again. There's only one concern I do decide to share. "Does anyone know what month it is?"

I receive a few seconds of silence before Jason speaks up. "Yeah, it's July something. Why do you ask?"

"Winter. If we get caught in a city or pretty much anywhere that isn't safe and winter rolls around, our chances of survival plummet. What I'm saying is that we have two months to travel to the island.

That would give us about two months to get situated before it gets too cold to do anything but huddle up and survive. As long as we keep up our pace, I think four months is more than enough time. Unless someone is in opposition, I think this is our best option. If anyone has any other plans to bring forward, this will be your last chance."

No one says anything. With a distinct goal in mind, we start our work. We pack the equipment we need and leave the stuff we don't on the roof.

Our journey starts and the weeks move by quickly. We stick to interstates and country roads as often as possible. We go through towns when we have to but find most of our food from abandoned homes in the country.

We rarely come across more than one or two Palemen in the country, and if it weren't for the occasional town crossing, I think it'd be easy to forget just how bad things are.

Our travel speed is acceptable, but we often have to go miles out of the way to avoid crossing towns and cities. The farther north we walk, the harder it is to stick to country roads. Eventually, we arrive at a city that would take weeks to avoid, so we decide to cross it. The city crushes our hopes of fast travel. The streets are filled with Palemen, and we can only travel house by house when there are openings. At this pace, it'll take weeks for us to make it across town, which is a huge setback.

After two weeks of painfully slow travel, we find ourselves stuck on the roof of a business in the downtown area. After being on alert for so long, trying to avoid drawing the attention of Palemen, we notice any change in the landscape immediately. That's why I notice the cloud of dust coming toward us even when it's miles away.

From my vantage point on top of the roof, I can see outside of the town. The dust cloud is probably about a mile away and closing in on us quickly. It's hard to be sure, but from what I can see, it looks like the dust cloud is being created by a car—and a crowd chasing the car.

My gaze doesn't leave the object, and as it comes closer, I become positive that it's a car. Looks of shock and disbelief are on the faces of me and my party. We see the car and can tell it's being chased by a horde of Palemen.

Suddenly, I have a powerful urge to grab one of our hunting rifles. The compulsion to aim it is so strong that I can't resist. As I focus the scope, I don't see the car I was expecting but find my crosshairs resting on a random Paleman.

Kill him now. My finger squeezes the trigger as I hear the voice of Chris in my mind. My vision fades, and I see myself from the perspective of my victim. Searing pain shoots through my mind as the bullet rips through my victim's head.

When my vision returns, I force myself not to scream. My vision is dark around the corners, so I struggle to my feet. I don't need to give my party something to panic about. Whatever's happening to me, I have to ignore it.

Wanting to distract myself, I look out into the horde that follows the car. What just seconds ago was a running mob has quickly broken down into a disorganized mess.

Someone in the car throws out several objects. I wonder what they are until I see the fiery explosions. The noise hits me a second later. The horde that was so recently pursuing the car is now walking in several directions. Several dozen Palemen lie on the ground, dead, their bodies helplessly mangled by the grenades. Palemen missing limbs and bleeding freely stumble around the dead bodies. Several wander around on fire, ignoring the flesh melting off their bones.

There may be some survivors in that group, but my best guess is that no more than one-tenth of them will survive that attack. Gas cans and grenades are terrifying weapons against crowds, and I make sure to add the idea to my arsenal.

With the threat of the horde gone, my focus moves to the car. It continues its movement, heading straight for us. Unsure of what might happen, I ready my weapon. As the car gets closer, I glimpse the people and items inside. From what I can see, the group is either an army group or heavily armored mercenaries.

Not wanting to start a fight where we can avoid one, I hold fire and let the car move down our street. As it comes closer, half of me hopes it goes past us, and the other half hopes it'll stop. When the car stops, I'm excited and scared at the same time.

Watching with bated breath, I see a man step out of the driver's seat. Aiming my gun at him, I ready myself but freeze when he pulls out a rocket launcher and aims it at the roof.

"Lower your weapon or I'll send you and anyone hiding up there straight to hell." I briefly consider firing my gun but decide it would be beyond foolish. As I lower my gun, I see a smile on the rocket launcher man's face, and a spark of recognition hits me.

"Kent, is that you?" The man looks at me, and he's obviously confused. He stares hard at me for a few seconds.

"Aaron? What are you doing here? I hardly recognized you." As Kent is talking, a Paleman walks around the corner nearby. Without missing a beat, Kent throws the rocket launcher into the car, pulls out a pistol, and fires. The Paleman drops to the ground, but several more come out from behind the corner.

"Well, I would love to chat, but I think we need to get out of here. You're welcome to come with me." I make my decision instantly. Kent is an old friend. I know him well enough to know he's trustworthy. Even if he isn't going north, I think we could convince him to take us past this infernal city.

Looking around the group, I see that everyone's waiting on me, so I tell them to move toward the roof's door. The others follow behind me as I open the door and start moving through the building. As I do this, I hear more gunfire.

When I get out of the building, I see around ten Palemen approaching the car, some on the ground, some standing. Most of them are bleeding from bullet wounds. Now that I'm down here, I help get everyone in my group situated in the car, counting off as I do so. When I'm sure everyone's in the car, I hop in myself. Fortunately, the car's a large military jeep, and even though we have a decent amount of gear and people, there's enough room for us.

The jeep starts moving, and after a second, Kent turns around from his spot in the passenger's seat.

"Normally, I'd catch up with you, but right now my primary concern is how the hell you knew which of those creatures the general was. Your group fired one shot, and I don't know if you have some insanely good luck or some other force on your side, but I want an explanation." For a second, I think Kent must know about Chris. I want to panic but force myself to stay calm.

"Kent, what are you talking about? What do you mean by a general?"

Kent lets out a heavy sigh. "Sorry, I forget that you wouldn't know what I meant." Kent starts to explain to me what a general is. Apparently, some of the Palemen have a higher level of consciousness. He isn't able to tell me why or how, but these Palemen are able to control and organize hordes of lower Palemen.

The thought that there's some organization among creatures we previously thought as devoid of intelligence is terrifying. Some of the things I've seen start to make sense. Apparently, the group that was chasing Kent's party was led by a general, and I managed to snipe it. Pain still lingers from when Chris directed me, and I saw the death of the Paleman.

The fact that some part of me was able to find the Paleman leader worries me. Whatever it is that lets a Paleman general control its soldiers has some sort of effect on me. While all this information rolls in my mind, Kent looks at me once again. I see a small seed of mistrust in his eyes.

"Well, I guess I'll chalk up what happened to a lucky shot. Either way, I appreciate you saving our tails. I'm not sure if we would have been able to take out that horde without you." While we drive, we find out that Kent's group stays at a base to the north. Luckily, it's about thirty miles north of the city, and the car ride will take a few days off our journey. If we're lucky, we might even be able to convince Kent to take us farther. We could make up the time we lost in that last town in a day if we used a car.

As we drive, Kent and I catch each other up on things that have happened since the power went out. Kent doesn't tell me much. About all I learn is that he got to the base after his family died. He won't tell me any more about it, and I know better than to argue. Even though I don't learn much about what happened to him, I don't care; it's nice enough to catch up with an old friend and tell him everything that's happened to me and the group.

As we get closer to the base, I start to become nervous, fearing that the people here will be unfriendly to outsiders. Once we're there, my worries prove false. Kent immediately leaves us, saying he has to go get someone, and while we wait, several men and women come up and greet us, asking all sorts of questions.

The people I see are used to fighting Palemen, but they've managed to hold on to their humanity and their community. Before long, I find myself happily chatting away with people, and it seems like only a minute before Kent is back with someone trailing behind him.

The man behind Kent is about six foot two and heavily built. His hair is shaved, and he has a very militaristic air about him. Instantly, I know that this man is the leader of the camp.

"So you're the people who are taking one of my star soldiers away?" As the man speaks, I become confused, and the confusion must show on my face because the man says, "So Kent didn't even ask you to join." He laughs. "Sounds about right. You want to tell me what's going on, Kent?"

Kent looks at the man, salutes him, and says, "Sir, I've seen too much and am ready for some peace. These people plan to go to a place where I can find some silence. I hadn't yet asked them if I could tag along, but since you promised me a car and provisions if I ever left, I figured they couldn't say no."

The mention of a car shocks me, and I know Kent is right. Even if I hated him, the offer of a car alone is tempting enough that I'd let him join. With a car, we could reach the coast much safer and faster. I find it hard to believe that someone would just let Kent drive away.

The leader nods and shakes Kent's hand. They start talking about supplies, and I'm lost. This place will make it through what's coming, and I briefly debate staying here.

As I think about what Kent said, about wanting quiet, I realize that this would be a hard place for Evelyn to grow up. True, she would survive, but at what cost? Places like this have death surrounding them at all times. The people may be friendly, but when I look into their eyes, I see it. There isn't a single person here who hasn't drained the life from a Paleman, and I imagine several of them have grown to enjoy it.

Once Kent finishes arranging things with his leader, several soldiers help load up the car with guns, ammo, gas, and, interestingly enough, C4.

Once the car is packed and we load up, no one in my group hesitates for a second. I'm sure they don't all trust Kent, but I know everyone came to the same conclusion as I did: travel with a car will go much more smoothly, and our chance of survival skyrockets.

The next few days pass by more quickly than I could've imagined. Our traveling up to and into Chicago is smoother than anything that's happened in a long time. It might have only been around half a year, but I've already begun to forget how convenient and easy everything used to be.

Even the journey through the city is smooth. We run into very few Palemen or people. At first, I find it strange, but I quickly become overly confident. After hours of running into nothing in the city, I find myself falling asleep.

I'm awoken when the car comes to a sudden stop and I'm jerked forward and thrown against my seat belt. My body slams back into the car seat, and I immediately force myself to look around, panicked. What I expect to see is dozens of Palemen gathered around our car. Instead, what I see is young children running around.

I'm so thrown by this that it takes a moment for me to see that all of the children are carrying high-powered rifles or shotguns. Several of them are pointing the guns in our direction.

I look into the eyes of one of the children, who's aiming her rifle at me, and I can see she's prepared to shoot us on the spot if she needs to. One of the children starts to walk forward. The boy looks older than the others around him. He walks with an arrogance that makes me feel like he's this group's leader.

Kent, our driver, slowly lowers the car window, and the boy comes up to it.

"You're trespassing in the Orphanage. If you give us your weapons, ammunition, car, supplies, and food and come with us silently, we might allow you to live." As I listen to the demands, my jaw drops. This kid wants to strip us of everything but our clothing, and then he *might* let us live. Anger swells in me and I find a part of me screaming for this foolish boy's death. Fighting back my anger, I force myself to remember the promise I made to my father to keep everyone safe.

Opening the door to the car, I slowly stand up with my hand in the air. As I do, several guns follow my movement; I look around and see that about half of the guns have their safeties switches on. All the guns are on me, but I think I can kill the leader before a single shot is fired. If I kill him, I bet half of these kids would run. The other half would hesitate, and I could scare them into letting us go.

I start preparing to take out the leader when I hear shouting; a boy is running through the crowd, shoving people out of the way.

"There are thousands of them! The boogie men are coming. Move the hell out of my way. I have to get to Ted." The newcomer runs up to the boy threatening us—Ted, I think his name was. The boy tries to catch his breath, and after a momentary glance at us, he starts talking.

"Ted, sir, I was scouting, and I ran into a group larger than I've ever seen. There are thousands of them. They're headed straight for us, sir. I've never seen them act like this. It's like they know where we are."

"They do know where you are, you little shit," Kent booms behind me. "They've come to kill you off. I don't know what you did to attract a general's attention, but it was the stupidest mistake you've ever made."

I look at Kent and see that he must have gotten out of the car during all the commotion. What he says is rough, but I see it has the effect he was hoping for. Most of the children, who only seconds ago looked like they could kill us, now look frightened. Several of them have already lowered their weapons. Ted looks at us with anger in his eyes before turning to his runner.

"How far away are they?" Kent asks.

The runner replies. "No more than fifteen minutes. They're moving faster than normal. I had to run as hard as I could to give you a heads up."

Ted looks at us and smiles. "Alright, it's your lucky day. You're free to go." I stare at the boy and realize he's being serious. Seconds ago, he was ready to strip us and send us to our deaths, and now he's ready to let us be a distraction. Fed up, I'm about to say something when I hear Kent's voice coming once again from behind me.

"If you send us away, you'll all die. If you let us help you, you might stand a chance of making it through this. We know how to kill generals, and I have a plan."

Children crowd around us, and I can tell they're looking to us for help. Ted looks angry, and I think he's going to say no. I only see a change in Ted when he notices all his people around us lowering their guns. They're telling him with their actions that he doesn't have a choice but to use our help.

"Fine," Ted says, "but after the fight, I want you the hell out of here."

Knowing we aren't going to get a better offer, we start to discuss a plan, and slowly, one comes together. It's risky but has a decent chance of working. Melany and Dawn will take the high ground in one of the surrounding skyscrapers, while Jason will man the battlements, which are the old subway rails. Ted, Brian, and I will act as a distraction for the front lines of Palemen.

We'll use some modified bikes that Ted said they found. Though I doubt it's true, I don't question it. Kent will drive around the back way and bring down one of the buildings nearby with the C4 we packed. The hope is that we take out the generals and use the noise of the collapsing building to draw the leaderless Palemen away. Then the threat to Ted's group should diminish significantly.

I run over the plan one last time as I stare down the handlebars of the motorcycle. As I look at the bike, I admire its design. It has several spikes and blades positioned on it and two extra wheels in the back for stability.

Whoever modified this bike made it to drive through hordes of Palemen. The original windshield has been replaced with thick Plexiglas, and it's been heavily reinforced along the sides with jagged metal to prevent any Palemen from getting close enough to bite or grab the rider.

I'm still looking over the bike when I see a flare go up, and I know it must be my signal. I look out of my alley, and sure enough, the street is full of Palemen. My bike kicks to life on the first try, and I shift my engine into the fastest speed I can in the hundred feet of alleyway.

The impact with the first Paleman shakes through my body, but the bike doesn't slow. Bodies are shredded, impaled, and sliced to pieces as my bike cuts a path of carnage through the street. As blood rains down on me, time slows. A smile comes to my face, and I feel Chris emerging. One hand revs the engine while the other pulls out a gun and fires wildly into the crowd.

I can feel the other motorbikes. With each life that's destroyed, I feel their pain and agony join in me, and my anger grows stronger. I almost lose myself to the feeling until Jason on the battlement starts raining Molotov cocktails into the front line of Palemen.

Finally, I find myself in the opposite alleyway, and I hear the gunfire start. It's only seconds before I feel the generals of this group. Time starts to have no meaning, and I feel the life of two of the generals fade. The mental focus of the entire horde of Palemen latches onto the last general, and I feel his mind shatter under the strain. The horde mind focuses on me, and for a second, all of their rage and pain is bombarding me. The thousands of screaming voices is too much, and I fall into unconsciousness.

Chapter **11**: Melany/Kent

July 25th

*

Melany

*

As I look through the lens of my camera, I find myself wishing for a cup of coffee. My nose almost picks up the smell as I imagine the last cup I had at the apartments. The coffee grounds used for that cup were a week old, but I didn't care. Even now, I'd trade almost anything for those same grounds.

Feeling Dawn tap my shoulder, I leave the view of my lens to look at her.

"What do we do?" Not knowing what to do, I sigh and look through my camera again. We're at the top of one of Chicago's high-rises. Bellow us, a fight is about to break out between the orphans of the city and a Paleman horde that's larger than anything I've ever seen.

Dawn and I were instructed to come up here and sharp-shoot. I'm not sure how shooting one or two Palemen could be of any help.

"Dawn, I have no idea. I'm starting to think Aaron might have had us come up here to keep us safe."

Dawn looks at me, and I can tell she's thinking very hard. "No, that can't be it. Aaron and Brian had a reason for us to be here. Otherwise, they would have had us watch over Evelyn."

Dawn's right. I look back to the crowd of Palemen and watch its movements. As I do, I start to notice patterns. From my height, it's almost like the Palemen move as a single unit. Suddenly, I have a thought.

Opening both eyes, I look through the camera lens with one and at the crowd with another so it's easier to follow the movement of the Palemen. They're in fact moving together. It's subtle, but there's an order to their movements.

As I converge on the center of the movement, I hear a loud crash behind me. Dawn shouts out in shock, and I'm about to turn around when I hear, "It's only a few Palemen. I'll take care of them, and you take care of shooting."

Trusting Dawn to protect me, I continue feeling that if I don't act soon, I'll miss my opportunity. Putting down my camera, I grab the rifle. My brother taught me how to hold a rifle when the power first went out. This will be the first time I fire one.

As I look through the scope, I pretend it's my camera. Following the movement of all the Palemen, I'm led to the center of the group. When I find the center, I see a Paleman and I can tell that he's my target. My hands shake, and I wish again for a cup of coffee to steady them. Holding my breath, I force my hands to be still.

"You're taking a picture," I whisper as I focus my scope on the creature's head and pull the trigger. The gun recoils into me, knocking the breath from my chest. I throw the gun aside and pick up my camera.

My camera lens moves to where I fired, and I can immediately see a difference. The Palemen's movements went from synchronized to chaotic. Before long, though, the Palemen once again start moving as one. This time, it's more chaotic, like whatever's controlling them is having a hard time doing so.

Following what I learned earlier, I look into the center of the group. First, I spot my next target with my camera, then my rifle. I take my shot. When I look at the scene with my camera, I see that I missed the shot this time. My bullet didn't kill the general, but I hit him in the arm. It's bleeding, and I know he's dying. My camera snaps as I take a few pictures. Then the Paleman looks straight at me and screams. He lifts his one good arm into the air and flips me off.

My instincts kick in, and I take a picture. Once the camera clicks, I let it fall to my neck and turn around in shock. Dawn looks at me, standing beside the body of a dead Paleman, and asks, "What's wrong? Did you not hit what you were aiming at?" Dawn comes closer, and I see blood on her hands and clothes. The blood brings a flash of the general to my mind.

"No, I hit him. He's probably dead by now. Something strange happened, though. He looked right at me and flipped me off."

*

Kent

*

My nerves are buzzing and my hands are shaking because I know what I must do. Everyone's relying on me, and if I fail, there's a good chance they'll die. When I volunteered to take down a building, I didn't think it through completely. Even if I'm successful at finding an empty building and making it fall, if the others don't kill the general, my efforts will be pointless.

As I drive through the city, I see several Palemen. They all walk toward the battle I left. I've seen generals before, but I've never seen them have such a wide effect—or such tight control.

The more I learn about this disease, the more disgusted I am and the more fascinating I find it. Such a complex and deadly sickness could only be manmade and amplified by nature.

Most of the buildings I pass are full of cars. The infection must not have hit the city immediately. There's no way these cars would have been moved if it did. When I look at the skyline, my gaze falls on a building. Smiling, I know I've made my choice.

The Sears Tower—or Willis Tower, as it was called before the power went out—looms in the skyline in front of me. The idea that I'm about to bring down one of America's landmarks feels right. America has fallen, so why not make one of its monuments fall as well?

Feeling like my plan will succeed, the drive is almost relaxing now. When I reach the Sears Tower, I find my way into the underground parking garage. Once I'm there, I start unpacking the C4, blast caps, fuse wire, and the homemade battery to set off the blast caps.

After everything is unloaded, I walk around the garage and survey the area. I have roughly sixty pounds of C4. With it, I want to bring the building completely down. The only question is how, since I have more than enough explosives to get the job done.

Never having taken an engineering class, I have to guess which support beams are most important to the structure. In the end, I pick the four corner beams, what seems to be the main center beam, and three more random beams from around the parking garage.

Using my car, I manage to get the C4 planted and all the wire set up to a central point about twenty yards from the exit to the parking garage. When I finish tying all the line together to my final wire, I'm ready to detonate. My plan is to set the explosion off with a gravity-powered timer.

We practiced this at the base, and I know that I'll have between thirty seconds and two minutes to escape before the C4 explodes. Setting the trap up, I ready myself to run. My concentration is broken when a sharp pain in my shoulder freezes me.

I push back, feeling the resistance of a body, and I know it's a Paleman. The teeth sink father into my shoulder, and I know there will be no way to dislodge them. Instead, I reach down and grab the legs of the Paleman behind me, then jump back with all my strength.

The maneuver is successful, and for a brief moment, I'm on my back, floating in the air. The impact with the ground smashes the Paleman's face deeper into my shoulder. Pain surges throughout my body. There's a loud snap as the Paleman's jaw is broken. Satisfied, I roll over, my vision blurry, but I see the Paleman on the ground.

Without hesitation, I jump on top of him and start slamming his head into the ground. It isn't until I'm sure the Paleman is dead that I stop.

Standing up, I look at the wound. There's no chance I'm not infected—and no chance for amputation. I'm a walking dead man.

Sighing, I turn around to set the bomb. Might as well finish what I started. As I turn around, I see the worst thing I could: the homemade battery is lying on the ground, broken, with its fluids leaking all over the pavement. It must have broken in the fight.

The battery breaking pushes me over the edge; I scream profanity and fall to my knees, broken, defeated, and dying.

*

Melany

*

Sweat drips down my brow, but I force myself to continue running. Dawn is running ahead of me, and her movements make it look like running is effortless for her. She looks calm, but I can tell that she's on edge. After I took out the second general and told Dawn about what I saw, she said she had to go to Brian. I think I know why she chose him to go to.

Dawn has been careful so far, but there was one day I saw her coming out of Brian's tent. It wasn't hard to put together what was going on. Dawn and I haven't known each other very long, but I find that I'm happy for them. They are a ray of hope for me. If they can find some normalcy in the midst of everything, there's no reason the rest of us can't.

Their relationship is part of what motivated me to start taking pictures again. Before the power outage, I was well known in my community as an amateur photographer. After the power went out, though, there was no use for my skills. Without digital cameras and photo editing suits, all I had left was talent.

I picked it back up a few weeks ago when we were stuck in a building in town. I found an old camera and a box of unused film, along with a book on how to develop pictures. Ever since then, I've been documenting our journey in hopes that, someday, I'll be able to make a book from the pictures and memories.

Being so absorbed in my thoughts, I almost run into Dawn when she comes to a sudden stop. I look around to try and find out why we aren't running anymore.

Gazing out onto the battlefield is too much for me. Seeing it from afar on a camera was bearable, but seeing all the gore up close is too much. I gag and throw up onto the street.

Dawn looks at me. "I'm sorry to say this, Melany, but you need to pull yourself together right now. Brian and Aaron are out there, and they may need our help."

Dawn is right. I force myself to stand and look back out onto the battlefield. Bodies lie everywhere, littering the streets. The stench of death and blood is all-consuming.

"Are you okay?" Dawn asks. As I nod, she continues talking. "Good. Follow me, and make sure to be careful. Not all these bodies are completely dead." The thought that some of the Palemen and people lying here are still alive haunts me, so I try to focus on Dawn's back as we walk through the crowd.

The minutes tick by, and I hear the ricochet of gunfire grow louder. As we enter a narrower street, the bodies become denser, and I'm forced to hold on to Dawn's shoulder for balance. After several minutes of struggling, we find our way to a clear spot in the road, and Dawn comes to a stop.

"Brian, oh thank God!" Dawn runs forward, and I let her go. She should have this moment to embrace Brian. Even among all the death, I smile when I see their embrace.

"Boy, I'm glad you found me. We took out the last general. He was much easier to spot after the first two were shot down. Was that you, by the way?"

Dawn shakes her head and points to me. "No, I would have to give Melany the credit for that." Dawn's words are cut off by a loud explosion that shakes the ground. Everyone falls, including me. Fear fills me until I remember that Kent planned to blow up a building. Sure enough, a dust cloud comes down our street, and I close my eyes and hold my breath while it passes over us. Once the cloud is gone, I open my eyes and look around. Everything's covered in a layer of dust, but when I see Brian and Dawn, they both have smiles on their faces.

"He did it," I say. "He actually managed to pull it off. Without the generals, most of the Palemen are bound to go to the site of the explosion. The battlefield should thin out." Sure enough, the gunfire that was so frequent a second ago has slowed to an occasional shot.

Smiling, I join my friends in a hug. It hits me then: Brian and Aaron were supposed to be riding bikes together.

"Brian, where's Aaron?"

Kent

The car's horn is blaring, and I scream alongside it. Dozens of Palemen are inside the parking garage now. The electric lines are hooked into the alternator. All I have to do is turn this key and I'll see all these bastards die. Tears stream down my face, and when I look in the mirror, I see my eyes have turned red.

Finally, hands shaking, I turn the key and rev the engine to life. The explosion is instant and all-encompassing. Time slows, and I watch as the Palemen around my car vaporize and my ears rupture. Images flare in my mind. At first, they flash by too fast to comprehend, but then they start to slow down.

The images are all I see. Even as the fire crawls across my skin and singes my eyes, I still see them. They are memories of my childhood and my friends and family. The memories are bittersweet, and I enjoy watching them. Before long, though, they reach a point I don't want them to. My memories of after the power went out start playing. No matter how hard I resist, I'm forced to watch them, a victim of my own mind.

I watch myself sitting on the couch. I know this memory well. It's haunted me ever since it first happened. There's a noise in the garage and I follow it.

My father stands in twilight with a Paleman biting his neck. The Paleman's eyes are as red now as they were then. Inside of them, I see hatred, fear, and death. I try to say goodbye to my father as he lifts the gun, but he's in so much pain I don't think he can even see me.

Blood spatters the walls in the garage. He missed. My mother screams and runs out to my dad.

All I could do was stand there, frozen in shock. Watching, I see my mother run to my father. She's attacked by the same Paleman who attacked him. Half of the creature's face was torn off by the gun blast that killed my father. That doesn't stop him from biting a chunk out of my mother's arm.

Even now, I'm ashamed of what I did. Tears stream down my face as I run from my mother and go into my room. Locking myself in, I cradle a crossbow I had for decoration and cry.

Even when I heard my brother's screams, I did nothing. I just hid and cowered. My own memories disgust me; my weakness and fear are what stopped me from saving my family. These memories are why I worked so hard once I found the military base.

Only now that I'm dying do I realize I was hiding my grief in my hatred for the Palemen. All along, I was trying to make up for letting my family die.

Realization hits me: I don't belong in this world. Some insane luck made me survive that first night when the rest of my family died. The fire burning away my body is a blessing.

Accepting death, I beg that the images of my memories go away, but they won't. Even when I see memories of me killing Palemen, I feel no joy. Only with the wisdom of death do I understand that they are the true victims. Palemen are diseased, and it's easy to forget when they're coming to kill you. Fact is, they're unable to control themselves. Their sickness forces them to kill those they love and be slaves to the generals who are stronger than them.

Death must be a gift to them; I can only imagine what being forced to stay inside my mind while my body kills others would be like.

Even now, I'm growing tired of these memories, tired of living. Emotions leave, and I no longer care if I was a coward or brave. My memories still play, but I'm finally able to close them out and fade into a welcoming blanket of nothingness.

*

Melany

*

From behind the glass windows of a bank, I see that the battle didn't reach this far. Brian is in the sick room with Aaron. I haven't seen my brother yet. After what Jason told me, I'm not sure I want to.

He said he found Aaron half-conscious atop a mountain of dead Palemen. He was drenched in blood but didn't have a single scratch on him. There was more, too—I could feel it. Something happened, and Brian couldn't tell me.

It's hard to believe that the brother I grew up with has become someone who could kill Palemen without remorse. After all, he's never been a violent person; he still isn't. His ability to kill Palemen helped keep us alive, but I'm still worried about him.

He tries to hide it, but I'm starting to see the strain of protecting us wear on him. Every fiber of me wishes I could help him, but I know that doing so would go against the person I am.

Many people would call me brave, but the truth is, I'm not. True, I left the apartment and am risking death because of it, but I don't provide much to the group. The most valuable thing I'm doing is documenting our existence. And that's only valuable if we survive all this.

A tap on my shoulder interrupts my thoughts. Startled, I turn around to see Dawn behind me.

"Hey, Melany. How are you doing? I'm sure everything that's happened is hitting you hard. Look, I'm sorry about earlier. I forget that not everyone can kill a Paleman without remorse."

"Don't be sorry, Dawn. If it weren't for you, I wouldn't have made it through today. You're so strong. I wish I could be half as strong as you."

Dawn comes closer to me and grabs me by my shoulders.

"You're stronger than I'll ever be. What I have isn't true strength. The only time I'm brave is when I'm backed into a corner and forced to act. That's instinct; it doesn't take bravery or strength to rely on instinct. Even Aaron relies on instinct, but not you. You stare into the face of what terrifies you, and yet it doesn't stop you. You look into the future, even if it's only a few weeks or months. I've seen you take photos, and I'm telling you it's the bravest thing I've seen any of us do."

What Dawn is telling me confuses me. How can she think taking photos is brave? What I take photos of might be horrifying, but at the end of the day, I'm not confronting what's in them. I'm only documenting.

Maybe that's what she's talking about. She must admire that even though the world has crumbled, I've held on to a piece of me from before. Or she might think that when I take photos, I'm choosing to remember everything that's happened to us instead of moving on.

My personal feelings don't matter if I'm giving others hope. If Dawn wants to believe I'm brave, I won't correct her. To her, I could be like the storytellers and historians of old. My pictures tell tales of what we once were and what our journey has become.

That's what I am to this group. Telling the stories about those who fight must be my task. Smiling, I hug Dawn and say, "Thanks." The hug catches her by surprise, but only for a second.

After the hug, our moods change. The situation we're in right now isn't a good one. Aaron is in a sickroom, unconscious. Ted is tolerating our presence, but I have a feeling that our opportunity to leave will expire soon. To top it all off, Kent hasn't returned, and considering he had the car, the chances he will return are slim.

As if she's reading my mind, Dawn says, "So what are we going to do now?" The time for feeling bad or good is over. The way Ted has acted so far, if we were to ask him to leave, I doubt he would say yes. But I've noticed that ever since the battle, I haven't been asked what I'm doing.

The security is such a joke here we could literally walk out and no one would even bother stopping us. The only thing stopping us is Aaron being unconscious.

For the briefest second, I ponder leaving him behind. But I immediately realize how foolish that would be. Aaron is my brother, and beyond that, he's a huge part of why we're still alive. The group looks to him as our leader, and without him, we would fall apart. No, whatever we do will have to wait until Aaron wakes up.

Dawn's question rings fresh in my mind. What will we do?

"Dawn, let's go see Aaron."

Chapter 12: Dawn

My eyes open. Forgetting where I am, I look around, panicked.
Brian shushes me, and I remember that we're in Chicago. Even now,
weeks later, I wake up afraid. I never thought I would grow to miss the
tube playground that was my home for months. Even though I hated
sleeping there, it still became home, and now I'm always scared when I
wake up.

Brian's relaxed breaths calm me down and keep me from panic.
He lies against the wall, and I lie against him, my ear to his chest. The
slow rhythmic beating of his heart calms me down, and I remind
myself that I'm safe with him here. Even though I know he may be
uncomfortable right now, nothing I could say would convince him to
have it any other way.

Ever since the first night we spent together, Brian has tried to
appear strong for me. He and I both know he wouldn't last two
seconds in a fight with me. He has me beat in a lot of ways, but I'll
always be a better fighter and survivor than him. Looking up, I see
Brian sound asleep. Trying not to wake him, I look at our
surroundings.

They seem unfamiliar until I remember where I am.
Disappointment hits me as I realize that Aaron must not have woken
up during the night. Guilt sets in, and once again, I consider
convincing Brian to leave with me. Tension is so high right now, and

I'm afraid that it's only a matter of time until it comes to violence. We aren't welcome here, not in Ted's home.

While thinking these things through, I lie against Brian and wait. After several minutes, I start to drive myself crazy, so I decide to wake him. Leaning up to him, I kiss him on the cheek. Brian rustles, and when he opens his eyes, they lock with mine. We both smile, and after a few moments of happiness, Brian looks more serious. Knowing what he's thinking, I ask, "He isn't up."

"No, I suppose he isn't. If he was, Melany would have gotten us and we would have left. Things are getting pretty tense here. I'm not sure Ted has much more patience."

Even with my short time in this group, I've grown to trust Aaron. There's no way we'll leave here without him. If we still had the car, we could sneak him out of here, but last I heard, Kent hadn't come back. Presumably, he died when he detonated the explosives that destroyed the building. If he wasn't far enough away when the explosion went off, there's no way he made it out.

"Hey, Brian, I realized I haven't seen Melany since last night. Do you know what she's up to?"

Brian looks around. Then, seeing no one is near, he whispers to me. "She's scouting out the best way to leave. We're getting out of here the second Aaron wakes up, and we'll need to know how to escape."

Melany was smart to think of escaping. She beat me to it. I wish I'd thought to scope out an exit strategy first. My muscles ache, and I decide that I want to stand. Getting up, I stretch, yawning as I do so. If we're waiting on Aaron anyway, we should do something to keep our minds busy.

"Brian, come on a walk with me." Brian stands, and we start walking together through the old bank. It's still pretty early, so we don't run into many people. When we get to the front, I decide I want to walk outside. Even though I know it might be dangerous, there's something we should check.

"Brian, let's go outside. We should try to go to where Kent brought down the building. There's a chance he's still alive, and we owe it to him to check. Besides, if we can find the car, escaping from here is going to be much easier."

"Okay. By the time we get back, Aaron might be awake. Let's find Melany and check in with her first. In case Aaron does wake up, we should have a backup plan." We get moving, and it isn't long before we find Melany and tell her what's going on. Together, we all decide on a meeting spot a little north of the bank. With everything arranged, Brian and I head out.

After walking in the city for a few minutes, I realize that I have no idea which way I'm going. When the building collapsed, I didn't see it—only the dust cloud that came after.

"Hey," I say, "do you know where we're going?"

"Um, sort of. I saw the building collapse from my vantage point. Only problem is, I've never been to Chicago, so I have no idea what building it was." Laughing, I have Brian describe the building, and it becomes clear it's Willis Tower. Strange how Brian, who's lived in

Illinois his whole life, never managed to go to Chicago. It makes me think that his parents were always reluctant to leave their bubble.

We travel along the old elevated rails as much as we can. The wide spacing between the railroad ties makes it impossible for Palemen to traverse them. We see plenty on the ground but know we're safe.

As we walk, I notice more of the city. When we were driving, it was easy to notice the small details. Now, I see that the city is in bad shape. Old trash, shattered windows, and graffiti are everywhere. From the looks of things, the city decayed long before the Palemen arrived.

Living farther south was something I took for granted. Fewer people and more arable land made survival and organization much easier. The fact that Ted's group survived through it all is astounding. The people in the city were no doubt at war shortly after the power went out.

In all likelihood, one in a thousand people is all that survived. After the Palemen hit, I imagine most of those who'd survived were wiped out.

Seeing the city like this forces me to respect Ted. He's faced things we couldn't even imagine; he may be an idiot, but he knows how to survive. The fact that he's let us stay with him and his group this long is astonishing, and I see him in a new light. He might not be the bad guy we thought he was.

When we reach Willis Tower, the destruction is obvious. Rubble and dust cover everything for blocks. The remains of the building are still smoldering, and as I look at the twisted steel and concrete, I'm humbled.

The idea that such a massive structure has crumbled like this terrifies me. The building that used to stretch hundreds of feet into the air is now a large pile that I could climb to the top of in two or three minutes.

Curious, I look over at Brian and see that he's also staring in awe at what lies in front of us. He notices me looking at him and says, "Kent is dead. If he didn't make it out of the collapse, there's no hope that he's still alive."

Part of me knows he's right, but I still want to believe he has a chance. "Couldn't he be alive? I mean, isn't there a chance he's in the rubble?"

Brian looks at me, and I can tell he's struggling with what to say next. "Yes, I suppose it would be possible that he survived, but for his sake, I hope he's dead. Think about it: even if he's alive, he's trapped under the thousands of pounds of unsteady metal and concrete. What could we do for him? We don't have cranes or machinery to lift anything. We don't have sonar or surveying tools to see where it's safe to dig. On top of all that, even if we did try to uncover him, all it would take is one Paleman to come up on us while we're working. That would be the end for us. We would both be dead. If Kent was trapped in the building, he's either already dead or doomed to die from dehydration."

Brian's words are blunt and raw, but they're true. He's right, and I too hope that Kent didn't survive the explosion.

"Should we head back, then?" I ask.

Brian nods and we start to walk back to the bank. About halfway there, Brian stops and sits down. He motions for me to do the same, so I sit next to him. He reaches for my hand and intertwines his fingers with mine.

"Dawn, the world is all messed up and I don't know what to do about it." Brian looks into the distance as he speaks to me. He's opened up to me before, but this is the first time I've seen him admit weakness. As I look at him, he hunches over, and I see despair on his face.

"Everyone's looked to me to be someone who's level-headed and knows the answer to things," he continues. "They aren't wrong, and I understand why they look to me. I know I'm able to look at things in a way no one else can, but I'm worried. We've been lucky so far, but what happens when we come across something I can't answer? Or what happens when our luck runs out? It's only a matter of time until someone's hurt or bitten."

Brian looks at me, and I know he's asking me for help. He's never turned to me like this before, and I realize that I've always been the one who turns to him for help.

Even Aaron, our leader, relies on him to provide ideas and strategy. Brian's the brain of our group, and that pressure must be intense. Brian must be under a lot of strain now, but I'm not sure what he needs.

"Brian, you have been strong up to this point. I haven't seen you waver when you give input. Has something changed? What are you worried about?"

Brian looks at me, and I see there's a tear on his cheek. "Dawn, I know I've done okay so far, but what happens when I have to make a hard decision? When we get back, I'll have to decide whether Aaron lives or dies. We've spent too long here, and we need to leave—for the safety of the group. If we stay one more night, we won't make it to the morning. No one else will decide, and everyone's looking to me for the answer. Even if by some miracle Aaron does wake up, there will still be questions I don't know how to answer."

Brian cries as he tells me this. He isn't wrong; everyone's waited on him to decide what to do next. He might be the brains of the group, but I don't think he's ready, willing, or able to lead us.

Brian has become more important to me than anyone else, and I feel like I'm closer to him than the others. Even with all the love and respect I hold for him, I know he isn't capable of leading our group. He's one of the strongest and most honest people I've ever met. What he isn't, though, is a leader. His way of talking and presenting himself is too gentle.

From what I know of Brian, I don't think he'd be able to make a decision that would determine if someone lived or died. After sitting in silence for a minute, Brian calms down and wipes the tears from his eyes.

"As I lie awake at night, I try to think what I would do if someone in our party is bitten. Or how we would respond to cannibals or other deranged people. I never find any answers. On top of the other worries, I'm always thinking of you. What would I do if I had to trade another person's life for you? What if you were bitten?"

Interrupting Brian, I say, "Don't worry about me. Nothing's going to get me any time soon. Besides, you haven't even known me that long. You shouldn't worry about me or things that haven't happened. No one can control the future." I say all this to reassure Brian. He's the most important person to me, but I can tell that isn't what he needs to hear right now.

"You're trying to protect me. I know that because I'd do the same thing in your shoes. Dawn, you should know that you're the most important thing in the world to me. My biggest fear is that I'll have to make choices between you and the group. If I had to face that, I know I'd always choose you above everyone else, even if that choice was the wrong one. I want to spend my life with you, Dawn."

Tears well in my eyes as Brian speaks. He looks at me, and I can tell he's unsure why I'm crying. He might think I'm sad or upset, but I'm happy. I pull him close to me and kiss him.

We fall back together. At first, he hesitates, but then he gives in to me. We kiss each other passionately, and the rest of the world fades. After a few seconds, though, Brian gently pushes me off of him.

"Sorry, there are Palemen around here. I don't want to take the chance of letting any sneak up on us."

"You're right. I should've been more careful, but I wanted to kiss you right then." Brian smiles, and I smile with him. The fear and worries have left him for the moment.

Never in my whole life would I have thought that I'd fall for someone like Brian. The fact that I not only fell for someone but fell for them so quickly, and in the worst possible circumstances, is a miracle. That miracle is something I wouldn't trade for anything. The time I've spent with Brian has been the best in my life, Palemen and all.

"We should get going," Brian says, and I nod in agreement. We stand up together, holding hands, and make our way back to the bank.

The walk back goes by much more quickly than I want, and I find that I'm dreading our return. A loud pop echoes, and a sharp pain slices across my arm. Instinct kicks in, and I drop to the ground. Brian falls with me.

"Dammit, I missed her. You two run around and flank them, now!" The voice screams commands to an unknown number of people, and I recognize it. Ted's patience must have run out, and now he's trying to kill us.

Brian looks at me and mouths, "Are you okay?" Remembering the gunshot, I look down at my arm, and the pain hits me. Examining the wound, I see two holes in my upper arm. My arm is mildly bleeding, so it must not have hit anything vital. My wound burns, but I'm pretty sure I'll live.

"The bullet went through," I say. "I don't think it hit anything vital. We need to see what's going on. My guess is that Ted fired the shot, and I bet his lackeys aren't as willing to kill us in cold blood." We creep to the edge of the railway platform we're on. We're lucky; if we had been on tracks, we would have been full of bullets by now. When I peek over the edge, I see Ted alone below me. He's looking away for some reason, and I decide now is the perfect time to attack him.

Hoping that I'm right and the other kids won't shoot me, I pull myself over the edge of the railway and fall feet-first into Ted.

The fall would've hurt if Ted hadn't absorbed the impact. We both crumble to the ground, but I manage to roll to my knees and leap onto Ted's back. He starts screaming, but I ignore his desperate cries. Using my good arm, I slam his head into the pavement. He stops moving, and that's when something cold presses against my neck.

"Listen to me and don't move. You should realize I could've shot you by now. The others will be here soon, and you don't have much time. Many of us at the bank are grateful to your group. We wouldn't have survived if you hadn't come along, so I'm going to let you go. Run, now. The rest of your party already left. They were heading north."

Hearing that the others made it out is enough for me, so I nod and stand. The gun stays against me, so without turning back, I run, screaming, "Brian, run!" I follow the tracks, running until I'm exhausted. When I stop to take a breath, Brian climbs down from the railway. I explain what happened, and we agree to try to find our group. Alarmed, he also looks at my arm, and when I look, too, I see why. It's covered in blood, and that's when the pain hits me.

Brian pulls a shirt from his backpack and tears it into strips. He does his best to clean and wrap the wound while I wince in pain. Shortly after he finishes, we hear a moan and see several Palemen coming toward us. Gritting my teeth, I grab Brian's hand with my good arm, and we start running again.

After we put a few hundred feet between us and any Palemen, Brian helps me climb onto the railway. Once on top, we rest for a minute and check my wound again. It's still bleeding, but the flow has slowed considerably, so we decide to start moving toward the meeting point we set up with Melany.

The walk there is painful, and each step sends new waves of fire through my arm. When we arrive at the billboard we said would be the meeting place, I'm in a stupor. Brian tells me he sees Melany and guides me down off the railway and into a building. Melany rushes to us.

"Melany, she needs help. Get the others." I'm so tired that I collapse. Brian catches me and guides me into a lying position. He cries and tells me it'll be alright. My eyes close, and I mumble that it'll be okay.

On the edge of consciousness, I float, knowing at least that I'm still alive. Something pricks my arm, and I open my eyes. When I do, I see Brian standing behind a woman I've never seen.

"Melany, Brian, I need you to make a stretcher so we can carry her up the stairs. Aaron, Jason, you keep watch. I'm going to suture her arm. She looks like she's lost a fair amount of blood, but she should be okay if I clean and stitch her wounds." Even if I don't know the woman, the fact that my friends are here keeps me calm.

Coldness moves up my arm, and the pain fades. The woman cleans and stitches my wound, but there's almost no pain when she does. Euphoria grips me and clouds my vision and thinking. Even when I'm rolled onto something and feel myself lifted into the air, I don't panic.

Trying to force my mind to stay conscious, I'm aware that I'm being carried over what feels like stairs. Fading in and out of consciousness, I'm not sure how many there are. When I'm set down, someone strokes my good arm and tells me that it's going to be okay, that I'm safe now.

Looking up, I see Brian. Smiling, I let myself relax. If he's with me, everything will be okay. My eyes close, and I finally succumb to the overwhelming feeling of tiredness.

Chapter 13: Marcus

July 26th

As I stand on the window ledge, an occasional Paleman walks
by. The Palemen aren't what worry me. I know we are plenty secure up
here in the apartment. What worries me is the increasing hostility and
isolation between the families. It's only been a few weeks, but the
absence of Jason has led to his family losing any sanity they had. Jason
was a close friend of my son, Aaron, and I liked the boy. How he
could've been so different than his family will always be beyond me.
His family has always been dysfunctional, and I never trusted them.

Since the power outage, Jason's family has broken down
completely. Before the outage, they were crazy but manageable. Even
after, they could be dealt with, but now that Jason is gone, the
floodgates have opened. They act erratically, and I'm worried about
what they might do. The first thing I noticed was them stealing food,
but lately I've seen some strange things.

The grandmother, and matriarch of the family, has started
muttering. She's built a shrine and worships the Palemen. There are
bowls crusted with blood all around where they stay. I confronted her
once, and she told me it was paint.

After I confronted her, I finally shut my family's living space off
from theirs, moving our food away from the group stockpile to our
own. The day I did that, I could hear the screams and curses. Part of
me is still surprised there wasn't a firefight that day.

Alexis moved in with us around that time. Her parents had moved their food and secluded themselves long before that. She finally gave up on them. She doesn't talk about it much, but from what I understand, her parents sit in the dark all day, afraid that if they leave the room, a Paleman will kill them. Her parents became so paranoid that they walled themselves into the room with their supplies. No one has heard from them since.

There have been late-night murmurs lately—and frantic shouting. Tonight, I'll start to build a wall. It'll only take a few days, but I'll feel much safer when there's something protecting my family. After I seal us off, the only concern is our food supply.

We have about six months of food remaining. We would have more, but Jason's family ate a year's worth of our food supply before we moved it. Even if we went down to half rations, we'd run out in about a year, and I know that isn't long enough.

A dog runs through the streets. It's clearly feral now. Dogs might make a good food source, but hunting them might prove challenging. Alexis has already started exploring outside, and if I asked her to, she would figure out how to trap them.

If we catch one dog a month, the population should remain stable. Doing so would stretch our food supply out another three months. No matter how I look at it, the only way we'll be able to get more food is by growing it.

My concern with growing is the danger. Anything we grow on the ground would leave us exposed to the Palemen. Anything we grow on the roof by Jason's family would pilfer. We have the seeds to grow for a season, but if they steal too much, there will be no way to grow food for the next season.

My mind races and I try to think of a solution. The thought of executing the family comes to my mind, and I push it away. The Palemen have taken my way of life, my friends, and almost everything I had. I won't let them take my humanity as well.

My mind is so lost in thought that when someone taps my shoulder, I jump, almost losing my balance and falling out the window. Whoever tapped my shoulder grabs onto my arm and helps steady me. When I turn around, I see an apologetic look from Alexis.

"Hey, Mr. Grey. Sorry to startle you, but there's something you need to see." Alexis has become a member of my family, but she's always worked to be unnoticed. In the few months I've known her, she's earned my respect, and I know that if she's asking me to look at something, something serious is going on.

She turns before I can reply, then walks away. Trusting her, I follow as she walks through the apartment.

Before long, we're on the side Jason's family lives in. I wouldn't normally come here, but with Alexis leading, I have little choice. She leads me to a window and motions for me to look through it. When I do, what I see is so shocking that all I can do is stare. After I stand there, watching for a few seconds, Alexis speaks to me.

"I don't know why they're playing in the street. I saw them from the roof and came straight to you." In the street are Jason's younger siblings. They're running and playing around a Paleman. They're acting like the Paleman is completely harmless. Close by, their grandmother looks like she is chanting.

I can only describe what I'm seeing as a pagan ritual. The family looks like it's whipped itself into a religious frenzy. The horror of what's happening hits me as I hear frantic screaming. The grandmother has gone into a full-on frenzy and is moving with a crazed vigor while yelling into the air.

Her skin is pale, and I catch a glimpse of blood-red eyes. She's turned, but she still seems to be in control of herself. The Paleman at the end of the road is standing still. From the looks of it, I'd say the grandmother is controlling it.

My mind rejects what's happening in front of me, and I try to back up, bumping into some furniture behind me. To my horror, the grandmother spins around and looks at me. When she does, I see the Paleman at the end of the ally lunge for one of the children.

Pulling out my gun, I take aim, but I'm too late. By the time I fire, the child's shoulder is already in the creature's mouth. My bullet hits the Paleman in the eye all the same, and the child and creature fall to the ground together.

A second later, I hear gunfire, and pieces of drywall and glass hit me in the face. Alexis and I drop to the ground and crawl a few dozen feet before standing and running back to our living quarters. Once there, my wife comes to me, and I tell her to help me set up a barricade. She does so without further questions.

My wife, Alexis, and I work on building a barricade and setting up some basic perimeter traps. After it's set up, we sit behind an overturned metal file cabinet. For the first few minutes, there's nothing but silence. After those minutes, my wife asks me what happens, and I tell her everything that went on.

After I tell her, we spend the next several hours waiting for something to happen. As the hours pass, my tension lessens. Once darkness falls, I tell my wife and Alexis to get some sleep and check on Sarah, who I'm sure is hiding.

As the hours crawl by, I start thinking of what we can do in the future to seal ourselves off. Even though I know it's likely pointless, I try to focus on what to do to seal ourselves off. The bitten child has turned by this point, and I'm guessing it's only a matter of time until he infects his whole family.

A few more hours pass. I'm considering going to bed when I hear cans moving. For a second, I'm confused, until I remember my perimeter traps. Moving myself, I peek over the file cabinet and through a hole in the barricade.

A figure lies on the ground, injured. I debate helping him for a second, then realize that I have to. Even if it is a trap, I have to help the man I see in front of me. When I look at Alexis, she nods, and I know she understands what I'm about to do.

As I stand, my heart starts pounding and my palms sweat. I move through the barricade, expecting to be shot. When I get out, there's a brief second when I'm sure I'll die. The second passes, and I realize there's no danger.

Going over to the man, I see him look at me with his red eyes. Thinking he's gone, I pull out my gun, but the man speaks.

"Please, hear me out. I want to try to explain things to you. All I want is to tell you how my family led themselves to where we are now."

No hostility emanates from the man, and I decide to listen to his story. "Alright, I'll listen."

The man relaxes a little, so I sit down a few feet away from him. My gun stays by my side in case he turns, but I don't point it at him. Now that I'm closer, I recognize this man as Jason's grandfather.

"Thank you for letting me speak," he says. "Lesser men would have shot me without a second thought. To be honest, I deserve to be shot. The guilt is too much. I'm damned, and I know it. I watched my family descend into insanity, and I let fear get in the way of helping them." Tears are in the man's eyes. The fact that he thinks himself damned makes me sad. Nothing he could've done would have put him past salvation in my mind.

I would tell him this, but I decide to let him continue his confession, since I'm not sure how much time he has left. If there's time, I'll console him after he's told me what he wants.

"It started with my wife. She had dementia before the power outage. No one wanted to admit it, but we all knew. Things were okay when Jason was around. He was the only person brave enough in our family to tell her she was wrong. You see, my wife has always been a pushy woman. With the dementia, though, she often pushed us to do things that made little or no sense."

Dementia helps explain things. It doesn't explain how Jason's grandmother became infected or how she retained control, so I continue listening. "It was only a matter of time before she was bitten," he continues. "She would wander off and leave the apartment so often it's surprising it took so long. She hid the bite, but her eyes and skin gave away the infection. It was madness, but she manipulated our family into hiding her. Funny thing is, she never finished turning. She stopped partway, and though her dementia was worse than ever, she was in control of herself. She was even able to control Palemen. Our family started listening to her out of fear, respect, guilt, and cowardice. Before long, we were worshiping the Palemen as the next step of human evolution."

The man's voice cracks and he sits for a while. His confession is shocking and disturbing, and I'm not sure I can find forgiveness for him. After a few minutes, he continues, and I try to listen and maintain my calm.

"Tonight was the last straw. I tried to tell my wife we needed to end this, and she snapped. She killed the children first; when I tried to stop her, she bit me and threw me into a wall. I tried to get up, but Palemen appeared and pinned me down. Those poor children, their parents were so far gone. When they were told to sacrifice themselves to feed my wife and her children, they did so without hesitation. She made me watch it all—every second. When she finished eating my grandchildren, my son, and his wife, she had those filthy henchmen of hers throw me out." The man is shaking, and I can tell he doesn't have long. He looks at me, and I know what he's asking for.

My limbs burn as I give the man a final blessing. I've never had such a difficult time being a pastor. Part of me feels this man is worthy of salvation, but the choice isn't mine to make. As the blessing ends, I move the gun to his head.

"Do you have any last words?"

The man looks at me, and with the last of his sanity fading, he says, "Kill her." The gun fires, and the bullet passes through the man's head and into the floor.

"Don't worry. I will," I say as I start walking through the apartment, going to where Jason's family used to live. The situation is too dangerous not to act now. Not only has Jason's grandmother turned, but she's controlling other Palemen.

Even if I didn't feel the need to hunt her down, there's a reason she must die. She's endangering my family, and I know that if I don't kill the creature she has become now, they might perish.

Hearing footsteps behind me, I turn, aiming the gun. My trigger finger itches, but I stop myself from firing when I see Alexis. Realizing she heard the gunshot and came to help, I mouth, "Thank you." She nods, and we continue toward Jason's old area. When we get closer, I whisper to Alexis, "Stay back. I'm going to go in alone. If it's a trap, I'll need you out here to help me finish off whatever's in there." Alexis looks at me, and I see she is worried, but she nods, and I know she will do what I asked her to.

As I make my way through the final doorway and into the living area of Jason's family, my stomach turns. A propane lantern lights up the room, and blood is everywhere. In the corner is a pile of bones, I don't have to think long to know whom they belong to. The walls are painted with blood, as are the floors and ceiling.

Standing in front of a mirror and looking at herself is Jason's grandmother. She doesn't turn or even acknowledge me, but she knows I'm here. Four Palemen come from the corners of the room.

They don't get close enough to attack me, but they do get close enough to threaten me. So I didn't imagine what I saw earlier—she can control them. Earlier, she had to perform a ritual. Now she has a powerful control, even though she doesn't appear to be trying.

The cold steel of the pistol in my hand calms me, and I'm about to bring the gun up when I hear a voice.

"So you're finally here? I wondered how long it would take for that idiot of a man to whine his story at you. What did he tell you? That I beat him and killed his family while making him watch? He's a liar; they were not murdered, and they sacrificed their life energy to me. I absorbed them, and I've grown stronger. All this has to be done. I understand now. I've seen the future, and humans are no more! I'll lead my children into a new dawn! Their flesh will give me the strength to ascend! Bend your knee and become my slave, and I might spare you! I'm *your god*!"

Her voice builds until she's screaming with such force that I know Alexis can hear it from outside. Looking at the woman, I can tell I'd be able to throw her off if I kneel, but I know I can't. Even with the world how it is, I still consider myself a man of God. I won't bend my knee to anyone or anything claiming to be a god, no matter the cost.

"Go to hell, you hag." As I shout this, I hear Alexis move through the door, and I make my move. I lift the gun and fire at the closest Paleman. I manage to hit him in the head, and he falls to the ground. Before I can move, I hear two more shots, and bodies fall behind me.

There should be two more Palemen, one behind me and the other Jason's grandmother. My mind flies at a million miles an hour while I try to think of whom to go after first.

When I hear Alexis scream, my mind's made up. I turn my back on Jason's grandmother. Glancing at Alexis, I see that her gun's jammed. Running forward, I aim my gun and fire. It jams. Of all times, why must it jam now? The Paleman lurches toward Alexis with an open mouth. She looks shocked, and I know she's about to be bitten. Pushing myself forward, I tackle the Paleman in time to save her.

My mistake was forgetting Jason grandmother.

"Idiot, you killed my children, and now I kill your wife." Turning toward Jason's grandmother, I see her standing about ten feet from me, holding a gun. She points it toward the door, and I'm confused about what she's doing—until I realize she mentioned my wife.

The gun fires and hits my wife, who's standing in the doorway. She looks surprised as she falls to the ground, holding her stomach.

Floodgates break in my mind, and anger pours out of me. I punch the Paleman beneath me in the neck with an inhuman amount of strength, and something in his neck snaps. Without stopping, I stand and charge Jason's grandmother. The gun goes off several times, and bullets rip through me, but I don't slow.

When I reach her, she's squeezing the trigger of her gun, but there are no more bullets. For the briefest second, I see fear on her face. My fist slams into her throat, and my hand cracks from the blow. She falls to the ground, choking for breath.

"Take it back! Take it back!" I scream as I kick her in the sides, then the head. My kicks continue until she stops moving. Even then, it takes a few more kicks before I can stop.

Anger pulses through me, and with each pulse, all my wounds pump out blood. She must have shot me at least eight times. On top of that, I received a bite from a Paleman and broke my hand.

Anger fades as pain takes its place, and I fall to the ground. My vision is hazy, but I see Alexis over my wife in the distance. Crawling, I'm desperate to reach them. Every movement I make is full of pain. My body screams in agony, but the desperation forces it to be silent. My life is fading, but I won't allow myself to die. Not yet.

Alexis is yelling something, but I can't hear it. She isn't looking at me, and I continue to crawl. Sarah comes into my view, and when she sees her mother, she cries. When she looks at me, it's even worse. Alexis grabs her shoulders and yells something at her.

She nods and runs over to me. Seeing Sarah saps my remaining strength, and my crawling comes to a halt. As I cough, blood comes out of my mouth. Pain screams at me from all over my body, but I ignore it. The soft touch of my daughter's hand in mine is the only thing I focus on. She looks at me with tears in her eyes, and even though I know she's here for me, I want to hold her in my arms and comfort her.

My wife is still on my mind, and when I look toward her, I see Alexis moving around her. She leaves and comes back with a medical kit I've seen Stephanie using. It's then that I remember that Alexis has been learning about medicine from Stephanie.

The fact that she's working on her tells me that she's still alive. A smile comes to my face, and I look at my daughter. Her eyes are full of tears, and she's mouthing incomprehensible words.

"Honey, come here," I mutter, unable to raise my voice. For a second, I'm worried that I was too quiet for her to hear me, but luckily, Sarah comes closer. "Honey, I love you so much. You're the joy of my life, and what you have given me is beyond anything I ever could've known existed before we had you."

My words come out slow and painful, but I force myself to speak, stopping only when I need to spit the blood from my mouth. As I speak, a hatred boils inside me, and I know it's the infection from my bite spreading and taking over my mind.

"Listen, honey, I'm dying, and I need you to be strong. Your mother is going to need you to help her move on. She'll be angry and she won't understand. It'll be hard, but you need to be there for her, okay?" Sarah cries, and I see her nod. Relieved, I sigh, which turns into a coughing fit. More blood comes from my mouth, and I realize that my time is soon.

"I love you, Dad," Sarah says, and I try my best to smile.

"I love you too, honey. Can you get Alexis for me, honey?" Sarah looks at me, confused for a second, but goes over to Alexis. I can't hear them, but I see Alexis nod, and together, the girls come over to me.

"Your wife is going to be okay. I was able to stabilize her. Luckily, the bullet passed through and missed her organs. She's in shock now, so I don't have long, but you deserved to have peace before the end." I smile and try to thank Alexis, but she hushes me.

"Your eyes are red, and we are out of time. Save your words, unless there's something that has to be said." As Alexis finishes her sentence, she pulls out her gun. "Sarah, you might want to leave now." Sarah's crying but she shakes her head.

"No, I should be here." In this moment, I'm prouder of my daughter than I've ever been. Alexis looks me in the eyes, and a tear escapes as I nod.

I'm not afraid of death. In fact, I'm looking forward to joining God. Soon, I'll be watching over my family and awaiting the day they join me. As the cold steel of the gun rests against my head, I smile and say my goodbyes to the world. A loud pop slams into my head, and the world goes black.

Chapter **14: Aaron**

July 27th

A blanket of darkness surrounds my consciousness. It feels like I'm floating in a lake, but I'm not cold. My body feels numb, and my mind is sluggish. Worries are gone, stress is gone, and here, I'm all alone.

When the fog starts to fade and my mind starts to clear, I become afraid. I feel pain as my mind clears, and worries and responsibilities return. My will tries to fight to stay in the abyss, but it's hopeless.

When my last memories start to surface and I remember where I am, I stop fighting. At first, I'm afraid that I was bitten and have changed into a Paleman. It isn't until my eyes open and I see a dirty ceiling in what looks like an abandoned office that I know I made it through the battle uninfected.

When I try to take in my surroundings, I see someone unfamiliar sitting in a nearby chair. Alarmed, I freeze. She catches my gaze and stands up.

The first thing I notice about the woman is a deep scar on her face. The second thing I noticed is that she's attractive. If it weren't for the scar on her face, I would say she's one of the most attractive women I've ever seen.

When I notice her getting closer, I try to speak, but the words lock up in my mouth. As she reaches her hand over and puts it on my forehead, I tense up.

"It looks like your fever broke. You're lucky. I didn't think you were going to wake up. How do you feel?" Her questions confuse me. Trying to sit up, I'm stopped when I become dizzy and have to lie back down. The last thing I remember was the awful pain and pressure from the Palemen at the battle. My weakness tells me I've been asleep for more than a few hours.

"Not so good. How long was I out?"

"Almost twenty-four hours. You're lucky you weren't bitten. Your friend Brian found you unconscious." At the mention of Brian, I remember the others and am struck by a slight panic.

"Are my friends okay?"

The woman looks at me and nods. "Look, I know you have quite a few questions for me, but we don't have much time. Ted is getting close to breaking down and trying to kill you and your friends. If you want to live, I'd suggest getting out of here."

As the woman speaks, I find myself looking at her face. Her eyes are a beautiful purple color, and her brown hair's cut short. She looks like she's in her mid-twenties, and she holds herself in an educated manner. The scars on her face go from the upper left side of her forehead all the way down to the right side of her jaw. The scars are ragged, and they look like something scratched or tore across her face.

"You can stop staring at my face now." Embarrassed, I look away, and I can feel myself blushing. The woman continues to speak as

190

if nothing happened. "If you want an explanation, I can tell you while you eat something. After that, you need to get your friends and leave."

At the mention of food, my stomach rumbles, and I realize that I'm famished. The woman grabs a tray from behind her. There are some canned goods on it.

She opens the cans and sets them on a nearby table. I try to sit up but find I need the woman's help to steady myself. She gives me the tray of food and a water bottle. Opening the water, I take a sip. The water rehydrates my mouth and gives me strength. This whole situation reminds me of when I woke up in the car after the power went out. The memory is equal parts bitter and sweet.

If I could go back to that day with the knowledge I have now, I would. My thoughts halt when I take my first bite of food. The canned goods are normally flavorless, but right now, they're the best food I've ever tasted. I eat the rest of the food and finish the water.

When I'm done, my spirits improve, and I'm even able to stand. After I'm standing, I look to the woman and smile. She smiles back, and I'm about to ask her name when I hear the door crash open behind me.

"You're one lucky son of a bitch to still be alive!" Before I turn around, I recognize the voice as Ted's. When I see Ted, I can tell he isn't a sane person. His pupils are small, and his eyes dart around.

"Why hello, Ted. What can I do for you?"

Ted gives the woman a look of utter hatred. "Shut your mouth, whore. I told you to kill this bastard, and how do you thank me? You nurse him back to health. Before I'm done, you're going to wish you—

" As Ted screams at the woman, he gets closer and closer. When he's within my reach, I decide I've heard enough. His sentence is cut off when I throw a punch and hit him square in the jaw.

His reaction is immediate. He drops into a fighting position and looks straight at me. His form is steady and calm, and I can tell this isn't his first fight. My first punch would have knocked him out had I been at full strength.

Ted lunges at me and feigns a left punch, following with a right swing. Even though I catch it in time with an arm guard, the blow still makes me dizzy. From there, the blows start hitting me fast. Each hit bounces off my guard, but they're coming in too fast to attack back.

My head starts to swim from the pain. I'm losing. When I see the nurse woman standing behind us, she moves so fast that my eyes have a hard time following. The side of her hand slams into Ted's arm, and I see a syringe sticking out. He looks at his arm, confused for a second, and I see my chance.

Jumping forward, I wrap my hands around the back of Ted's neck and pull him down toward me. My knee shoots up and connects with a powerful thud to his diaphragm. Ted falls to the floor, gasping for air. Before he can catch his breath, I see him starting to lose consciousness. Whatever the woman put into that syringe must have knocked him out.

She looks at me, and I see that she's one of Ted's captives. Now that she's attacked him, I doubt she'll stay here long.

"Well, I think it's about time we left. How long would it take you to pack up some supplies?"

The woman looks at me, and I can tell she's confused. "You want me to come with you?"

"Only if you want. I know I haven't known you for very long. Anyone who can take care of a total stranger is trustworthy enough for me. Besides, you can't stay here after what you did to Ted. It would be safer for you to come with us."

The woman smiles and grabs a bag she has behind her. "I'm already packed and ready to go. I was going to leave when your group did, but I'm glad you asked me to join. My chances of making it on my own were slim."

We exchange smiles, and then I turn around and walk into what looks like a hallway. When Melany sees me, she runs up and gives me a hug. I explain what happened. Jason and Melany tell me where Dawn and Brian went and where we're supposed to meet them.

With a plan in place, we start our travels. It takes around an hour of walking to reach the meeting place. Melany tries to convince me to stay on the bottom floor of the building, but I refuse, and we end up climbing up to the top floor.

The stairs are particularly taxing on me, but I refuse to show weakness or admit that I'm tired. When we finally do reach the top of the building, I find an old office chair and collapse into it. The others follow my lead and take a minute to rest. After we catch our breath, we do a quick check for supplies and Palemen.

We're lucky, and we find a five-gallon plastic water jug and an untouched vending machine. As we feast on chips and candy bars, the woman introduces herself as Sophia and tells us her story. In exchange, we tell her our stories.

Jason and Melany look a little hesitant about Sophia, and I can tell they're wary of her. To be honest, I don't blame them. Trusting a person you just met can be very dangerous. Something tells me that Sophia is trustworthy.

It's hard to understand why. There's something that draws me to her. I feel like I can trust her with anything. Of course, I'm hesitant to follow those feelings, but I give her more trust than I typically would.

After we finish eating, Melany and Jason start a patrol, hoping to find Brian and Dawn. Seeing this as a good opportunity to learn more about Sophia, I decide to question her.

"There's something that doesn't make sense to me, and if you don't mind, I'd like an explanation." Sophia nods her approval, and I continue. "You told us about what happened in Georgia, but you failed to mention anything before that."

Sophia sighs and looks at me. "Look, I left out some things because I didn't want the others to know. You should know everything. It'll make what I tell you next easier to understand."

I'm a little confused about what she means, but I keep my silence as she tells me her story. This time, though, she tells me about her captivity in the CDC building and how she's immune to infections. She tells me about how she's been bitten twice and weathered it, infection-free. She also tells me about how the bites changed her, made her able to sense the Palemen, and made her stronger. When she tells me this, I wonder if I experienced the same thing. Before I can think too long, though, she asks me, "Are you the same? I noticed something different about you. Can you feel the Palemen?"

Realizing there's no point in lying, I nod and say, "Yeah, I can hear them and feel them in my mind. It first happened a few weeks ago, but it's gotten much worse lately." Sophia looks a little concerned. Memories of Chris come to me, and I decide to tell Sophia about him as well. She doesn't seem surprised by what I tell her.

"I was afraid you might say something like that was happening. The research I found on the Palemen told me that there's a small percentage of people like you. There's some chemical released by the disease that has no effect on most people. The people who were afflicted were shown to have increased adrenal output, hallucinations, mania, and insanity." My heart drops as I realize that there's no escaping what's happening to me. Sophia looks at me, and she senses my despair.

"There's one way to avoid what's going to happen to you. We can get far away from any Palemen, and you should be okay. My condition is similar to yours, so I'd be willing to go anywhere with you if it meant an end to hearing the Palemen's voices."

Hearing her say this gives me hope. Maybe we can make it to the island and things will be okay. I tell Sophia about our plans. She seems somewhat excited—or at least less stoic—when I tell her where we are going.

Before we can talk any more, I hear a commotion. When I stand up and investigate, Sophia follows me. We find Dawn and Brian. Dawn is in pretty rough shape. Blood drips down her right arm, and she's sickly pale. Her eyes are clear of any red, so I figure she is infection-free.

Sophia takes commands and starts shouting orders. To my surprise, the others follow her direction without hesitation. Even if the others don't trust her, they understand that she's a capable medical technician. Jason and I keep watch while Brian and Melany make a stretcher. Evelyn keeps close by my side, staying silent. She's been so quiet lately that I'm starting to worry. She's been spending more time with Melany than me. It's not that I'm jealous; I'm happy that the two are bonding. I only miss her a little.

Sophia pulls some supplies out of her backpack and starts cleaning Dawn's arm. The blood makes me a little dizzy, and I look away, focusing instead on making sure nothing comes into the building and surprises us.

After a few minutes, Sophia has us help set Dawn onto the stretcher. Still feeling weak, I let Jason and Brian man the stretcher and watch the rear of the party as we climb the stairs. My demands to be on the top floor seem like a poor decision now. Despite this, we make it up the stairs and manage to get Dawn set down.

"Don't worry. Your friend is stabilized. She's lucky the gunshot did very little damage on its way through. She should be at full strength in a few days. As long as she stays free of infection, she should make a full recovery."

We all sigh in relief, and I'm thankful we were lucky enough to find someone who can take care of our medical needs. After everyone calms a bit, Sophia pulls me, Jason, Brian, and Melany to the side.

"Aaron filled me in on the plan and invited me to join. From what I observed of your group, though, I wanted to make sure it was okay with all you that I join." Melany and Jason look at Sophia, and I can tell they're still cautious of her. Brian seems to be trusting.

"You saved Dawn's life," he says. "We're all in your debt for that. I can't speak for the others, but I'd be glad if you joined us. Having someone who can patch up wounds would be very valuable."

After Brian's comments, the others agree that it would be a good idea. Like that, our group accepts Sophia. They may not trust her as well as they trust the others, and I can't blame them. At least they accept her as part of the group.

"Okay, I'm glad everyone's okay with me joining. Now, I wanted to talk to you about your plan. I know I'm new to the group, but something bothers me that I wanted to bring up. The island idea is brilliant, and I know it could work. My only concern is the local population. Think about your own town when the disaster struck. I imagine it became very tightly knit. As I traveled through the country, I saw plenty of towns like it. Luckily, I had enough skills and medical knowledge that I could earn some food from them, but I don't think I would have lasted long at all without those skills. My worry is that the Beaver Islanders won't be as accepting as you hope."

Looking around, I see that the others aren't that surprised by her concern. The worry that we would be rejected from the island has crossed my mind, as I'm sure it's crossed theirs. Of course, I already have a backup plan for the group.

"Luckily, I have a plan, Sophia. Even if the people on Beaver Island reject us, there's an uninhabited island right next to it. The island is about five hundred square miles large. It's unsettled land, or at least should be, and there's even an old forester's lodge we can winter in. To be completely honest with you, I want to work on making it livable, even if the Beaver Islanders do accept our group."

Jason and Brian look at me, perplexed. After a second, Jason speaks up. "The town might not be welcoming, but checking it out is worth the risk for me. We could live in the wild, but I don't want to. When it comes down to it, living in the wild could be harder than surviving among the Palemen. If this town is open to healthy newcomers, I'm ready for a return to society. Aaron, I respect you, but why would you isolate yourself?"

"Even if we are welcomed on Beaver Island, having a backup plan isn't a bad idea. If I made the island livable, it would always be a second option for us. It's not like I wouldn't visit and take advantage of food and supplies there. It's simple; I would enjoy having the peace and quiet for a while. If others want to join me, I won't argue. You may want to be immersed in civilization again, but as for me, I want silence, and others might want the same."

"Okay, you're going to do what you want, and I can respect that. Don't expect this to be the last you hear about it from me."

Jason's comments bring a smile to my face. It's good to have a friend who cares enough about me to bug me about something he sees as foolish. For a few seconds, there's silence, but then Brian steps forward.

"There's one more option that I don't think any of you have considered. I could care less what island you plan to stay on; I respect both of your desires. As for myself, I could never settle down on either island. Once all of you are safe, I plan on using the islands as a base of operation to rescue other survivors. Aaron, I understand the desire for peace, but I could never live with myself if I sat there while others were dying."

Brian's words shake me, and for a second, they make me question everything I've decided. The thought of leaving the islands once we got there never crossed my mind. The fact that my selfishness overtook my desire to help others shames me. As I remember Evelyn and what Sophia told me about insanity, though, I realize that staying put is my only option. When no one speaks up, Brian nods and turns around. The meeting comes to an end when he walks away. Jason follows behind him shortly. Evelyn gives me a small hug, then follows Melany.

When the others are gone, I look at Sophia and decide I want to ask her a question.

"You went over it, but I want to know more about the disease, and I want to know how you discovered the information." Sophia tells me about the file she received from Charles, as well as the trail to Chicago she took to find a man who could answer her questions.

When she did find the man, he was changing. She wasn't too late and was still able to get some information from him. That information led her to discover more files, which explained how the infection might have started.

"About a year ago, there was a group of soldiers who found a biological weapon from a terrorist cell. The weapon was broken down and analyzed by a team in Chicago and a group in Georgia. They discovered that the weapon contained a modified strain of bacteria. Through the use of animal testing, they found that the bacteria were capable of taking over brain stems and the motor cortex. It controlled its host to further propagate the disease. The primary symptoms of the disease were blindness, slowed heart rate, increased adrenal output, and loss of muscle control limits. They also found increased hearing perception, lowered dexterity, and extreme rage."

Since my mother is a nurse, what Sophia says makes some sense to me. I know enough to realize that there's no cure for this disease. If the bacterium takes over the brain stem, the damage done would be too severe for recovery. Even if the infection were to be eradicated, the infected person would likely become an immobile vegetable.

"There were several precautions taken to avoid cross-species infection. One of those precautions was regular health checks on all employees. So when one of the workers had strange cardiovascular activity during a routine exam, he was isolated. After it was confirmed he was not infected, the heads decided that he should be the focus of the study. Instead of trying to find any other remnants of a dangerous disease or creating a cure, focus shifted to the military benefits it could provide."

The fact that a dangerous disease was ignored frustrates me. America deserved to be struck down. It makes me sad that we could've become so inflated and corrupted that such an obvious threat would be ignored.

"Of course, they didn't know the influence would cause mania and insanity at the time. All they noticed at first were the heightened strength responses and adrenal levels. What I believe happens is that the chemical causes your brain to go into survival mode. What I mean by that is, it puts you in the same state you would be in if you knew you were being hunted by an animal, like a bear or mountain lion."

When I think about it, Chris starts to make more sense. Sophia did tell me hallucinations were part of the side effects of being exposed to Palemen. It might go deeper than that. What if Chris is a manifestation of my desire to survive at any cost? Besides, visions of the Palemen are real. I know they are more than hallucinations.

Whatever's happening to me, it feels like I have a psychic connection to the Palemen. Their pain and thoughts echo in my mind when I'm close. It might be all in my head, but something tells me it's not. Sophia continues talking as I ponder everything.

"Since there were several hundred people working in the lab at the time and only one person was affected, it was deemed a rare reaction. One of the main focuses was to study the man and try to find what caused the reaction. The hope was that we could produce something in the lab that would allow this reaction in every soldier. The power went out before that discovery was ever made, but the research shows that they were very close." Sophia finishes speaking, and I take a second to process all the information.

"There's one thing that still confuses me," I say. "How do the generals exist if the disease cripples the mind?"

"Like I said, I can only guess, so I could be wrong. The people who become generals are the ones who are sensitive to the disease. That's my theory, so people like you become generals. For some reason, they are able to fight off the bacterium or remain partially uninfected. This causes them to keep some control of higher thought processes."

It takes a minute for everything to sink in, and only then do I realize what she's telling me.

"So what you're saying is that if I'm infected, I'll become a general?"

She looks sad and nods. "Sorry, but like I said, it's a guess, and I could be wrong."

The fear that I could turn into a killing machine and influence other Palemen terrifies me. The thought that I could use Palemen to kill hundreds of others is almost too much to bear. Feeling the holster at my side, I look at my gun, debating whether it would be better to end my life now. It might be hard on my friends, but my future looks bad. I'll either go insane and kill people or turn into a general and kill people.

When I look up, I see Sophia watching me, and somehow, I know she understands what I was thinking of doing. With her here, I decide there's another option.

"Alright, I'll cope with what's happening to me, but I need you to make me a promise. If I get to manic, or I'm bitten and start to turn, I need you to kill me without hesitation. Can you do that for me?"

Sophia looks at me, and I can tell she's serious when she says, "Of course I can do that. I'd already planned on it. Also, Aaron, if Chris takes over, I'll do the same. I don't understand what he is, but I know his takeover wouldn't be good."

Feeling some relief over having someone willing to take care of me if I break, I relax.

"Alright, thank you, and I don't think I need to ask, but will you stay silent about everything we have talked about?"

Sophia smiles at me.

With the others gone, I find myself looking at Sophia. She looks at me, and I see there's something wrong. She looks uncomfortable, and I can tell she's struggling to speak. It's odd to see her like this, since she was able to have a complicated and difficult discussion unhindered.

"When I looked over the supplies, I noticed that you don't have any spare air mattresses. I hesitate to ask, but I understand that a good night's rest is important to avoid any mistakes being made. I would ask your sister, or Dawn, but I don't think either trust me enough to say yes."

Sophia's blushing, and I'm confused by what she's babbling about. "Sophia, what are you asking?"

Sophia looks at me and says, "Could I share a mattress with you and your daughter while we travel? Don't misunderstand me: I'm not your girlfriend or your woman. All I'm trying to do is be practical."

Laughing, I say, "Of course you can share my mattress, and don't worry: I'm not the kind of guy who would try anything. Even if I was, I would never dream of doing anything with my daughter so close. There's no issue with you staying with us, but I do have one condition. You have to befriend Evelyn. If she doesn't agree to you staying with us, there's nothing I can do."

Sophia nods, and without another word, she walks away. Taking advantage of the moment, I close my eyes, trying to process everything that's happened to me in the past few days. When I've gone through everything, I feel better, so I start looking for the others.

It doesn't take me long to find them. The office cubicles have been moved around to form a sort of barricade with one entrance and several partitioned rooms. It doesn't take me long to find Evelyn and Sophia. The two are chatting away, and I can tell Sophia has already won Evelyn over. I'm about to join them when I see Brian walking toward me.

"Hey, Aaron, we decided on a watch schedule, and you and I are first."

I sigh. At least first watch will give me some time to think about everything. "Alright, sounds good, Brian. But first, I'm going to check on Evelyn. I'll be right back." I make my way to the partition Evelyn is in. When I get there, Evelyn runs up and gives me a big hug. I start to help her get ready for bed, but she keeps asking for Sophia to help her.

After a while, I agree and let Sophia take care of her. I hug her goodnight and thank Sophia before starting my watch.

While I walk around the empty office building, I try to think of what I'm going to do. That's when I decide that everything I've learned changes nothing. The only thing I can do now is take things one day at a time. It's all I've done since the power first went out, and it's gotten me this far. My only hope is that taking things one day at a time will lead me to tomorrow.

Chapter 15: Stephanie

The grave of my husband lies in front of me. It's only been a few weeks since his death, and the pain is as fresh today as it was the night he died. My anger and pain over my husband's death may never go away, and I'm not sure I want it to. It isn't in me to let it go. If he had died naturally, it might have been different, but my husband's death was caused by Jason's grandmother, and I'll never forgive that.

There's nothing in this grave but ashes, but that's more than enough for me. His body wasn't the only one I cremated. I also cremated the children. Alexis buried them in a nearby lot. We cut the rest of Jason's family into pieces and used them as bait for dogs. Originally, I wanted to leave them in a field somewhere, but Alexis convinced me to find a use for their bodies. If I hadn't been so angry, I probably would have been disgusted at the idea, but looking back on it, I'm glad we did.

Alexis was able to bring down a half dozen of the dogs, and using a survival book she found in a nearby home, she gutted and skinned them. We got about fifty pounds of meat and a bedspread that will help keep us warmer through the winter.

When I examined the meat, just to make sure it wasn't contagious, I discovered that dogs' immune systems are extremely efficient at eliminating the bacteria that causes the Paleman disease.

When we discovered this, Alexis started working harder to track and hunt dogs.

She says she does it to build up our food supply. We both know she's lying, but I leave it be. With the food we added from Jason's family, and the fact that we have half as many mouths to feed, we're set up to make it a few years on our current supplies. Alexis is probably just looking for an escape, and I can't blame her.

The last few weeks have been lucid for me. I walk around and work, but underneath it, I'm depressed. Everything I do hurts me, and it isn't getting any easier. At night, between sobs I find myself wishing I could've died with Marcus. When I wake up every morning, my first feeling is disappointment that my prayers were not answered.

The only thing that's kept me from ending my own life is my daughter Sarah, who still depends on me—that and the hope that someday Aaron and Melany will return to me.

As I take a last look at my husband's grave for the day, I debate lying down next to him and just waiting for death to take me. Alexis is watching nearby, though, and I don't want to put her in any danger. When I stand up, I wipe away the tears on my face and start walking toward the apartment building.

Alexis is tailing me, and I know better than to argue. She has really changed since the night my husband died. She doesn't talk much now; I think Marcus was more of a father figure to her than her own father. Her parents are hidden away, and I have no idea if they are even alive. I doubt she does, either. Ever since Marcus died, she's been actively exploring the areas around our apartment and killing any Palemen she encounters.

At first, I thought what she was doing was pointless, except for the dog bait it provided. After the first week, though, I noticed a significant decrease in the number of Palemen I saw every day. Before long, it wasn't surprising if I didn't see a Paleman throughout the whole day. Because of her, I feel safe traveling to and from my husband's grave.

Alexis has become a very skilled fighter and medical student. She doesn't know this, but I've seen her use her spear and bow, and she is very good. The times I've watched her, she usually kills two or three Palemen with her bow before they even notice she's there. There was only one time I saw any Palemen get close to her, and she killed them with her spear before they came to within arm's reach of her.

Even though she isn't my daughter, I still feel proud of her. Marcus and I started watching out for her, and it's surprising to see what she's becoming. While I'm thinking this, I hear Alexis's voice, and I'm startled until I see her standing next to me.

"Stephanie, I need to talk to you when we get back." As I try to catch my breath from being startled, I respond to her. "Okay?" She looks at me with an awkward half smile, then walks away. This is the first time she's approached me while I was visiting Marcus's grave, so I know she must have something important to tell me. The way she acted seemed uncomfortable, though, so I'm not sure what she wants to talk to me about.

The walk to the apartment is a short one, and there are no Palemen anywhere nearby, probably thanks to Alexis. When I reach the apartment, it isn't long before Alexis approaches me.

"Stephanie, I wanted to talk to you about scavenging." Alexis looks very worried, and I'm not sure why. There's never been an argument about her scavenging. Personally, I don't see any reason for it, and though she's brought plenty of food and supplies to us, there hasn't really been a need for any of it.

"Alexis, you know I don't care that you scavenge. As long as you're safe, you're welcome to continue scavenging if it's what you want." Alexis sighs, and I can see that she's trying to gather courage.

"Well, you see, I've looked at our supplies, and we have around eight years' worth of food and supplies. If I continue to hunt and start a garden, I think it's more like ten to twenty years of supplies. By your own estimates, the Paleman infection should die out long before that. That's why I want to start looking for other survivors." Alexis pauses, and I'm shocked by what she's said. After everything, why would she want to find other people? We are safe here; we have food. The last family we trusted to live in our home with us killed my husband.

Why would Alexis think it would be okay to connect with and trust others? Even though I'm angry, I let Alexis continue, hoping she has a good explanation for herself.

"There are people who need help. I know you're wary of helping others, but think of me. If it weren't for you and Aaron, my whole family would have been dead by now. Stephanie, you're like a mother to me. You've taught me how to heal and help others. I'll always be grateful to you, but I know there are people out there whose lives I could save. I want to go out there and help them, and I want you to come with me."

Alexis is one of my daughters in my eyes. Her real parents abandoned reality when the power outage hit, and she's struggled to keep them alive since. Now they remain hiding, locked away and cowering in fear.

Even if she is my daughter, what she's asking is too much. I taught her what I know about healing so she could help others here in my absence, not help possibly dangerous strangers.

"Even if I was willing to go with you, what good is helping others if it only brings us more sorrow? People are unpredictable and dangerous. You help someone, and they might turn around and stab you in the back just because they think it will make them live longer." Alexis looks at me, and I see a brief expression of sadness and pain.

"The thing is, I don't just want to help and find other people. I want to bring them back with us and build a community. If there are people who try to take advantage of that, I'll deal with it. A community needs laws, and I've learned in this world that you cannot afford to be lenient." Alexis is silent, and so am I. As I consider what she's saying, I realize that she's adamant about this, and I'm fairly certain that if I refuse to help her, she'll go out on her own and try to do what she wants without me.

My trust in others isn't restored, and I don't think it ever will be completely, but I love Alexis. If I don't help her, she could die. Putting my feelings aside, I resolve myself to help my adopted daughter. All I can hope is that she comes through on her promise of taking care of those who want to harm us. Hopefully she realizes the full meaning of that promise.

Memories of the oaths to heal return to me, and even though I made them in what feels like a different world, I don't think I can escape them. Perhaps Alexis is right; if we can help heal and build a community, it would be wrong not to try.

"Okay," I say. "I can't say no to you. You have backed me into a corner, and I think you know that, but I'll help you all the same. If anybody in our family is hurt, I'll hold you personally responsible. If you can live with that, I'm willing to help." Alexis looks at me, and I see a look of calm calculation.

"It's a deal then. And don't worry; I won't let any harm come to anyone. I have no intention of stopping until I see a community full of hope again." With that remark, Alexis turns around and walks out of the room. She's probably gathering her things and will want to leave immediately. Reluctantly, I decide to find Sarah and quickly explain the situation to her. She helps me pack for the trip, and after we're done, I find Alexis and find that she's ready to go as well.

Seeing no reason to delay any longer, I say goodbye to Sarah, and Alexis and I leave the apartment.

As we move through the abandoned town full of trash and memories, I force myself to stay focused, knowing that a single mistake could lead to my death. The town is quiet and empty, and I realize as we walk that this is the farthest I've been from the apartment since we first came here.

We run across several Palemen, but they are always distracted and oblivious to our presence. Using her spear or bow, Alexis kills every one she runs across. She's very effective, and I can tell that she's been practicing. The sound of dogs howling at night suddenly makes sense. I'm sure they've been very well fed thanks to Alexis.

Suddenly, Alexis stops and holds her hand up to her mouth in a gesture of silence. Stopping instinctively, I look toward an abandoned theater that Alexis is moving toward. Before I can wonder why we've stopped, I hear a crash come from inside.

Not knowing what's going on, I follow Alexis as she shimmies her way through the partially blocked theater door. The squeeze is tight, but we both make it through a gap and into what looks like manmade fortifications. Both Alexis and I stand still, letting our eyes adjust to the dim light.

As I look around, I see trash, graffiti, and decay. This theater was closed long before the power went out, and I can tell. Cracks line the walls and foundations. Trash is everywhere, and in one corner, there's a mattress. Before I can take in any more of my surroundings, there's a high-pitched feminine scream that echoes through the lobby. From the sound of the scream, it seems like it might be coming from the back of the lobby on the left side, and instinct tells me it's coming from one of the theaters.

Both Alexis and I start moving toward the source of the scream as quickly as possible. I'm glad she realizes how foolish it would be to run through the trash and junk of this lobby. A single prick from a needle, or even a rusty nail, would spell death for us.

Luckily, when we reach the back of the lobby, I can see that there are only two theaters—one on the left and one on the right. We come up to the theaters' doorway. Around it, lumber that looks freshly broken is scattered on the ground. Through the door, I can see five Palemen moving toward a woman and man at the back of the theater. I freeze, but thankfully, Alexis doesn't. She brings two down with arrows and runs a third down with a spear as she makes her way toward the people in the back of the theater. I follow, not wanting to be far from her protection.

As we approach the two people, I notice that there's a man using the woman as a shield. Two Palemen are closing in on them, and Alexis will only be able to get to one before they reach the couple.

"Wouaaa." The sounds of a baby crying fill my ears, and I realize that the woman is fiercely hugging a bundle that must contain her child. What I must do hits me, and without even thinking, I run past Alexis and slam my body into one of the Palemen, hoping Alexis will be able to kill the other one. My hope was to knock it over, but I feel the creature grab me, and I lose my balance.

We both tumble to the ground, but luckily, it loses its grip. It is only inches away from me, and I only have seconds to react. I fumble with a knife pouch and pull out my knife. I flip my body to face the Paleman and see it above me, about to lunge. As the creature swings its mouth down toward me, I throw my knife up under its jaw and feel the blade slide into the soft tissue. Blood seeps out as I watch the creature stop moving and the life drain from its eyes.

I twist as the body falls, forcing it to land by my side instead of on top of me. Sliding the knife out of the creature, I stand and see Alexis with her bow drawn and pointed at the two survivors. She looks at me out of the corner of her eyes.

"You okay?"

I nod and am about to ask her why she has the bow pointed at the couple when she says, "Alright, I want you two to separate and stand against the wall. Tell me your story. I have no intention of hurting you, but if you try to rush me, I'll fire." The two people stay frozen, and a whimper of pain comes from the woman holding a child.

"Please," the woman begins to say, but her sentence ends with a soft cry, and I see the man has her arm twisted behind her.

"Shut up, bitch! You ain't doing nothing," the man says. "Here's what's happening. You're gonna give me the baby, and I'm g'tting' out. Shit, this ain't even worth the meal."

As he says this, I'm confused until I see a man's body lying a few feet from us. He's obviously not a Paleman. A pool of what looks like fresh blood lies under the body, and I realize this man must have been murdered by the person now holding the woman and her child hostage. I don't understand why he would want to take the baby or why he made a comment about it not being worth a meal—unless the two were connected. My stomach sours, and I'm filled with unbelief and horror.

Twang. I hear the bowstring and see an arrow sprout from the man's neck. He instinctively reaches up to his throat, and when he does, the woman runs from him. The man wears a look of confusion as he falls to his knees. Before he understands what happened, Alexis drives her spear through his eye.

When she said she would take care of people who tried to hurt others, I didn't think she meant this, but it makes sense. This world has no jails, and you can't banish someone and trust that they'll leave. The only way to handle someone who's harmful to others is by execution.

As I look over to the girl, I can see that she's quite clearly terrified. I realize that both Alexis and I are armed, so I put my knife back into the pouch.

"It's okay. We are here to help. I promise we won't hurt you. Is your baby okay?"

The woman still looks hesitant, but I think she realizes that there's nowhere else to go.

"He's okay, but he's been a bit yellow for a few weeks. My husband found someone who said they could help, and he brought him here, and now he's dead." The woman starts crying, and I approach her. She no longer seems afraid of me, so I step forward and look at her baby. From what I can see of its face and pupils, I think the child has some jaundice. Simple enough to treat. All she needs is a few hours of sunlight.

The woman leans into me, and I find myself hugging her, the baby now silent between us. She weeps openly, and all I can hope is that Alexis is watching the door.

We help the woman move to another room so she doesn't have to be next to her dead husband, and over several hours, we share our stories. Like us, the woman and her husband found shelter. They ran out of food around the same time the child was born and became desperate for help, which led the husband to look for others. After telling her our story and what happened to my husband, she agrees to come back with us to the apartments. The baby quickly recovers with Alexis's and my care, and after a week or two, the woman starts to recover as well.

As the weeks pass by, Alexis and I find more and more people to join our community, and it slowly grows. We start to use the building around us, and bridges connect us to the rooftops and upper floors of the former downtown area. After a few months, the place becomes a little raised town with around fifty inhabitants.

Things run smoothly, and Alexis even creates a police force of sorts, which protects everyone. It's hard to believe that not long ago, we were all alone and there was no hope. I find that I'm becoming happy again, and I hold pride in what I, Alexis, and the others of this town have built. I know my husband would be proud of what we have done.

That's why when Alexis tells me she plans to leave, I don't understand. After she explained that she wanted to go looking for her brother and the others, and possibly create more communities like this, I understand. Looking at my adopted daughter, I'm filled with pride. We share our final goodbyes, and I see her off. Half the town is with us, so there's no time to say private words.

She's younger than me, but without her, I would never have held hope in my heart again. Now I know I was wrong, and I know that, someday, I'll see her again. So maybe this isn't a goodbye so much as a farewell for now.

Chapter 16: Aaron

August 5th

The bright sun shines through the colored vinyl of my tent. I stare at it for a while, not quite wanting to get up yet. Next to me, Evelyn sleeps and I hear her calm, steady breaths. When I look to my other side, I notice Sophia and am confused until I recall the events of the past few days.

I turn onto my side and look at her. As she sleeps, she twitches, and I can see that she's in the grip of some dream. When I look closer, I notice she's sweaty and looks upset. Thinking she's having a nightmare, I'm about to try to wake her up when her eyes shoot open. They are like the gaze of a snake hunting its prey. Pure hatred and blood lust emanate from them, and I'm frozen in fear as I lock eyes with Sophia.

After a second, though, her gaze grows softer and confused. Quietly, I whisper to her, forgetting the murderous gaze she gave me a second ago.

"Are you okay?"

Sophia looks around and takes a deep breath. She nods, telling me she's fine. She smiles and rolls over. I decide to give her some space and leave the tent to avoid waking the still-sleeping Evelyn.

Once outside of the tent, I decide to look for whoever was on last watch. If I remember, it should be Melany and Jason. The search takes almost no time, and I find them next to the camp stove. A pot of something that smells like pine needles is brewing. When I get closer, they offer me a cup. Wanting something to warm me up, I take it.

When I sip the tea, I taste what seems like pine needles. The warmth spreads through me and chases off the morning chill. We sit around the camp stove, silent in the somber mood of the morning.

After about thirty minutes, I'm more energized than I've been in weeks. The feeling seems somewhat familiar, and I realize I'm getting a caffeine rush. I look at Melany and Jason, and they seem wide awake despite having been up for hours.

"What did you guys put in this tea?"

They both look at me and laugh as if they are part of some joke. "One of the things Jason's picked up along the way was a field and plant guide. In it, he found that some varieties of holly have caffeine in them. We found one of the plants, and Jason and I worked on drying and preserving it into this tea. It's a combination of holly and pine needles. It tastes pretty good, and the effects are the same as coffee, if not better. We have a cutting of the holly plant that we took, so when we do make it to the island, we'll be able to farm it. We have about two pounds of the tea to last until then."

I smile and take another sip. This is good. We've all missed the effects of caffeine. Having it again should increase our ability to do late-night watches. Having heightened awareness is always welcome.

We spend a few minutes talking and joking, the mood lightened by the holly brew. After talking for a few minutes, though, the conversation veers when Jason says, "So, it's time we map out our route, make copies, and pass them out to everyone. We've been lucky so far that we haven't been separated from each other, but we should plan for that possibility." I agree and pull out an atlas. Not until I have the map out in front of me do I realize that I have no idea where we are.

"Do you know where we are?" I ask.

Jason points at the map while talking to me. "Well, we walked about ten miles north of downtown Chicago, so we would be about here." His finger points to the town of Evanston, Illinois.

When I study the map, I see that Beaver Island is far to the northeast, and there's quite a bit of water between us. Going across the lake and into Wisconsin and then following the coast until we can't anymore would be the best way to do it. As I look at the map, I realize how foolish it was for us to go through Chicago, but there's no changing that now.

"Alright, so I'm thinking that we want to avoid all major cities, am I right?" Both Jason and Melany nod their agreement. "We should follow this coast and try to find a boat that will get us across. We'll avoid going into Milwaukee unless it's the only option for a boat. From there, we'll cut northeast and land far north of Grand Rapids. From the look of the atlas, we should be able to walk along the coast or even sail up to this town here." I point to a small town called Northport at the very edge of a peninsula.

Jason seems hesitant and asks, "Even if we do find a seaworthy boat along the coast, do you think we'll be able to get it to the Michigan coast? The lake is about fifty miles wide, and I'd rather not take a huge gamble getting across."

"It's our only option. We don't have the time or luck to go the long way back through Chicago. I'm sure we can find some sailing books where we find a boat. Even if we do horribly and move at a snail's pace, it's not like we'll be in any danger. There's no way the Palemen are coordinated enough to swim. They would drown in any water deep enough to submerge them."

"But do you think we can go fifty miles without running into trouble with the lake?" Jason asks. "What if there's a storm? None of us have experience handling a boat in any kind of water, much less in rough conditions. Yes, the lack of Palemen is nice, but the lake is a fearsome adversary."

Jason is right: Melany and I have both been on the ocean in several different boats, though we were too young to take part in their operation. "We don't have zero boat experience," I say. "Both Melany and I have been on the ocean on several boats. True, we didn't operate the boats, but you're afraid of the unknown here. I'm telling you there's nothing to be afraid of."

"Aaron, there are huge differences between being on a boat and operating one. If we get caught in a storm and don't know what we're doing, we could end up slammed into rocks or shipwrecked in the middle of the Great Lakes. We wouldn't be the first ship to be sunken by the lakes. Most of the others were sailed by experienced sailors."

Jason isn't wrong, but he's overreacting. Fifty miles might seem like a long way, but we could paddle that far in a few days. "You're right. Weather is a danger on the open water, but we can predict the weather for at least one day. As long as we move a half mile an hour, which I'm pretty sure we could do, we'll make it across that fifty miles in two days. We'd only have to risk not knowing the weather for one day, and I say that's safer than we've been in months." Jason still seems apprehensive, but I can tell that I've won him over to some degree.

"Okay," he says. "It's a good plan. I just wanted everyone to be aware of the risk. I suppose we should make some copies of this route and pass them out to everyone."

We get to work mapping out our route. After we're all happy with the first map, we make enough copies to pass out to everyone. We pass them out with a cup of hot holly tea, and everyone is excited about both. Soon after everyone finishes their tea, we pack up and get moving.

The journey through the outskirts of Chicago is uneventful. We rarely run into any Palemen. The city is empty and eerie. I imagine that the three generals and the battle in Chicago must have all but wiped out any population in the area.

For the first time since the epidemic, I'm left to wonder what we'll do after the Paleman threat is gone. Without power and with a fraction of the population that we once had, there will be no returning to our old lives. Sophia and I talk while we travel, and we grow closer.

She's the only one I'm not worried about showing weakness to. She's seen my dark side and still trusts and respects me.

As we travel up the coast, we have a difficult time finding a ship that's in sailing condition. When the infection started to spread, I'm sure people panicked. Trying to escape, they must have taken any boats they could. Luckily, the extra days we take in finding a ship help settle our worries about sailing. Though we don't find any sailing-worthy boats, we manage to find several dry-docked and broken boats, along with some sailing how-to books. We manage to learn everything we need to by the time we find a ship that's seaworthy.

In a town called Kenosha, we finally find a boat that's viable. The only thing it's missing is a sail. After talking, everyone decides that making or finding a sail would be easy enough. As we search for the sail, we fix up a few minor issues with the boat.

Today is the day we plan to launch it. We found a sail in a warehouse but wanted to wait until the daytime to break into it. Dawn and Sophia decided to be the ones who grabbed the sails, while the rest of us did the final checks on the ship. As soon as they return, we'll raise the sail and be on our way.

After a final run-through, I take up watch, waiting for the girls to return. Someone startles me by tapping my shoulder, and when I turn around, I see that it's Melany.

"Hey, Aaron, do you have a minute? I want to talk to you." I don't know what she could want, but there's no reason for me to say no.

"Yeah, no problem. What's up, sis?"

"Well, I was thinking. What happens when we get to the island? What I mean is, say this place is safe. Won't the people have been sheltered from the chaos? If so, won't they think we're a bunch of kids?"

I'm a bit confused. We've been through so much that it hadn't dawned on me that others might only look at our age. "You could be right," I say, "but what's the alternative? If we want to rejoin civilization, we'll have to blend in."

"But, Aaron, can you go back to being a kid? I mean—" Melany is cut off by Brian, who's shouting from the other side of the ship.

"Aaron, Melany! Sophia and Dawn are in trouble. Hurry!" Our conversation ends immediately, and we look out to where Brian is pointing. Around three hundred yards out from us, there seems to be a group of people. In front are two figures who I'm certain are Dawn and Sophia.

"Melany, I need you to use your camera. Tell us what's behind them."

Melany nods and grabs a camera and lens from her bag. After a second, she focuses and starts to tell us what's going on. "It looks like they might have run into locals. There's some people chasing them." She pauses and lowers her camera before looking through it again. "I don't know how or why, but one of the men is holding on to a chain with a Paleman on the end. The man is so pale."

Without thinking I jump. The boat isn't far from the ground, only five feet or so, so my momentum doesn't stop when I hit the ground. I'm alone but notice that Brian is ahead of me. I didn't see him jump, but he's so far ahead of me that he must have gone long before me.

Running faster, I try to catch up, but Brian's running as fast as he can, and I have a hard time gaining on him. Even when I push myself as hard as I can, I only match his mad pace. Brian reaches the group about ten seconds before I do. He whips out his rifle and aims it at the man holding the Palemen on chains.

Now that Brian's still, I catch up and unsheathe my two pistols and aim one at the same man as Brian. The other I aim at another of the men in the group. The men look upset and one screams out.

"You dare point a gun at a god!" The situation is tense, but we're outnumbered. Without knowing what's going on, I hold my fire, and luckily, so does Brian.

"Wha—" I try to speak but am cut off by the man who I can only presume is a zealot.

"How dare you speak in God's presence. He is a virtue among men, and a dirty outsider like yourself has no right to speak in his presence. He has descended from heaven and provided protection from the evils of the world. He does what is right by chasing those vile women. He sanctified them with his own flesh and gave them his greatest blessing." The man's insane rambling falls on deaf ears; whoever these people are, they think the Paleman general is a god. His ability to control other Palemen isn't a divine gift—it's a fluke of a disease.

Sadly, I know there's no changing a zealot's mind, and because of this, I see only one course of action. My focus shifts to the gun pointed at the Paleman general, and I aim, knowing I'll only have one shot. The gun fires, and the false god drops.

"Brian, grab Dawn and run!" I scream as a chain reaction hits the general-worshipers. Some drop to their knees; some stare in shock. Brian follows my advice and grabs Dawn, helping her run. Ignoring the chaos erupting around me, I run toward Sophia. When I get to her, she mutters sorry and collapses onto the ground. Standing over her, I curse to myself. Where there was some semblance of order before, there is only chaos now. The Palemen, chained and controlled a second ago, are ripping, biting, and tearing into their captors.

A few stragglers come toward me, but I pick them off. As I stand guard over Sophia, I'm forced to watch as the other men are torn apart. When it's all over, there are around twenty bodies, Palemen and human. I empty my gun magazine into any of the men or Palemen who were unfortunate enough to survive. With the crises past, I pick up Sophia and move her to the boat.

As I walk back, a slight twinge of guilt hits me, but I brush it away, feeling that I've become a cold, emotionless monster, snuffing out life after life. But at what point will I finally confront it? At what point will I admit to myself that I enjoy the horror I'm inflicting?

Tears stream down my face as I walk back toward the boat. There's no returning from the things I've done. Sophia moans and shifts. Thinking she's coming to, I set her down. She starts to stir, and I wipe the tears from my face.

She doesn't come to, but when she shifts, I see a wound on her neck that I know is a bite mark. Tears return to my eyes, and I put my gun to her head, knowing that she's now doomed. My guilt for the man I killed turns to hatred, and I'm now glad they're dead and in the depths of hell.

I'm about to pull the trigger when Sophia mutters something. It's soft and I don't hear it, so I move my ear over her mouth.

"Don't shoot. Immune… I'm immune." My resolve to kill her collapses. Remembering her telling me she was immune, I curse myself for forgetting. I still doubt it's true, but it would be wrong of me not to trust her. If she turns, I'll kill her myself.

From past experience, I know that I have about thirty minutes before she turns, so I decide it would be better to wait here with her. Holding her hand, I set the gun down next to us. She falls asleep, and I do my best to make her comfortable on the cold concrete.

As I watch her, the time passes, and though she grows paler, her eyes stay purple and she remains herself, as far as I can tell. Even after thirty minutes, I wait. Only when an hour has passed and the sun is starting to set do I decide to bring her back to the ship.

When I reach the ship, Jason helps bring me and Sophia on board. Once we're on deck, the others come toward me. Evelyn runs up and hugs my leg.

"Dawn is gone," she says as she weeps into my leg.

I see Brian approach, and he has a look of dark fury and sadness on his face. "Why have you brought her aboard?" he asks. "She's infected like Dawn, isn't she? Why is she alive? Are you so dumb that you're willing to risk all our lives for nothing? Could you not kill her?" Brian waves his gun around as he screams at me. Dawn's death is having more of an impact on him than I would have thought. I step between him and Sophia.

"Brian, please trust me. She's been bitten and infected, but she'll be fine. She's immune. This isn't the first time she's been infected."

Brian stares at me for a second before collapsing. He starts to scream. He's past his breaking point. "What do you mean? Can people be immune? Did I kill Dawn when she had a chance to live? Why, why, why, why, why!"

Brian moves his gun toward his head, and I'm sure he's about to end his life. Before he can pull the trigger, I see Jason kick the gun out of his hand. He must have snuck around when Brian started to break down. Brian starts to thrash around, and Jason, Melany, and I all have to fight to subdue him.

"There's been enough death today, Brian," Jason says before turning to me. "Aaron, even if what you say is true, we can't risk having an infected person on a moving ship. There will be no escaping her on the open water if she turns. By the looks of her, though, she seems like she might be about to turn."

"I… I can't, Jason. Please, give her a chance. We'll get off the boat until she's come through, but please give her a chance. I can't kill someone who has a chance of pulling through. She should've already turned by now, and if she does end up turning, I swear I'll end it."

Jason nods, and with his help, we move Sophia into a nearby houseboat. Before Jason leaves, he pulls me to the side. "Aaron, I only want to risk it until morning. If she isn't better by then, we have to leave her. I'll look after your daughter if you want to stay here."

I nob my consent, and Jason leaves. He's right, and I know that if I made everyone stay longer, it would only ruin the trust the group has in me. Even so, a part of me hates him for what he's doing.

When I return to Sophia's side, I see that she's even paler than she was before. Despite this, I can't help but be mesmerized by her. In the moonlight, she looks so beautiful. I realize then that I'm in love with her. Growing up, I always thought love would be something simple, not something like this. Sophia is someone I never want to see die, much less kill by my own hand. Tears stream down my face as I leave Sophia to check my perimeter.

On one of the laps I make around the boat, I see someone walking toward me. The darkness of the night shades the figure, but I know it isn't a Paleman by the way it's walking. My hatchet and guns come out of their sheaths, and I ready myself. When the figure gets closer, though, I recognize it as my sister Melany, so I help her onto the boat and we embrace.

"Aaron, it's all so wrong. This world is wrong." She starts to cry, and I hold her closer as she cries into my chest. All these people I'm with are suffering, and I want this hell to end for them.

Tears stream down my face as I say, "I know, Melany, but soon, it will become right again. Soon, we will be safe."

Melany quiets her sobbing a bit and continues speaking. "Aaron, I need to go back soon. I needed to see you. Please don't hate Brian. He was in love with Dawn. He didn't know what he was doing. He was the one to end her life."

The realization slams into me. I can't imagine how it felt to find some measure of happiness in this post-apocalyptic world, only to have it ripped away. Part of me understands now why he was in so much pain.

After everything Brian has been through to find love, having to kill the person he found happiness with would be shattering. His actions make sense. That's why I understand why he's so upset to hear that someone might be immune. There's no doubt in my mind that he would have traded Sophia's life for Dawn's, and I can't blame him.

"Don't worry, Melany. I could never hate him. I can only hope he feels the same about me." She smiles and starts to walk away. Suddenly, I remember our conversation earlier about us being treated like children. I realize I have an answer to her question.

"Hey, Melany. You know how I know it'll work out when we get to the island? Nobody can go through as much pain and trials as we have and still be considered a child." She looks at me, and I see a small glimmer of reassurance—and sadness.

"Yeah, I guess you're right." I help her off the boat and watch as she walks away.

A part of me feels bad for lying to her, but hope is all I can give her. We've all learned firsthand how little people can see. When we reach the island, it's possible that the survivors will see us as children who somehow made it there. They'd be wrong. There's no going back to being a child after you've taken someone's life.

As I walk into the houseboat and sit down on the bed, I put my arm on Sophia's forehead. Noticing that her fever is down, I begin to hope. When I look closer, I see that her skin is also starting to regain some color. Encouraged by this, I sit by and watch her. After a few minutes, she stirs into consciousness.

"What? Where am I?" Relief at hearing Sophia's voice floods into me. My relief is so great that, without thinking, I lean down and kiss her. Before I can regret my decision, I notice that she's kissing me back. After a few minutes like this, we stop, and Sophia looks at me.

"Not that that wasn't nice, but where am I?" Flushed with embarrassment, I catch Sophia up on everything that happened. Part of me feels guilty for kissing her and letting myself feel some measure of joy. With Dawn's death so fresh in my memory, I understand that any of us could die at any moment. I didn't want to risk never letting Sophia know how I felt.

When I explain this to her, she agrees with me, and though we're sad, we also find happiness and warmth in each other. It's only when the sun comes up that we realize that we have to return to the others.

As we walk to the boat and I look at the sunrise, I realize that the world we live in now is cold and it is dark, but there's always hope found at the dawn.

Chapter 17: Brian

It was only this morning that I woke up happy and full of hope; the person I loved most in all the world sleeping in my arms. How did I not realize that things could change at the flip of a coin? I was foolish to believe that I could find any lasting happiness in this hellish world. Why didn't I realized that any joy I found could just as easily be lost?

My presumption that our luck would last was idiotic, and I can see that now. Dawn shifts in my arms, and I remember what I have to do.

"Brian," she says, "I'm not ready. I don't want to die. Not now. Why now? Six months ago, I could have, but now, I finally found a reason to live." Every word she speaks lashes out against me like a whip. My heart hurts, and there's a knot in my throat.

The seconds tick by, and I know I'm that much closer to losing her and that much closer to having to say goodbye. She begs me to live, but there's no way I can fulfill her wish. If I could give my life for hers, I would.

The others gave us privacy, but I know they didn't want to do what I must. No one wants to end the lives of friends or loved ones. Even so, I can't forget or forgive what I saw on my friends' faces when they saw the bite on Dawn. Their faces showed sadness and sympathy—but also fear.

Before the power went out, I had no purpose, and even after the power went out, I had no purpose. Not until after the outbreak did I finally start living for myself. I stopped being a slave to my parents' fears and found that my life was better under my own control. The freedom I found was the sweetest thing I'd ever experienced until Dawn came into my life.

She made the purpose of my life clear. Or so I thought. Without her, I'm not sure what to do. She stirs, and I force the knot out of my throat.

"I know, Dawn. I know, but what can I do? I want to save you—I do—but how? Tell me how." My nerves fray and I realize that I'm starting to break down and panic. My life is collapsing all around me, and I can't think of what to do to stop it.

The desperation is thick in my voice, and it's killing me. Dawn moans in pain, and I'm immediately worried. Without realizing how futile it is, I try to think of ways to lessen her pain, but I remember there's nothing I can do to help her now.

She's dying, and I'm worried that she's feeling some pain. Even if it would be a waste to the others, I debate going to Sophia's room and looking for morphine when I hear Dawn speak.

"I'm sorry, Brian. I know this can't be easy for you. I forgot that I wasn't the only scared one." I calm down a little when she talks.

"Brian, can you do something for me?" she asks. My anxiety returns. I'm scared to know what she wants from me. Mostly, I'm scared to let her go; I don't want to move past this moment. Even with the fear and anxiety right now, at least I have her in my arms. At least she's still alive.

"You know I can't say no to you, Dawn, especially not now."

When Dawn laughs, I'm shocked. Her laugh is beautiful, though it's the last thing I would expect to hear right now. How could she laugh, knowing that she's about to die? If I was in the same situation, I would only feel anger and grief, not joy. The laughter goes on, and I can only listen and wait.

"Yeah, I was kind of counting on that. Brian, I know it's hard, but I want you to spend the next few minutes with me, pretending everything's fine. I want our last few minutes together to be happy ones. I don't want your last memories of me to be ones where we're sad, miserable, and scared. There's nothing I can do to stay alive, but I can make sure you'll still want to live after I'm gone."

Dawn is putting on a strong face for me, and it hurts. Like always, though, she's right. It would be better to spend the next few minutes enjoying her in my arms. The pain is boiling, but I force it down my throat. It burns as it goes down, but I ignore it and wrap my arms tighter around her.

"Yeah, let's do that." I force a fake smile, but when I see Dawn smiling at me, I can't help but smile back. Dawn hugs my arm, and we lean back against the wall of one of the many abandoned building in town. Even now, as our time runs out, I can't help but feel happy with Dawn in my arms.

"Brian, do you remember that first night we talked how hostile I was toward you? There's no one else in the world that could've charmed me as fast as you did. I don't know what it is about you, but I swear, after that first night, I would have followed you to the ends of the world."

As I remember the night, I smile. Dawn had just joined the group and we were on watch together. Before that night, I'd thought nothing of her. Somehow, we understood each other, and before the end of that night, we were in love. It only took two hours for me to become closer to her than to any other person I'd known before.

She's wrong about me charming her, though. Words were never something I was good at, and I was a pretty big fool that night. By some miracle, though, she understood who I was. Or rather, she understood how I thought. She made me want to open up to her. Never before had I felt the desire to let someone know who I was.

Before that night ended, we both knew each other's life stories—and more. Dawn learned my insecurities and desires, and I knew hers. We fell in love before either of us had a chance to realize what was going on. When I think about it, I suppose we charmed each other somehow.

"After that first night, I knew I'd do anything to spend my life with you. I'd never been so sure of anything in my life, not until that moment."

Her words fill me with happiness—until I remember that her life is almost over and I have to pause to regain my strength. My eyes burn, and I have to force back tears. She won't hear me cry, not in her last minutes. I try to distract myself with happy thoughts and happy memories.

"How about the day I taught you to shoot a gun? You were so afraid. Remember how you shook and how you were scared you might hurt one of us? You always acted tough in front of everyone. You never acted like that with me. I'm glad I got to see a different side of you."

When I look at Dawn, I hope to see a smile, but I notice her skin becoming paler. When I stroke her head, hair comes out in my hands. Even so, her smile tells me she's happy. It's so beautiful, and I capture it in my mind, never wanting to forget it.

"Yeah, I remember that. I also remember how you were scared for me. You tried to hide it—you always do. I can't remember the first time I knew what you were feeling. All I remember is being glad I could understand you. Brian, you always act so calm and collected, but I know you have as many doubts as the rest of us."

Right now, despite myself, I'm happy, and Dawn knows it. She's the only person in the world who could make me feel anything but pain right now. I love her more than I can comprehend, and I don't know what I'm going to do without her.

Thinking past today is hard for me. Never have I thought about what I'd do if I lost Dawn. The possibility had never crossed my mind. While I suppose I should have, considering how dangerous this world is, Dawn has always been so strong, so I always thought she would make it.

"Brian, I don't think I have that long left. I want you to make a few promises to me before I go, okay?" Fear grips my stomach. I don't know what promises she wants from me, but knowing her, they'll be hard to fulfill. When I look at her, I know she understands that I'll do anything she asks.

"Listen to me. I want you to move on. You aren't the only one who's going to lose loved ones from this disease. You've talked to me so many times about your desire to help others once you reach Beaver Island. Don't change your plans to save people like us. Let someone find a happy ending through you. Even if you save one couple, it'll be worth living for it."

I'm not sure how, but she knows that, deep down, I was planning on killing myself after I killed her. Why would she make me promise to live? She loves me, so how does she not understand that without her, there's no reason to live?

She's so kind. Even when dying, she still thinks about others. I could search the world a hundred times over and never find anyone as special as her. If I'm going to live, it can't be for myself. The only way I can honor her wish is to save others, but the moment she dies, so do I.

"Brian, one other thing: I want you to live for yourself, not others. You may want to die, or you may want to save others. I want you to promise me that your life will be more important to you than the lives of others."

Dawn's intuition was always sharp. Even now, in the midst of everything, she's reading my mind. Dawn is my world; it doesn't matter that I've only known her for a few months. This disaster has brought us close, and without her in my life, I have a hard time imagining ever being happy again.

The promise she wants me to make means I'll have to try to become happy again. Even if I try my hardest, I don't think I'll feel any happiness for a long time. If it's her dying wish, I'll have to fulfill it, even if I don't believe I can ever be happy again. Dawn was always better at these things.

Dawn looks up at me. Her eyes are starting to turn red, and I know she doesn't have long. She stares at me, waiting for an answer, and I know I have to give her one.

"Yes, I'll do everything, Dawn. I'll save every person I can for you. I promise. Though I don't ever see myself happy without you by my side, I swear I'll try. Every morning, I'm going to wake up wishing you were in my arms, and no matter what you say, that's never going to change. I love you, Dawn."

I lean over and kiss her as I say this, and despite my best efforts, tears stream down my face. Dawn smiles. She gives me a look that tells me she loves me. Her eyes were so beautiful before, but now they're red and full of fear.

"Brian, I'm so tired. I want one last thing from you, though." Waiting a few seconds, I watch Dawn. "Wait until I'm asleep. I don't want to have to know it's coming. Going in my sleep would be so nice."

I nod and run my fingers through her hair, ignoring the clumps that fall out as if they're nothing.

"Of course, Dawn. I'll wait till you're sleeping. Dawn, please remember: I'll always love you."

Dawn's tears roll down my chest, and somehow, I know they aren't all tears of sadness or fear—but of happiness. She's scared, but I also think she's ready for the end. Rocking her and running my fingers through her hair, I hum to help Dawn fall asleep.

My nerves are tightening. They feel like they'll explode. I don't want to do what comes next. What feels like an eternity passes before Dawn's eyes start to close. Her mouth moves, and I hear her muttering, so I lean closer to her.

"Goodbye, Brian. I love you."

The tears stream down my face, and I kiss her one last time. When I'm sure she's asleep, I lay her down and look at her one last time. She's pale and missing clumps of hair, but to me, she's still beautiful. Memorizing every detail of her, I burn her into my mind, knowing that whenever I go to sleep or close my eyes, I'll see her like this.

I pull my gun from its sheath and place it next to her head, making sure to line it up for a clean shot. The last thing I want is for my hesitation to cause her any more suffering. She'll feel nothing. In the blink of an eye, it'll all be over for her.

"Goodbye, Dawn. I'll never forget you." My eyes want to close, but I refuse to let them. Pulling the trigger, I end Dawn's life with a loud bang. Thankfully, I'm spared seeing her brains splatter across the concrete since I make sure to turn the other way, knowing I'm not strong enough for that sight. I rise to my feet and manage to take two steps before I throw up. It feels like I'm being torn apart. Dawn is dead. I'll never again talk to her, laugh with her, or cry with her. Never again will I kiss, hug, or spend the night with her. We'll never have children or a home. All I'll ever have with her now are memories.

Dawn deserves to be buried, but I know I can't do that. I'm not strong enough to look at her. Not with gore and brain everywhere. I don't want anything to mar the memory of her beauty.

Struggling to the boat, I realize that I have to make sure she's dead. If I don't, I'll spend the rest of my life thinking she lived or that I caused her pain. Taking a deep breath, I turn around and see her. If it weren't for the blood to the side of her head, I'd think she was sleeping. Her eyes are closed, and there's a soft smile on her face. When I check her pulse, I find none.

Knowing the job is done, I turn from the love of my life and walk to the boat in a grief-filled stupor. When I get there, the others approach me. Melany is the first to reach me, and I tell her where Dawn is and ask her to bury her. She has tears in her eyes, but she nods.

The others leave me alone, and I find a quiet section of the boat and collapse into unconsciousness, hoping that the stillness of sleep will give me some rest.

Even in my dreams I find no relief. I dream of Dawn and see her lying there on the concrete, pale skin and red eyes. Over and over, she asks me why as I shoot her in the head, ending her life. The pain of having to watch her die again and again causes me to scream in pain for what seems like an eternity.

At some point, I realize I'm no longer sleeping, and I have to force the screaming to end. The nightmares I was having seemed to last forever, but it looks like the sun has only been down a few minutes at most. My nerves are frayed and my body is exhausted, but I know better than to try and sleep.

The others on the boat are silent. They might be grieving as well, but more likely they're avoiding me. Even in my state, I realize how crazed I am now, and I can't blame the others for staying away.

With nothing else to do, I look toward the town, hoping there is a Paleman I can kill. Killing them is the only satisfying thing I can do. It may not be the carrier's fault, but I don't care. I want to tear apart anyone with the Paleman disease. To me, they're no longer people; they're the infection that killed Dawn, an infection I want to wipe out.

There's movement in the town, and part of me perks up in the hopes of slaughtering a Paleman. Even now, though, my rationality remains intact, and I know that any moving figures might mean danger.

I raise the alarm. The others join me to see the incoming figures.

When the others come, I notice that Aaron and Sophia are nowhere to be found. Only now do I realize I never stopped to think if he made it or not. Now that I see the figure in the distance, I can't help but think it must be him. When the figure gets closer, though, I see by the way it is walking that it's indeed a person, but it seems to be carrying a body.

The body might be Sophia. If she was infected like Dawn, he must have chosen to spend her last moments by her side as well. Why would he carry the body all the way over here, though? It makes no sense.

"It's Aaron. Looks like Sophia is on his back," Melany says, staring down the lens of her camera.

Our group can do nothing but wait. If Sophia is dead as well, I'm not sure I can bury her. If she was infected, seeing her might remind me of Dawn. Since I can't do anything else, I wait for them to approach.

Why would he bring her body here? What is he doing with Sophia? She's either dead or turned. There's no way she could've made it this long without being bitten. There's no surviving the infection, no delaying it. A single bite means certain death. If she's still alive and infected, I have to be ready to do what he can't.

When he reaches the boat, I notice that Sophia is still breathing. I ready myself for what I have to do.

"She's immune," Aaron says. Is it even possible that someone can be immune? I realize then that the infection is a disease. It may be incurable, but that doesn't mean it always infects. Just because I haven't seen it before doesn't mean it's impossible to resist the disease.

Those three words sever what remains of my nerves. My mind snaps, and I fall into a dark fog, unsure of who, what, or where I am. There is only darkness, grief, anger, and hatred. The darkness eats away at my soul, but I refuse to let it destroy me.

"DAWN!" I scream over and over into the fog, remembering my promises to her and trying to still the rage emanating from every fiber in my body. There's no answer, and there never will be.

Chapter 18: Aaron

The water is calm, and I watch my reflection move as the boat glides through the water. So far, moving on the boat has been slow with spurts of movement. The boat itself has held together, but our inexperience has blinded us to many issues.

When we first found this boat, we thought it was in great shape, but the sails are barely working and the boat sprung leaks almost as soon as we started moving. Jason was right to worry. Luckily, we haven't run into any storms, or his fears of sinking might have been well founded.

The boat may not be in the best shape, but it's still moving fast enough that, even in this boat's condition, everyone's decided that moving along the coast was a better plan than walking.

We all agree that it's best to take it along the coast, but no one wants to try to sail to Garden Island. The boat needs a full, around-the-clock crew to bail out the water and keep it afloat. Even so, the lack of fear and danger from Palemen has done everyone good.

Even if we make it to the island, I'm not sure what I want to do. Ever since the night Sophia and Dawn were bitten, I've felt a bit off about everything. The people that died that day were on me. True, they might have killed my friends, but they were uninfected, and it's been tearing away at me.

Rationalizing killing Palemen was always easy. The infected are beyond help. Rationalizing killing the uninfected hasn't been as easy. Even though I know those men at least in part led to Dawn's death, I still have difficulty rationalizing it.

Who am I to play God with the lives of others? Whenever I sleep, I see the faces of those I killed, and I hear them ask me why. They tell me their stories, and I feel guilty for causing their deaths.

The thing that sickens me most is that I don't regret killing them. Chris no longer talks to me, but I always feel him under the surface, waiting for me to relax. One day soon, I'll fail to stop him from breaking free, and that thought terrifies me. For now, I want to reach the island.

My reflection in the water ripples and changes until I see Dawn's face. It should surprise me, but I've been seeing her everywhere. She's either haunting us, or it has something to do with the guilt of her death. Every time I see Brian trying to hide his pain, my guilt increases.

The pain has almost crippled him, and I know that it's my fault. I grew too careless. We didn't know the town. Sending two people to search for a sail wasn't enough. My confidence in our luck got to my head. I figured nothing could happen to us, but I was wrong.

Brian tries to hide his pain. He still moves and acts like he's expected to, but everyone sees the truth. Even though I see his pain, I'm amazed at how well he's functioning. If it had been me, I doubt I could've done the same. If Sophia, Evelyne, or Melany were to have died, I don't think I'd still be leading our party.

Someone taps my shoulder, and I'm startled. When I turn around, I see Sophia. We only had the chance to talk a little since we started sailing. It's always been with the others around, though. There's no privacy for anyone on this boat.

Since the night she was bitten, we've grown closer. I've been a bit scared to approach her. My feelings for her remain, but everything has been so complicated that I haven't figured out what to do.

"Aaron, it's time we talked. I'm sorry I waited so long, but I wanted to think it through." Though I have some idea what she wants to talk about, I'm a little worried all the same.

"Sure thing. I've wanted to talk to you, too. I haven't found the right time."

Sophia smiles, and it brings a smile to my face. It's the first time I've smiled since the night Dawn died.

"Aaron, things are complicated right now, and I don't remember my life before things were like this. I know that I care about you, but I've found myself in a conundrum. While I know have feelings for you and you have feelings for me, I don't know if we'll both make it out of this alive. The night we had together was wonderful, but if we keep perusing things, it might affect our judgment. Our focus needs to be on the group's survival, not each other's."

A few weeks ago, I would have seen her coming off as cold. After Dawn's death, though, keeping my head and heart clear is the best thing to do. She's right: I need to focus on the whole group. If Sophia were hurt and I only focused on her, we could all die. I need to set aside my feelings for now. Besides, if all things go according to plan, we'll only have to wait a few weeks at most.

"Yeah, that's a good idea. We can't let personal feelings get in the way of our judgment. We need to keep our wits clear. The last thing anyone wants is any more tragedy. For the record, though, I hope we both make it."

Sophia laughs, and I find myself smiling. We can talk all we want about what we should do, but no amount of words will change my feelings. It will be tough, but I'll have to force myself to focus on the whole group, not only her, if we get into trouble. Sophia smiles at me and grabs my hand, holding it in hers.

"Okay," she says. "So I want you to tell me about your life before everything happened. In return, I'll tell you everything that I remember. Is that a deal?"

Nodding, I talk to Sophia about my life. She has to stop me a few times so I can explain some things from the past, like the Internet or electronics. I forgot that her amnesia makes these things seem impossible or strange to her. She's lucky; I wish I didn't remember the luxuries of the old world. It would make it so much easier to live in this one.

It takes a while, but I manage to tell her quite a bit about my old life. After I finish, she fulfills her promise and tells me everything she remembers. It's then that I realize how dark her life has been. What I thought would be a blessing is actually a curse. She may not remember the luxuries, but she has no happy memories of the past, either. Until she met our group, there was only misfortune for her.

246

Until now, I didn't realize how horrible it would be to not remember anything but the world as it is now. Chaos, anarchy, and Palemen rule the world. The only happiness for many is our memories of the easy, peaceful lives we all once lived. Part of what keeps me going is the hope that, someday, things will return to the way they were. Life is hard and bitter now, but at least I have happy memories to go back to. They give me hope for the future. They make me feel that if mankind could make it to that point once, we could reach it again.

Sophia and I continue to talk as we go about the tasks of running the ship. With her company, it feels like minutes, but before I know it, the sun begins to set. She tells me that she starts a bailing shift soon, and I want to sleep while I can, since I drew a night shift. She kisses me goodnight, and though I'm confused why she would do that after saying we should hold off, I don't complain.

Knowing that I have to watch the boat in a few hours, I fall asleep. My sleep is sound until Brian wakes me. Together, we head up to the top of the ship to keep watch.

He tells me that Jason and Melany are working on bailing the ship. After he tells me this, I notice them throwing water over the side every few minutes. As we're making our watch rounds, I feel a headache and try to ignore it. Headaches have never been a problem for me, but in the last few days, I've been getting them almost every day. It feels like something is buzzing inside my head. My attention is diverted when we make it to the ship's wheel.

Brian takes the helm of the ship, and Sophia, who was piloting, goes under the ship to get some rest. Keeping Brian company, we pilot the ship around a hundred yards from the shore. As the coast goes by, I keep my eyes open, scanning for boats.

When there are stretches of land that have no docks or signs of civilization, I have time to think. As the night goes on, my headache worsens. It becomes almost unbearable. Wanting to distract myself, I start up a conversation with Brian.

"Brian, I have a question for you."

Brian looks at me, and I can tell he isn't sure what I'm going to ask. "Okay, go ahead."

Sensing his hesitation, I decide to try to relax him with a casual question. "If you could have any food in the world right now, what would it be?"

Brian looks at me, and his mouth opens. I can tell he's at a loss for words. My question caught him off guard, and it takes him a second to collect himself. A smirk appears on his face before he answers me.

"I figured you were going to ask me about Dawn. Your question caught me off guard. If I could have anything at all, I'd have a peanut butter and banana sandwich."

Asking about Dawn was my original plan, but I thought better of it after detecting his hesitance. His answer is much simpler than I would have expected. When I ask myself this question, it's always something extravagant, which makes me wonder why he chose something so simple.

"Of all the things in the world, why would you choose that?"

Brian takes a second, and I see a hint of a smile as he answers me. "It was always one of my favorites. I usually ate at least one a week. The last one I had was a week before the power outage. It was hard to come by any bananas after the power went out, since they have such a short shelf life. Eating one would remind me of how simple life was before all this happened."

Brian's response is simple, yet it makes more sense to me than my lavish ideas. His answer reminds me of why I trust and like Brian. He's rational and able to look at things in a fairer perspective. He might be the only person who could help me with something I've had on my mind for a while.

"I have one more question, Brian, and I'm warning you: this one is more serious."

Brian looks at me, and I can see a deep hesitation, but he nods.

"Listen, I need to know: do you think I'm losing it? Am I still capable of leading everyone to safety?"

Brian looks a little surprised, but he collects himself. He remains silent for several minutes. My headache grows worse every second, and I start to feel like there's an intense pressure pushing on my head.

"You might be, not because of what happened with Dawn. Lately, it seems like you're wearing thin. To be honest, though, we're all cracking up a bit. Even if you're starting to crack, you're holding us together. If you were to lose it, some of the others would as well. Aaron, please be honest. Are you worried you might break?"

The pressure on my head seems to lessen a bit as I think about it. I know I'm slipping a bit. Even so, I'm pretty sure I can keep it together until we reach the island.

"No," I say. "I know I can keep it together, at least as long as it takes to get everyone safe. After that, I should be able to pull myself together. Besides, even if I do break, on the island, everyone will be safe, so what does it matter?"

Brian nods, and I can tell that what I've said will stay between us. We stay quiet for a while. My headache lessens, and I continue the patrols around the ship. When we reach the next town, there seems to be a dock, and Brian and I decide to take the boat in closer for a better look.

When we're nearing the shores, I see some Palemen but think nothing of them. They're too far out to be any real danger, and unless we plan to dock, I see no need to even mention them. When I look at one around fifty yards out on the shore, I see that it used to be a man. He looks angry, and my headache worsens immediately, so I close my eyes. When I do, I hear someone scream at me from the shore.

"I'll kill you all! I'll rip, tear, devour. They killed them. They killed them all. Her face! I saw her face torn. I saw it ripped. I'll kill them all!"

The words are dark, and I'm disturbed by them. They wake something primal in me, and a shiver runs up my spine. I look back, and something tells me that the shout was from the man.

As soon as I acknowledge this, my mind is assaulted not only by the Paleman who yelled, but also by all the ones on the shore. Their screams are full of anger and rage, and I know I'm not hearing them with my ears.

The pressure of their collective rage presses on me, and my mind starts to crack under it. Somehow, I manage to stand and walk down to the cabin of the boat, muttering to Brian that I need to rest, but I'm not sure.

When I make it to the cabin, the voices get louder. If I don't find some way to block them out, I know I'll go mad. Chris wriggles under the surface, pushing to break free. Primal rage emanates from me, and I understand where the headaches are coming from. Chris did something to make me hear the Palemen, and I'm not sure I can fight it.

All my concentration goes into trying to control myself as I fight waves of anger. As I wander around the cabin, I stumble into someone.

When I look up, I see Sophia. She looks at me, and there's fear in her eyes. She tries to speak to me, but I can't hear her voice over the screams of the Palemen on shore. She grabs my shoulders and hugs me, and I become a little more grounded. The voices are still there, but she helps keep me in check with reality.

She puts a finger up, and I know she's telling me to hold on for a minute. I'm not sure what she's planning, but I can't afford the energy to argue. All I can do is trust her and believe that whatever she wants to do will work.

Putting my hands over my ears, I try to focus on my surroundings and push out the Palemen. It doesn't work. The more I resist and fight them, the more lost I become and the stronger my urge to kill the others on the boat becomes. When Sophia returns, my mind starts to fantasize about ripping her apart and about the taste of her flesh.

Before I lunge at her, I see she has my daughter, Evelyn, with her. At first, I'm mad and confused, unsure of why she would bring my daughter here. But I realize that it stopped me from attacking Sophia. There are those who need my protection. My mind cannot break now. I have no choice but to fight off the voices. I understand what Sophia wanted to accomplish. My desire to protect Evelyn and the others fuels my efforts to drown out the screaming and the pain of the Palemen.

When I think about my daughter's safety and the responsibility I owe everyone, the voices seem to lessen. Then I realize that I'm hyperventilating, so I force myself to calm my breathing and put myself into a meditative state. The Palemen and their voices are there, but I don't fight them. I accept them but refuse to let them affect me. The screams that blocked all my thoughts dull to a yell, and I accept it. I'm in control now, and I know that I can't lose control again.

Now that my mind is clearer, I question how I can hear the Palemen. It must be linked to what Sophia told me about being affected by the epidemic, even though I'm not infected. Regardless of what's happening, there's nothing I can do about it right now. There's no choice for me but to deal with it until I can go somewhere without Palemen.

"Dad, are you listening to me yet? Sophia said we could bail water for a while. She said it would be nice to give Jason and Melany a break."

Evelyne looks at me, and I smile to try and hide the worry inside. Sophia gives me a concerned look. She may partly understand what I'm going through. After all, she said she was sensitive to the Palemen as well. If she thinks physical work is the best cure, who am I to argue?

"Sure thing. I'm sure they could use a break, but are you ready to work hard?"

Evelyn smiles, and the voices quiet down a bit more. "Of course. No one's let me help yet. They tell me to watch. Hey, when are we going to find a new boat and make it to the island? The others say there are going to be other kids to play with on the island and that I'll have to go back to school. Is that true?"

She asks me so many questions that I'm not even sure where to start. There are some things, like the children, that I'm not even sure of. Like the rest of us, she'll have to wait for answers and see when we get there.

"Honey, slow down. Let's take care of one thing at a time. Now, if you want to talk about all these things, that's fine. If you want to bail water, then we better get moving."

Evelyn pauses for a moment before running off to find Jason and Melany.

"Aaron, what's going on?" Sophia asks me when Evelyn is out of earshot. "Are you going to be okay? Has Chris come back?"

"No, Chris is still silent, but the Palemen aren't. All their pain and rage press into me every second, and I don't know why. Sophia, I don't know what's going on. But I have it under control now, thanks to your quick thinking." Sophia looks at me, and I know I can trust her.

"Aaron, remember, I won't hesitate if you turn rabid. You remember my promise to you, right? Even now, I'll put you down if you're beyond saving." After I nod, she continues.

"I do care about you, and if you need me for anything, let me know. You need to keep it together for a little longer, okay? We will be far away from any Palemen soon." Sophia hugs me tightly, and we embrace for a while before breaking apart and going to find Evelyn.

We find her and start working to bail water from the ship. The bailing is hard work, but it helps to keep me distracted. After a while, the voices fade to a near buzzing. Every once in a while, there's an outburst from a strong Paleman, but after the first few, they become easy to manage.

As I work alongside Sophia and Evelyn, we laugh and joke. My mind wanders a bit, and I fantasize about us on the island. My hope is that we'll make it there together. In my fantasies, we're on the beach in summer, and in the winter, we're in a cabin, reading books by the fire.

There needs to be more than promises for me to make it to the island. If I don't have a reason to live after we make it to Garden Island, what's the point? My decision to live away from the others seems foolish. Being in a civilization with others is exactly what we all need to move on.

Besides, the Palemen can't last forever. They may be mutated, but they're still human. At some point, they'll die out. After that happens, if I don't have some contact with others, it will be much more difficult to rebuild and rejoin what remains of society. The damage to the electrical system is extensive, but I bet that, without the Paleman threat, we could have lights and other utilities within twenty to fifty years, if not sooner.

These thoughts distract me until I see Sophia stop her work. When I look up, what I see terrifies me. On the shore, I see a multitude of Palemen. Among them, one stands out, and I hear him screaming orders with clarity. He's commanding the Palemen around him to destroy the boat. That's when I realize what's about to happen, but it's already too late.

Before anyone can react, Molotov cocktails start hitting the boat. The fire spreads over the outside of the boat immediately. Filled with desperation, I pull my gun out. Before I can fire off a round, though, I hear a single shot. I look toward the source and find that Brian has fired his rifle. The bullet strikes the general, and he falls down.

His mind issues a last command before it's silenced. All the Palemen now see us as the cause of their rage, and they're told to pursue us until we're dead. There's nothing we can do that will make them disperse now. Their sole focus is our destruction.

With frenzied desperation, I go to the wheel of the ship and turn the boat toward the shore. While I do so, I scream for everyone to gather supplies and abandon ship. The others hear, and everyone gathers as much as they can before jumping off the ship.

Before I jump off, I find Evelyn and grab her hand. Together, we rush to get some food in a bag before jumping ship. Luckily, the

Palemen aren't in the water. Instead, they're focused on the incoming ship.

Everyone gathers in a circle, and we scout out a small shack nearby, which we can swim to. The boat collides with the shore and shatters into a flaming wreck, distracting the Palemen.

When we make it to the shore, I take point and use a hatchet and Dao sword to dispatch any Palemen in the way. Since most of them are distracted by the boat, only two or three fall to my blades.

When we get in the shack, we start fortifying the doors and windows. We all go into the bathroom, which only has a window in the roof, and block and lock the door. The door is solid steel and looks strong enough to hold back the horde.

When I look around, I see that the bathroom is large. I guess that this was likely a place to shower after hitting the beach. After a few minutes, we hear Palemen on the outside walls, and their voices assault me. There are hundreds, and they're accompanied by scratches on the walls. Like a damn being broken, the voices rush in on me, and it's too much. Around me there is only rage.

Chapter 19: Jason

August 24th

Aaron twitches while I watch him. It's obvious that he's in a tremendous amount of pain, and I'm not sure he'll ever wake up.

As I listen to the scratching noises coming from the walls, I can't help but feel exposed. There's no telling how long we can hole up in this place. We have food and water, but even with what we salvaged from the boat, we have a week before supplies run out.

This situation looks hopeless, and to top it off, Aaron has collapsed and lies unconscious. When I look around, I see that the others look as panicked as I do. None of us seem to think we'll survive this.

Evelyn screams and yells as tears roll down her face. She's been screaming at Sophia ever since Aaron collapsed.

"Help him, Sophia! You're not a good doctor if you can't help him! He'll save us. I know it!" My ears close to her pleas for help. It hurts not to listen, but I'm not sure what we can do for her. The poor girl has driven herself into a frenzy, and there's nothing any of us can do for Aaron right now. The only thing we can do is wait and hope he comes out of it.

As I watch Sophia, I notice her grab something from her bag. Whatever she grabbed, she forces Evelyn to take. Thinking of what I would do in that situation, I figure she must have given her something to put her to sleep.

The pill has no immediate effects, and Evelyn, angry at being forced to take something, lashes out at Sophia. After a few minutes, though, she becomes silent and falls asleep.

Sophia did the right thing by drugging Evelyn. The girl was past calming down. I envy her a little, because it might be better to not be awake tonight. If these walls don't hold, or the Palemen make it inside, we'll all die here. Going out in your sleep would be the best way to die.

When I look back to Aaron, I see that he's still twitching. Brian is sitting near him, and he has his gun ready. Something has been up with Aaron lately, and I figured this has something to do with it. Seeing Brian ready to shoot him tells me that it's something dangerous.

I'm so focused on watching Aaron that I don't see Melany approaching me. Only when she taps me on my shoulder do I realize she's there. Though I'm a little startled, I manage to maintain my composure.

"Jason, we need to do something. Everyone's anxious and afraid. Brian's determined to watch over Aaron, and Sophia's determined to watch over Evelyn. Everyone's starting to lose hope. You and me need to do something to help give everyone hope again."

Melany's right: the only thing sitting around is going to do is make things worse. Though I'm not sure what we can do to help, anything is better than sitting and waiting for death to take us.

"Yeah, you're right. What do you want to do?" Melany pauses and I can tell she doesn't have a plan. She was expecting me to have some idea of what to do. I can't think of anything, though, and we sit in silence for a minute. When I'm starting to think there's nothing to do, she speaks up.

"I wish there was some way to scout out things. If we could get a look at what we're dealing with, we may be able to find a way to run past this mob."

Her idea is simple, but I realize she's right: we can't give up without scouting. It might seem like we're outnumbered now, but we might be wrong. For all we know, we could slip through the Palemen. The only way to find out would be to go through the building and check the windows.

When I listen to the scratching, it seems like it's only coming from the outside. As far as I can tell, no Palemen have made it inside yet.

"What if we checked inside?" I ask. "I doubt the Palemen have found a way in yet. Even if a few have made it inside, I can shoot them." Melany nods, and I can tell that she's excited about the prospect of escape.

"Why don't we grab a bag, too?" Melany asks. "This place could have some food. That way, even if we are stuck here, we'll have some more time."

For all we know, the Palemen might calm down and leave in a week. If we find extra food, then it might keep us supplied long enough to make our getaway. The more I think about it, the more reasons I find to scout the building. We could also find tools to better barricade the door to the showers—or even weapons and things to set traps. As I ponder the possibilities, I'm excited to explore the building.

Melany and I start getting ready. I walk over to where the bags
are stored, then grab the one that seems empty. It's a little heavy, but I
figure it's as good as any.

Next, I grab Melany and we talk to the others and tell them our
plan. Everyone approves, and I can see it sparks some hope in them.

We make a few more preparations, and I get my rifle. After
checking to make sure everything is working, I load and shoulder it,
then go to the door.

Melany and I remove the barricades from the door. Then I have
her open it. I ready my rifle and look around, confirming my earlier
thoughts that the hallway is secure.

After triple checking, I step through, making sure to stay alert as
I do so. After I signal to Melany, she follows my lead and shuts the
door behind her. On our way through the building, we don't see any
Palemen. Oddly, I also notice that there's no scratching on the walls.
Somehow, they must know what room we're in.

How they're behaving is interesting. I would have expected
them to force their way in. There's no general, but the Palemen are
acting in unity. I've never seen them behave like this, and it's making
me uneasy.

When I look through the windows, we pass them, and I see that
we're surrounded. The bodies I see outside the windows are so thick
that I can't see past them. All I see is a literal wall of flesh.

As I catch Melany's eye, we both know that escape right now is
impossible, at least from what we can see. She signals to see if I still

want to continue exploring. Since the Palemen are inactive, I see nothing to lose, and I nod yes to her.

As we go through the building, I make sure to memorize every turn we take and make a virtual map in my head. If we get the chance to come out again, I'll have to remember to draw a map before we do so.

The search proves uneventful until we run across what appears to be a breakroom. It's then that I realize what this building is. It must have been a staff hut for the lifeguards who worked at the nearby beach.

As if to confirm this, I remember seeing a lifeguard tower nearby when we were swimming. Since this was a staff area, there's a good chance we'll find something useful in these lockers. I signal Melany to go through the lockers while I stand with my gun sight on the open door. Since I'm facing away from her, I can't see what she's doing. Every so often, she slips something into my bag. I enjoy the silence for a while and think about how well things are going.

As if to spite me, the sound of footsteps comes from the hallway. They're drowned out by a loud crash coming from behind me. When I look back and see that one of the locker doors has fallen off, Melany looks at me apologetically.

The footsteps I heard moments ago return, and they're much closer and moving with more haste. Whatever's responsible for the footsteps will be here soon, so I decide silence is no longer a concern.

"Don't worry about the noise," I say. "Something was heading our way anyway. After it's visible, I'll shoot it and then we run back to base. Does the plan sound good to you?"

Melany nods, and I turn my attention back to the door, preparing myself. A few seconds later, a Paleman peeks through the door. In such close proximity, the shot to his head is an easy one. He's dead before the echo of the gunfire ends.

Whatever was keeping the Palemen calm breaks, and I hear slamming on the outside walls. Melany and I start running. We both sense how important it is to get back immediately.

As we run through the recently silent halls, I look at the windows. Every one we pass is smashed open, and a multitude of hands and bodies are struggling to come through. The halls are wide, and we manage to go past them unscathed.

We turn down the last hallway and are greeted with a worrying sight. The hallway is much narrower than the others. Besides, there are two windows on either side. Like all the windows, these are broken and hands are reaching through. Unlike the other windows, though, there's no way around these ones.

Surely I can divert the Palemen's attention long enough for Melany to get through. After that, I might be able to slip underneath the horde's grasp. I hear footsteps approaching from behind us, and I know that we don't have much time. I explain the plan to Melany, and we ready ourselves.

Motioning for Melany to go, I start firing into the window. My tactic works, and the hands retract enough for Melany to run and slip under their grasp. She turns around and looks at me. The shower room door behind her opens, and Brian appears. Looking at the arms, I know I can't fire and run without drawing attention to myself.

If I crawl, I can make it through the hallway unscathed, but not with this bag on my back. The footsteps from behind me are getting closer, and I know I've run out of time. With only seconds to think, I decide that a brute-force run might be enough to break through the sea of arms. The Palemen have no way of expecting it, so it might work.

I drop my gun to the floor and kick it to Brian. Taking a deep breath, I run toward the arms with all my strength. Memories of the childhood game of red rover come to mind as I run past the multitude of arms. Déjà vu hits me when my body is slammed to a stop.

My shoulders scream out with pain, and I realize that one of the Palemen must have grabbed my backpack. Before I have time to panic, though, someone from the other side of the horde grabs my arm and pulls. I slip off one strap of the backpack, and luckily, the other rips.

As soon as I'm free of their grasp, all three of us dash into the showering room. We shut, lock, and barricade the door behind us before taking a second to breathe.

Pain radiates from my shoulders, but I'm glad to have escaped unscathed and alive. It's too bad we lost the things we found and the bag, but at least I'm still breathing.

Smiling, I look at Brian, expecting to see some relief, but when our gazes meet, all I see is anger. I'm confused by his reaction. We did nothing wrong. If we hadn't had such bad luck, we would have made it back here with more supplies, as well as a good understanding of our situation and surroundings. Only when he speaks do I realize why he's angry.

"Did you idiots even check the bag before taking it? The one you took had all our food in it."

His statement is so shocking that I don't know what to say. I didn't check the bag before leaving. I figured it would be the best one to grab since it wasn't that full.

Now, because I failed to check the bag, I threw away our chances for survival. Without food, we have no more than two days before we're too weak to travel to Garden Island.

"I... I'm sorry. I didn't think. I didn't know I had it. Brian, I'm sorry."

Brian looks at me, and I see him calm a little. "It doesn't matter. What's done is done. It doesn't change our fate much. I'm glad you two got back in one piece. Were you bitten anywhere?"

His sudden reversal of mood confuses me, but I nod no to him. Not satisfied, he checks over me himself.

"Well, at least you're infection-free. Now that you two are back, I need to show you something."

Without another word, Brian turns around and walks to the other side of the room. Once there, he points to the skylight in the ceiling. "What you need to see is on the roof," he says. "I'll boost you and Melany up there."

Brian helps me get up through the skylight and onto the roof. While I'm climbing up, I wish I'd thought of this before we went on our adventure. When I make it up, I immediately turn around to help lift Melany.

Once I get Melany on the roof, we stand up together. Based on what I saw through the windows, I figured we were surrounded, but what I'm seeing now seems impossible.

All around us are hundreds—even thousands—of Palemen. There's no path through them or any way I can see of avoiding them. The mass of bodies is staggering. Their movement seems like that of a unified body. The view reminds me of pictures I've seen of rock concerts: walls of people moving back and forth to the beat of the music.

Now I see why Brian wasn't mad for very long. True, I lost the food, but all that did was shorten our lives by a week or so. As I look into this sea of Palemen, the realization of our defeat strikes me. There's no escaping this horde. Our fate and our deaths have been sealed.

Words escape me, and unsure of what to do, I sit down and stare at the masses. Melany sits by my side and lays her head on my shoulder. She's never shown any affection toward me, but I can understand her actions.

Right now, I'm so hopeless that I wish I had someone to hold me. Wanting to feel close to someone right now, I put my arm around her, knowing that if I were in her place, it's what I'd want. Meanwhile, I'm wondering who's supposed to comfort me.

"Hey, Jason," she says. "I'm wondering, what were you going to do if we made it to Garden Island?"

I don't know why Melany is asking, but I decide there's no harm in telling her now. "Well, I wanted to start a school. I wanted to teach kids and other people about how the world is now and how it used to be."

When I pause to remember my motivation, I remember what happened after the blackout. The vivid memory of the girl's death comes back to me, and I watch her murder in my mind for the millionth time.

Normally, I would push the grief away, but now that I know I'll be dead soon, I find no reason to. I decide to talk to Melany about it. After I tell her about the pain and grief that event has caused me, I begin to feel some relief. Like a dam breaking, I tell her all about my worries and pain throughout this journey. Even though I thought I was the one comforting Melany, it turns out she's ended up comforting me.

Melany listens throughout and only interrupts me to ask an occasional question. After I've finished, she's silent for several minutes, then says, "You know, Jason, I would have helped you. It's funny: I wasn't sure what I wanted to do until you talked to me. If I'd made it to the island, I would have taken all my photos and put them together. After that, I would have written stories for each one, forming a book of our journey and everything we know about the Palemen. With the book I created, I'd show people what happened to the world. If we had made it, I bet we would have ended up working together."

She's right; if we made it to the island, we would have ended up working together. For some reason, this thought makes me a little happy, even though I know it could never come true now.

When I take a moment to think about how much a book like the one Melany wanted to create could educate others, I realize that students would have tangible proof of how the world fell. Someday, this infection will die out, and there will be a need for stories. People will need to remember how horrifying this epidemic was. If they don't, there's no hope of avoiding another one.

History was never a favorite subject in school for me, but now I realize how important it was. What Melany would be creating is a history book. When I tell her about my realization, she surprises me by laughing.

"I always hated history," she says. "All I can imagine is some kid like me sitting in a class, trying not to fall asleep while being forced to study my book." The picture she paints makes me laugh. It feels good to laugh, and I forget for a minute that we're in a helpless situation.

We spend minutes laughing and only stop when our sides are aching and we're out of breath. It's been more than a year since I laughed like this. Thinking back to the last time, I realize it was before the world changed. Smiling, I'm glad that I shared some joy with someone before the end. We stare back out to the horde, and my mind slips back to history.

All throughout history are instances of some great event that changed mankind. It was foolish to ever believe that our generation would be an exception to the pattern. The best man can hope for is that it avoids causing the same tragedy twice.

Mankind was due for a great change. These Palemen might as well be the soldiers attacking Troy or the barbarians sacking Rome.

The world will be forever changed by this disease, and no one is to blame but humanity.

Who knows if the epidemic is worldwide or only in America? All I know is, if we don't die here, I'll teach anyone I can about this war and all the others. That way we can move forward and on to man's next stage. As I look over to Melany, I say, "Are you ready to go down yet?"

"Yeah, might as well. I suppose the others will want to talk about what to do."

We make our way down. I go first, then help Melany. Once we're both inside the building again, I take a quick look around the room. Little has changed. Brian's by an unconscious Aaron, and Sophia has Evelyn in her lap. I decide that I'll break the silence and speak up.

"I'm sorry I lost the food, everyone. It's robbed us of a few weeks of living and a way to escape. I wish I could find a way to repay everyone, but I know I can't. We need to move on, though, and figure out what we want to do. Aaron's collapsed and sick. He might not recover. We have a week of strength left before we're hopeless. It would be best if we decide how we want to die now, while we still have a say."

I stand, waiting for someone to speak up. After a few moments, Sophia stands.

"I don't see a way out of any of this. I don't have enough medicine to kill us all. In fact, I gave the only medicine I had to Evelyn, and that was only a sleeping pill."

Before Sophia spoke, I hadn't realized that suicide was an option. At first, I'm appalled, but the more I think about it, the more I realize how much better it would be than mauling or starvation. Before I can pursue my thoughts further, Sophia continues. "Whatever we decide on, it should be done before Evelyn wakes up. I don't want her to suffer a bloody death or die of starvation. It would be best to kill her now, regardless of what we choose."

Brian looks over at her, and I can see disdain. "So that's our only option, then? To kill ourselves? Why would we want to do that? I say we go out and kill as many of those bastards as we can. We could kill enough that the next group to come along won't end up in the same place we did."

Brian and Sophia stare at each other with disgust. Fearing an argument, I walk between the two. "So our options are to wait and starve, to kill ourselves, or to die fighting? The easiest way to decide is by vote. Can everyone agree to follow a majority?"

Looking at Brian, I can tell that he's angry. When he nods his agreement, I'm a bit surprised. Next, I look over to Sophia, and she nods as well. Finally, I look at Melany, and she nods.

I take charge and go through each option, telling people to raise their hands for the option they choose. The vote wins three to one for us to kill ourselves. Brian's the only one who wants to fight.

There was a second when I almost voted with him, but then I realized how tired of fighting I was. After all the pain caused by this journey, I decided I wanted a simple ending. The idea of a calm and painless end sounded better than more fighting.

After the vote, we decide that everyone will shoot themselves after Evelyn and Aaron are killed. After a while, Brian agrees to kill Aaron, and Sophia will kill Evelyn. We all prepare and say our final goodbyes.

Brian readies his gun, putting it against Aaron's head. We all take a final look at Aaron, and Brian starts his countdown. Before he can reach the end, Aaron pops up and looks around.

When I look at Aaron, I see that he's in absolute terror. Somehow, I know it's him there, and not something else in control. Aaron didn't become what Brian feared he would.

A flame ignites within me, and I want to survive. It makes no sense; Aaron being awake changes nothing. We're still doomed to starve or die. My mind tries to tell me that hope is pointless now, but as I look at Aaron, I know in my heart that this changes everything.

Chapter 20: Aaron

August 25th

When I wake up, all I hear are screams of rage and pain. There's so much hate that I can see it. It's like a hot summer day, and waves of anger are vibrating in the air. As I look around, I see my friends staring at me, concern on their faces. After I force myself to focus on them, the screaming around me lessens and the waves seem to dissipate.

"Aaron, are you okay? What's going on?" Melany, my sister, says, concern plain in her voice. She looks like she's close to panic, and I know that if anyone panics now, there will be no making it out of this situation. Our only chance of survival right now is to stay calm. The others in the room look panicked as well, so I force myself to calm down and stand up.

"Yeah, I'm fine. A bit tired from the swim, is all." No one buys my excuse, but they seem to calm down all the same. "How long was I out?"

This time, Jason answers. "About an hour. You would twitch or thrash occasionally, but Sophia told us to leave you be. We checked out the situation as best we could. There's no way I see of escaping since we're completely surrounded."

It doesn't surprise me to hear that we're surrounded. The multitude of Palemen screaming in my head is enough to tell me that. Even so, he seems so discouraged and it sounds like he's given up.

The last thing we need right now is everyone giving up. If we have any chance of making it out of here, we need everyone to be thinking straight. If all you believe is that you're going to die, then that's likely what will happen.

"Wait a minute. How do you know we're surrounded? Did you leave this room?"

"We got onto the roof through a skylight right over there," Jason says.

Jason points out the skylight, and I see how anyone could go through it with the help of one or two others. After that, you could lower a rope or pull people up one by one. Once you were on the roof, you'd be able to see for quite a distance.

Having nothing else to do, I decide I want to see exactly how many Palemen are out there. Even though I can feel their presence and I have a pretty good idea of how many there are, I want to confirm their numbers with my own eyes. Before I go to the roof, I want to know how bad it is inside.

"Have we been able to go into any other rooms, and do we know if the Palemen have made it inside yet?" My question meets with silence, but after a few seconds, Jason speaks up.

"We checked a few rooms for supplies, but the Palemen got in while we were looking around. Things were going well, but then we were ambushed. No one was hurt, but they got the bag we had for storing the supplies we found. I should've checked before, Aaron. If I had, we wouldn't be in this mess. I'm so sorry."

"What do you mean? Why should you have checked the bag?"

"The bag I lost had all the food in it."

This information is crippling. It means we only have a few days to figure something out. If we can't figure out a way to escape, we'll starve to death or become too weak to fight off any Palemen who get inside.

All I can do is wonder if we've come all this way only to die in a shack. The voices of anger from the Palemen are growing louder as I start to lose hope. Before my mind can slip more, Sophia speaks up.

"We have water, enough for quite a while, and the showers work in here. So if we find a way out of this building, we could survive for a few days."

When I look at Sophia, she has a pleading look in her eyes. She's telling me to pull it together. It's reassuring to know that at least she hasn't given up yet.

The screaming is so loud, and my head feels like it might explode into a million pieces. The group may have a few days, but I know I don't. Whatever plan of action we decide on, we'll have to carry it out tonight. My composure won't last for much longer than that.

Without anything else to do, I decide now is a good time to go on the roof. "Alright, I want to look around the roof. Brian, could you come with me?" Brian nods and boosts me onto the roof. With Jason's help from below, I lift Brian up after me.

When I stand up and look around, what I see confirms what I've felt all along. There are over a thousand Palemen surrounding us. Even though I'm confirming what I already knew, it's still discouraging to see how hopeless we are here. There's no path or gap between these bodies. All around us, there's nothing but bodies, dirt, sand, and anger. We aren't even near any power lines, trees, or other buildings. We're a tiny island surrounded by Palemen, and we're stuck without a boat.

The closest object I can see is a boat stand a few hundred feet away on the shore. Not sure of where to turn, I decide to sit down. After a while, Brian sits next to me.

"I'm not sure how we are going to get out of here," Brian says. "I promised Dawn I would live, but it looks like I'll be joining her." Brian sighs and pauses for a second before looking at me. "How are you doing right now? You were out a pretty long time, and I can still see you're struggling with something."

When I look at Brian, I know lying would be pointless, especially after I told him I was slipping on the boat. So I decide to tell him everything. I know he's strong enough not to panic—or at least I hope he is.

"I know I can't last the night with everything that's going on. I hear the Palemen screaming in my mind, and the noise is all-consuming. I'm struggling even now to stay sane. On top of that, I don't see a way out of this mess. Unless something comes to me, I plan on staying up here on the roof until my mind breaks. Then I plan on walking off the roof."

When I pause and look at Brian, I'm not sure what I expect out of him. I find him sitting next to me, no trace of emotion on his face. It's amazing that he can stay so calm, and I'm glad of it.

"Brian, can you make me a promise?" I ask. "Someone has to look after Evelyn. If the Palemen find a way inside after I'm gone, I want you to promise you won't let them get her. I can't bear the thought of her being torn apart by those monsters."

Brian looks at me in horror. I never thought I'd be able to crack Brian's composure, but it looks like I have. That's when I realize that what I'm asking is too much. Asking a friend to kill a small girl in cold blood is something that should never be done. We sit in silence for a few minutes, and I'm about to get up when Brian speaks up.

"Okay, I can do that. If I can't get everyone out, I'll make sure no one is turned."

Relief hits me. That shouldn't be something a person ever has to ask a friend. Now that I know someone will take care of things if there's no other choice, I'm relieved. As Brian and I sit in silence, I decide to tell him everything about Chris and my delusions.

I've kept my secret so long, but since it looks like we're going to die, I tell him. Beginning at the start, I tell him about everything. I don't expect him to reply, but talking about it helps to relieve some of the pain from the voices.

I'm surprised when, after a few minutes, he starts talking about Dawn. He tells me all about their relationship and all the promises she had him make. He tells me about how he hears and sees Dawn everywhere we go. He tells me that, even now, he can feel her with him.

After he finishes talking, we stay silent for a while. I imagine that, like me, he wanted someone to hear about his pain. We watch as the sun starts to go down. The beauty of the sunset on the water has a calming effect. Even now, without hope, I can admire how beautiful the world is.

The sun's glare catches on something, and as I look at it more closely, I see that it's a boat rack with two canoes on it. They're hung up with paddles and life jackets attached. An idea hits me.

It may not be ideal, and it would be a horrible journey with only water as a provision, but we could make it to Beaver Island with those canoes. All we need to do is divert the horde long enough to get the boats into the water. Then we'll be safe. We still have a sliver of hope left.

"Brian, look over there. Do you see those canoes?"

Brian looks to where I'm pointing and nods yes.

"Say we could think of a way to get to them. Those could be our tickets to Beaver Island."

"Do you think we could make it that far with no food?"

"It wouldn't be the first time someone made a long trip without food. I'm not saying the chances would be great, but we have a better shot on the water than we do here. This horde will follow us on the shore, so the way I see it, Beaver Island is our only choice. It's our best shot. What do you think?"

"You're right. It might be a long shot, but it's our best option. We need to figure out how to get those boats. Look around, though. How are we going to get through all these Palemen?"

Brian isn't wrong. There's no point thinking about the boats if we can't even reach them. Going through the building is impossible since the inside is flooded with Palemen, so I move to the edge of the roof and look down.

We're only twelve feet above the ground here. If we're careful, everyone could reach the ground from up here. The fall isn't that far, and avoiding injury from a jump would be easy as long as we're careful.

How can I distract this many Palemen long enough for the others to escape? There's no possible way I can think of at first. The only way to do this would be to lead the Palemen away somehow.

Then the revelation hits me. The only way to save everyone is for someone to sacrifice themselves. If a person were to jump off the roof and make it through the horde, they could lead the Palemen away. Whoever leads them away has no chance of surviving, but they would save the others.

The truth is painful, but I know it has to be me. These Palemen are fixated on me. If I were to be our distraction, there might be a way to get the others out alive. The sooner we start the plan, the better chance the others have. If I act as bait, my death will at least mean something. Besides, at the rate these voices are pulling at me, I'll be dead by morning anyway.

The horde is thick, but I might be able to get through. My chances will be even better if I don't worry about being bitten. If I know I won't survive anyway, who cares if I'm bitten? The idea of death scares me, but I don't see any other way to save those I love. I realize that I'm getting ahead of myself and think it would be smart to run my idea by Brian.

"Hey, Brian, what if I went off the roof alone. I could cut through all the Palemen before drawing them to me. It might cause a big enough distraction that everyone else could make it to the boats. After you guys got onto the water a ways, I could swim to you."

Brian looks at me, and I can tell he sees through me. He knows that if I were to distract the Palemen, there would be no surviving. He looks hesitant, but I can see that he knows it would work. He must have come to the same realization that I did: nobody will survive without someone sacrificing themselves. It doesn't matter how well someone can fight. There's no fighting off hundreds without injury and death.

"I don't know, Aaron. I don't think there's another way, but I could be wrong. We should ask the others. They can think of some way to make it to those canoes without you having to die."

For my sake, I hope Brian's right. I don't want to die. I want to see my daughter grow up, and I want to fall in love with Sophia. There's so much I want to do with my life, and if there's a way I can fulfill those desires, I will. Deep down, though, I know that sacrificing myself is the only way the others will survive.

Brian and I make our way back into the building. The first thing I see when we get back inside is Jason talking to Melany in a corner. When I look around for Sophia, I find her sitting next to Evelyn.

"Sophia, could you please come over here?"

Sophia looks up to me and sets Evelyn down before coming over. Brian and I tell her about the discovery of the boats. Together, we brainstorm for a while, but we fail to think of any way for us to get the boats unmolested. The only worthwhile idea we have is using the guns to pick off the Palemen in a concentrated area.

Even with all our ammo, we wouldn't be able to make a large enough dent in the horde. Also, the noise of the guns would likely draw as many Palemen to us as it would kill.

After a while, it's clear that we won't come up with a plan, so I propose my own.

"Sophia, there's one way I can think of that has a chance of working."

I see Sophia look at me. Brian walks away, and I'm grateful that he's giving us some privacy.

"Sophia, I can't make it through the night. I'm struggling even now to hold it together. Whatever we decide to do, it will have to be tonight. I can only think of one way to save anyone. If I jump off the roof alone, I can cut a path through the horde before they converge on me. Once I do that, I'd be able to fire my guns to draw them to me. If I did this, the rest of you might be able to escape."

Tears form in Sophia's eyes. The last thing I want is to see her cry, because I don't know if I have the strength for that.

I'm scared to die. I know I won't make it out of that horde. If I go, there will be no hope of living.

"Aaron, I don't want you to go. There's no way you could live through that."

Sophia starts crying and hugs me. Seeing her cry is more painful than any wound the Palemen could inflict on me. I wrap my arms around her and feel my eyes tear up.

"Can you see any other way?" I ask. "I'm losing my mind. I doubt I can last the hour. The rage is crawling in, and it's hard to resist it. Chris will take over any time. I'm so scared of what he'll do when he does. At least if I divert the Palemen, I'll save you. I promised my parents I'd keep everyone safe, and this is the only way to fulfill that promise."

As I hold Sophia, she cries into my chest, and I know she has no answer for me. If there was another way, we would have thought of it by now. Death scares me, but I'm strengthened by the fact that I'll fulfill my promise. Sophia and the others will live, and I can die happy with that knowledge.

We've made it so far, and now the island is in sight. When I look around the room, I see Brian talking with Jason and Melany. He's telling them and I'm relieved, since I'm not sure I'd have the strength to tell my sister and Jason.

Crying, Melany tries to walk over to me, but Brian stops her. I want to say goodbye to her, but first, I have to say goodbye to Sophia. Saying goodbye to my sister will be even harder, and I'll need to collect my strength.

"Aaron, not like this," Sophia says. "I'm sure you'll be fine. Let's wait till tomorrow. You said you can't, but you've always proven me wrong. Please, you can't do this. I don't want to leave you. I want to make it to the island with you and spend my life with you."

What Sophia's begging me to do is what I wish could happen, but it can't. There's no way I can hold out. Even now, my mind is starting to slip. When I look around the room, Chris sits at the corner of my vision. He laughs at me, and I know he's waiting until I'm too weak to resist him. He'll take over soon—I know it. I hold Sophia and kiss her.

"Sophia, I want you to take care of Evelyn for me." Sophia's crying, but she nods. "I'm sorry this had to happen, but we knew it was a possibility. Sorry to ask for more from you, but I need one last thing. I want you to promise not to kill me, even if I turn. Even though I made you promise you would, I want you to focus on getting out of here and not looking back, okay? You cannot afford having the horde's attention drawn to you."

Sophia's still crying, but she nods. When I see my sister walking over, I let Sophia out of my embrace. Melany takes Sophia's place, and she cries into my chest. Though I'm not sure what Brian told her, I know she realizes I'm going to die.

"I wanted to make it to the island with you," Melany says. "I don't want to lose my brother. We promised Mom and Dad we would live. Don't make me tell them I failed."

Everyone wants me to live, but I know I can't. I smile. I may be about to die, but seeing all these people sad to see me go makes me feel like my life has had a purpose. No matter how valuable my life may be to them, though, it isn't worth the lives of everyone else. One death is a small price to pay for saving five lives.

"Melany, where you're going, you'll finally be safe. You won't have to worry about food or water. You'll never again be in fear of Palemen hunting you. It's what I promised to do, and I'm glad that you'll make it. I know you've been keeping a journal of our journey.

Talk to Sophia on the island. She can answer some questions for you. I want you to tell everyone about the things going on. You can inspire the people on the island to help others like us. Our journey and our story need to be told so people understand what it's like out here."

Melany's crying, but I know she'll listen to what I said. Reluctantly, I break my embrace with Melany. Everyone seems to be watching me.

"Listen up, everyone," I say. "We need to get ready now. Whatever we do, though, we can't let Evelyn know what's going on. If she resists even slightly, it might put everyone in danger."

"Don't worry about that," Sophia says. "Before you woke up, I was worried we wouldn't make it through the night. I gave her a sleeping pill. Nothing will wake her up at this point. I can carry her on my back if we find a way to tie her there."

Normally, Sophia's confession to drugging Evelyn would be upsetting, but right now, it's a relief. Thinking, I come up with a way to secure Evelyn to Sophia.

"Use my shirt as a rope," I say. "If we cut it into strips, we should be able to make a rope strong enough to hold her."

Everyone gets to work. It doesn't take us long to make the rope. Once it's done, we test it out and find that it works quite well. We secure Evelyn to Sophia and she seems safe enough.

We gather everything together, and I strap all the extra pistols to myself. Where they're going, they won't need these. After I take all the extras, I have a total of six pistols strapped to me. They're all loaded and should give me enough firepower to divert the Palemen.

I decide to give one of my Dao swords to Sophia. At first, she refuses, but I insist. I want her to keep it as a memento. Some part of me should make it to the island. Once I'm surrounded, the extra one wouldn't do me any good anyway. Strapping my remaining Dao sword and a hatchet to my side, I do one final check over before I'm ready. Before we go to the roof, both Brian and Jason hug me and say goodbye.

Jason is in a lot of pain, but there's nothing I can say to him to make things any better. All I can hope is that the peace of the island will help heal him.

We all climb onto the roof one by one, starting with me. Once we're all up, everyone's demeanor changes. There are no more tears or hints of hesitation. After this journey together, we trust each other and work as a team. We all know that any hesitation or resistance could lead to everyone being killed. The only thing I receive before jumping off the roof is a last look of goodbye from everyone. I ready myself and start scanning the horde for an opening.

Spotting one, I sprint toward the edge of the roof. While flying through the air, I notice how free I feel. I don't regret where this journey has led me, and I'm no longer scared of dying for those I love.

Chapter 21: Alexis

May 25th

The first day after I left was the hardest. Leaving Stephanie was one of the hardest things I've ever done, but I'd done all that I could there. I knew I had to leave to be happy. Even though I feel a little guilty that I left Stephanie, I knew I had to. Honestly, I'll miss Stephanie more than my parents. For all I know, they died long ago. Even if they're still alive, they're dead to me now.

The reason I wanted to leave is to save people. The community I set up with Stephanie fills me with pride, and I want to build others like it.

While I'm out saving others, there's even a small part of me that hopes I'll find my brother. My hopes of finding him increase when I find some clues that they made it to the edge of town.

Among the clues there's a note from Aaron addressed to his father. The note is mostly sentimental, but luckily it also tells me where they were planning to go. I can't bring myself to go back and show Stephanie, since the note is to her dead husband. Someday, when I see her again, I'll give it to her, but not now.

I follow the trail the others planned out, hoping I'll find more clues along the way. Finding a map, I mark it and follow their route.

My journey goes well, though I run into a few groups. Most are resistant to me being near them. The only reason most would even talk to me is because I told them I was a nurse. Even though it's stretching the truth, telling people this seems to make them much less hostile toward me.

Even after everything that's happened, I still hold hope for humanity. There have been times when I've seen people who degraded into animals. And a few times I'm forced to put them down. Seeing these people makes me realize that civilization was a luxury. Without luxuries and a system to provide, everything falls apart.

Without power, food, and water, some people become vicious, looking out only for themselves. I would rather run into a pack of dogs or Palemen than humans who have fallen. At least the dogs and Palemen are only following their nature.

I remember my last few weeks and how I got to where I am now. I know I'm safe, but when I left, a holding cell is the last place I thought I would have ended up. Thinking back to how I got here kills time.

When I was walking along the road, I spotted something impossible. There was an old jeep driving toward me. If I had seen people approaching, I would have left the road and hidden.

Seeing a moving vehicle after all that time made me pause. In that moment, I understood how deer feel when they get caught in the headlights. What they see is so abnormal that it shocks and confuses them.

The car stopped, and the passengers aimed their guns at me. At first, I thought I was dead, but after they made sure I wasn't infected, they lowered the guns.

They told me they were mercenaries of sorts and that they could drive me to their base if I wanted to come with them. Surviving this long, I learned to be wary, so I tried to extract some information first.

They told me their base was north, and I knew that if I risked the ride, I could shave days off my journey. Brian had too much of a head start for me to hope to catch up. Any time I could shave off would help me reach them on the island that much sooner.

For the last three days, I've been confined to this cell. I'm starting to think that I may die here. Now I wish I'd never taken that ride. They told me they put everyone in a holding cell for twenty-four hours to ensure they're infection-free, so I agreed to be detained. As I look around my cell for the hundredth time today, I confirm that there's no way to escape.

When I hear footsteps outside my room, I tell myself they aren't for me. This time, I hear the click of a lock, and the door opens. A man steps through, and I'm so shocked that all I do is stare at him.

"Hello, my name is Ryan. I want to apologize for keeping you contained for so long. Recently, we had some violence on the premises. Because of this, I wanted to determine your motives. I hope you'll forgive me, but I took the liberty of reading your journal."

Ryan holds up my journal, which is a record of the time from the power went out to now. It was a foolish hope, but I wrote it so that if I died for some reason, I wouldn't be forgotten. I'm a little upset that this man read it, but at least I won't have to explain much to him.

"So what did you decide, then?" I ask. "Since you know everything about my journey, I'm sure you could determine my motives."

The man smiles, and it confuses me. "You're right. I do know everything about your journey, and I can help."

Not sure what he's planning to say, I expect that he's going to try and get something from me. "Brian and the others came through here," he says. "They left with one of my best men, Kent. I can give you a car and enough gas to reach them, if you want. We come across cars often on our trips, and I have a surplus."

The man's willingness to give me a car is shocking—so much so that I'm speechless. When I finally recover, I ask the man everything I can about Brian and what he was doing coming through here.

He tells me about when Brian was here and even about Kent, the person he left with. After that, he continues telling me about the base and himself.

His wife and children died shortly after the outbreak. He promised them he would save as many people as he could. Since then, he's set up a military camp and scouts for people and supplies. On these expeditions, they kill as many Palemen as they can and help those that want to be helped.

He tells me about Palemen who control groups and how their main focus has shifted to hunting them down. In the middle of explaining his last expedition, he says, "You know, I realize I've forgotten to ask your name. I'm sorry about that. So what can I call you?" This man has shared so much with me that I feel like I can trust him.

"I'm Alexis. Nice to meet you, Ryan."

Ryan and I both laugh, and I realize that the man isn't much older than me. At most, he's in his late twenties.

"Alexis, the reason I'm telling you all this is that I want you to stay here on this compound. You should know that the choice is yours to make and that I won't force you to stay against your will. If I didn't tell you that your chance of survival going north to Beaver Island is pretty low, I wouldn't be able to live with myself. All the same, the choice is yours. It's not that the journey itself is dangerous if you're careful and take your time; I'm sure you could make it. Winter's coming, and I doubt you could deal with the Palemen and the cold. Not at the same time."

What he says rings true, but I'm not sure that I want to wait a whole year. It might be worth the risk if it means I can see my brother again.

"It'll be winter in a few months, so the only way to make it to your brother this year would to be to go straight through Chicago. That's pretty much a death sentence. We've only come close to the city, and it's a death zone. People are at war with each other there, and there are more Palemen than you could count. Like I said, though, I'll give you a car and gas if you choose to go."

Ryan is clearly an honest man. It wouldn't be so bad to work with him for the winter. After all, it would be better to wait a year to see my brother than to die on the way and never see him again.

"Let me be honest with you, Alexis. I want you to stay. You wouldn't only be a good addition to our community as a person, but I also think your medical knowledge could be a huge asset to us. I know you were not academically trained, but your experience is more than anyone else has on the complex."

I know that he's right about the city. If I tried to go around, even with a car, it could take months. The last thing I want is to be trapped somewhere this winter without enough food and freezing to death. The idea of leaving my brother even temporarily is daunting. The idea that I may be able to help save people while waiting is too good to pass up.

"Ryan, could I leave at any time I want and still get that car and gas?"

Ryan smiles at me. He must be glad that I'm considering staying. "Of course. I don't keep anyone here against their will. You and everyone else here is free to leave any time without asking."

Ryan's smile is infectious, and I find I'm warming up to him. The hope that I can help others makes me a little more willing to trust what he has to say. Even if he's lying to me now, it'll be much easier to escape if he trusts me. My only concern is what he does with the people who have become animals.

"Ryan, I want to know something: what do you do with those unwilling to work with you or those who try to sabotage you?"

Ryan's smile disappears, and his face darkens. "Well, at first we tried to detain them, keeping them in these rooms, but we learned how counterproductive that was. This compound is no stranger to execution. From what I've read in your journal, though, this shouldn't be a problem for you." Ryan looks at me, and I nod.

Building the community with Stephanie taught me that as well. Some people aren't savable. There were a few executions after the first woman and child we saved. Some of the executions I was sorry to carry out, but I regret none of them.

"One last thing, Alexis. If you tell me you want to stay, don't feel like you have to be a nurse or help with the medical needs. What I read in your journal I shared with no one. I won't lie to you: if you're our nurse, you may have to do some gruesome things. My men and I go to the front lines. We're careful, but sometimes one of us is bitten. If possible, we amputate the bitten limb. If that doesn't work, well, we believe in triage. Every person who goes out on our raids understands the risk and is willing to sacrifice life and limb."

The idea of amputation startles me, but I suppose it would work. Even so, having it done must be excruciating. In the end, I can understand wanting it done, though. If my choices were death or the painful loss of an arm, I would choose to live despite the pain.

It's foolish, but I thought I'd be dealing with colds, scrapes, and bruises if I was the nurse. Ryan was kind to break this fantasy; more likely than not, I'd have to see several people die. There might even come a point when I'm forced to decide who lives and who dies. It's a scary thought, and I'm not sure if I'm experienced enough to be the one making those decisions. Even so, it would be wrong of me not to use my skills to help others, even if it means possible triage.

"If someone's bitten and we can't amputate," Ryan says as if to confirm the thoughts I was having moments ago, "they won't come back from the field. It's sad, but it's too risky to bring them back. Some end it themselves. Others aren't so willing. Understand that you'd have to deal with this as a nurse."

Ryan says this as if to confirm the thoughts I was having moments ago. I take a few minutes to think it over. "I'm willing to be your nurse," I say, "but I have one condition. I want to be a battlefield nurse and come along with you and your men on every raid possible."

"I can't promise your safety if you go out there. You understand that, right? True, it would be more effective to have a battlefield surgeon, but it'll be dangerous. If you want to come along, we'll be happy to have you. I just wanted to give you the disclaimer."

Ryan smiles. Part of him might have been hoping I'd want to go out on raids. Ryan surprises me when he says, "We leave in an hour. I'll take you to someone who can show you your room and get you some gear."

I didn't think that he'd be willing to let me go out so soon. After waiting in this cell for so long, though, going anywhere is fine with me.

"Alright, let's get going then. No time to waste sitting around here."

The next hour flies by as I'm given back everything I came here with, including my journal. Besides the gear I came with, I'm given some field surgery supplies such as sutures, tourniquets, and even some morphine. Most of the supplies they give me are typical first aid material. The only thing that's strange is a razor-sharp blade with the name "De-Limber" spray-painted on it. Whoever marked the blade must have a sick sense of humor, but at least I know what it's for.

Before we deploy, I'm given a choice to take any weapons I want. The only thing I add to my weapons is a pistol, much preferring the comfort of my spear and bow. My surgery kit goes on one hip, and I holster the pistol on the other. I hope that I won't have to use either, but it's better to have them on hand than regret not taking them. Once I finish gearing up, I find my way outside. The noise of a running jeep is all I need to find Ryan and the two other men inside it.

"Interesting choice of weapons, Alexis. I like the spear," Ryan says to me as he waves for me to hop in the car.

Once I'm seated, the car roars its engines and we get moving. The car is still somewhat strange to me. The noise and smell it produces were once familiar. After months of electrical solitude, the sensations feel new to me.

"Alexis, I want you to meet Robert and Mathew. They're some of my newer recruits." Mathew sits up front with Ryan, and Robert is the man sitting next to me. I shake both of their hands in greeting.

Mathew seems a little more battle-hardened, but I can tell that both men have been through their share of trials. They look like good men, and I'm sure they'll be able to watch my back. My only hope is that I'll be able to watch theirs.

"Nice to meet you two. Hope everything goes well today." When I stop to think about it for a second, I realize I never asked what the plan for today was. "So, Ryan, what's the plan?"

"Well, I'm taking you three to a place we clear out every few weeks. It's a large hardware store, and it's nice to provision our supplies from there. We shouldn't run into any trouble. There are no locals and usually only a few wandering Palemen. Nothing we should have trouble with." I nod, relieved that my first time out will be a low-pressure operation. I imagine Ryan planned it that way.

The ride lasts about an hour, during which there isn't much conversation. Both men seem nervous, and they aren't the only ones. My own nerves are starting to eat at me. My worry isn't about running into Palemen—I know how to deal with those. What worries me is having to watch others' backs. Being responsible for my own life is one thing. Being responsible for others is another worry altogether.

Everything will work out. I'll have to trust the others to have the same worries. I can't afford to be distracted. I'll have to trust them and do my best to earn their trust. There might come a time when these men need me at my full attention.

The car starts to slow down, and I look out the window. I see a large hardware store and realize that we're here.

We drive up to the front doors of the store, and I notice several Palemen at them. The doors are barricaded, and I'm not sure why we would risk getting out here. I'm about to ask Ryan when he speaks up. "Mathew, you're with me. Alexis and Robert, you two will be a team. We will take left, and you take right. After we've eliminated the Palemen at the front, we'll do a sweep of the perimeter on our respective sides. If anything goes south, get back to the car. There are enough heavy guns in here to hold back about anything. Otherwise, we'll meet on the back side of the building. Is everyone ready?"

Robert and Mathew answer with a yes, and I'm silent for a second before answering with a yes as well. We all move out of the car, and Robert comes over to me.

"Alright, I'm sure you know this, but no guns unless you need them. No sense drawing more to us if we can avoid it." Since this is my first time having a gun on me, I doubt I would have used it, but what he says makes sense. No reason to make a loud noise and draw any Palemen into the area. In one hand, Robert holds a large baseball bat with nails driven through the end. In his other hand, there's a hatchet.

The comfort with which he's holding his weapons tells me he's used to fighting at close range. For a second, I try to figure out the safest way to do this. After I've come up with a plan, I run it by Robert.

"Alright, Robert. I'll take point. I can strike with my spear long before any Palemen close in. If any slip through, though, I'll step aside and leave them to you. Any objections or modifications?"

Robert looks at me a bit strangely. He's not used to being told how to fight. I think he might refuse for a second, but then he nods. "Makes sense. If you think you got it, who am I to argue? One suggestion, though: use these."

Robert pulls something out of his back pocket and hands it to me. When I look to see what he gave me, I see a roll of quarters. Confused, I look at him for an answer. "Throw them in the air right before attacking, and it will confuse the Palemen for a few seconds."

True, the Palemen use noise to see, but I'd never thought to use that to my advantage. I split the roll apart so that when I do throw the roll into the air, it will split and the quarters will fall.

"Good thinking," I say. We look over to Ryan and Mathew, and they signal their readiness. All together, we run toward the targets. Right before we reach the Palemen, several turn toward us. I throw the coin roll into the air, and before the coins hit the ground, I drive my spear into one of the Palemen's hearts. He falls down to the ground around the same time the coins land.

We have four more Palemen, three about five feet in front of us and grouped tightly. One, confused by the coins, stands a foot or two from me. Taking advantage of the disorientation of the Paleman, I yank my spear from my first opponent's chest and drive the point into the second creature's neck.

The spear is wrenched from my grip as the Paleman falls, but I let it go and grab the bow off my back. The other three Palemen turn toward me, finally recovering from the quarter trick. I fire two arrows before the three Palemen close the gap. One arrow takes a Paleman in the eye, the other in the shoulder.

"Robert," I say as I back up, hoping he hasn't lost focus. Luckily, Robert comes to my aid. He brings the bat down onto one of the Palemen's heads. The creature's body crumbles to the ground. Before I can blink, Robert slams his hatchet into the soft flesh between the shoulder and the neck. He rips the hatchet out with a spurt of gore, then kicks the Paleman in the chest, sending it crashing to the ground. After a few seconds of struggle, the creature dies and the area is clear.

Robert looks at me with an expression of surprise and respect—a look I return for him. We check on our comrades and find that they are clear as well.

In that moment, I realize what I want. I may not survive long enough to reunite with my brother, but when I do, I want him to be proud. When we meet again, I want to tell stories of the hundreds I've saved, and in the end, that's worth all the risks in the world.

Chapter 22: Aaron

Aug 26th

While I fly through the air, I remember all the dreams I've had of flying. All my life, I've hoped that someday I'd be able to fly for real. For a second, I think this might be another dream. Then I start falling.

Time slows as I approach the ground, and I allow myself one last fleeting regret. I wish with all my being that I didn't have to do this, that I didn't have to die. Both my fantasy and my regrets end when my feet hit the ground.

I drop and roll to break the fall. Without hesitation and with the utmost focus, I start to run. There's no room for error, regret, or fantasy. There's only running or dying. At first, I dodge Palemen and make good progress. After they catch on, I force my way through. Slamming bodies with an adrenaline-fueled strength, I push them aside and slip by the ones who haven't realized what's going on yet.

Saying I'm surrounded by Palemen is an understatement. Everywhere I look, there are bodies around me. Luckily, I'm still making good progress. The sheer number of bodies might be confusing the Palemen or delaying their reactions.

When I'm about halfway through the sea of Palemen, I start to think this might be easier than anticipated. That's when the Palemen finally catch on, and the sea thins and stretches out. The Palemen form smaller, more independent groups.

The groups start to spread apart. As I continue to run forward, they constrict around me like a boa. I've never seen Palemen act like this before. They scream in my head and their collective rage is pointed at me.

"Good. Focus on me and forget the others," I think as I run. One group gets close and tries to snare me. Dodging it, I pull out my hatchet and Dao sword for the next group. When they try the same tactic, I make use of my Dao swords to swipe the hands away. Some blood spatters on me. I welcome it. Blood might be what I need to slip out of a Paleman's grasp.

I begin to fear that this has been too easy. Running harder, I try to get a look at the horde. By my best estimate, I'd say I have twenty yards left. Knowing the distance is so short pushes me to run harder than I've ever run before.

As I close in on freedom, the Palemen get so tight around me that I can't avoid them all. I focus on the ones blocking my path, cutting them out of the way and often using their lifeless corpses as shields. Untrimmed nails rake my bare chest, sides, and back as I run. Even so, the resistance is too light.

When I break into a clearing, I see why. A solid wall, five Palemen thick, stands in front of me. The Palemen link arms, so there will be no forcing my way through this. Knowing I can't slow down, I run headlong for them. At the last second, I jump into the air with all my strength, wanting desperately to clear the horde.

My momentum carries me over all but the last ring of Palemen, which I slam into and roll over. Two Palemen are broken away and tumble to the ground with me. Both bite down and wrap their arms around me, one on my leg and one on my left arm. Without hesitation, I take a pistol and fire two quick shots through their skulls.

There's no pain from their bites; I'm too amped up for it. Once they're shot, I roll away from their grasps and start running from the mass of Palemen. Even though I escaped, I'm still doomed to death now that I've been bitten. Even so, I smile when I feel the horde's anger over me escaping.

As I run, the horde chases me. There's no doubt in my mind that I'm pulling enough away to allow my group to escape. They're focused on me, and they are angry.

Excitement ripples through my body. My plan is working. My friends and loved ones will make it out of here alive. When I've run far enough to lead the Palemen away from the building, I turn around to face the horde.

Taking a few seconds to check over myself, I see several small bites and scratches, but none of them are very severe. The Palemen are fifty yards behind me. I drop my hatchet and Dao sword. I also pull my combat knife out of its sheath and throw it into the ground.

Forty yards. I empty two pistols into the horde, Palemen dropping with each shot. Thirty yards. I throw the pistols to the side and replace them with backups. Sixteen more shots, sixteen more dead. Twenty yards. I empty my last two pistols. Sixteen more dead, one thousand to go.

Combat knife in my left hand. Dao sword in my right hand. Ten yards.

"Ahhh!" I scream as a charge headlong into the Palemen horde. Behind the horde, I see my friends escaping.

"Live for me. Remember me!" The words leave my lungs with such fury I know that they reach them.

One yard. Bodies collide. My Dao sword cuts through one or two. It's torn from my grasp by the waves of Palemen. They grab me and I stab their eyes, throats, chests, and groins. They bite, and so do I. My fingers break inside the duster guard of my combat knife. I don't care. A Paleman bites off my finger. I cut open his jugular. Dozens grab me, but I won't go down. I must stay standing. I must buy time.

My world devolves into blood, flesh, and pain. Morality has no place here. Savagery is the only thing that remains. I gore as many Palemen with my mouth as I do with my knife. My elbow slams into a temple. A Paleman falls. Another takes its place.

The Palemen break from me. I frenzy and jump one who retreats, stabbing him three times in the face before jumping to the next. The horde rips my hair, flesh, and clothes as I stab into hearts, heads, and throats. They retreat more. Why? I push these thoughts aside. My bloodlust demands more.

Blood drips, some of it mine and some of it theirs. When I chase one down, he tries to grab me. His grasp slips on my blood-slicked body. Sanity leaves me as I continue my rampage. The Palemen try now to get away from me.

They can't. I'm faster. I'm death. I stab, he falls. I elbow, she falls. Over and over my dance goes on. The knife falls from the broken remnants of fingers, so I punch, kick, and bite those I catch. They fall to me like a lamb to a lion.

Laughter comes from my lungs. I won't stop.

"Hahahaha," I cackle madly as I hunt down Palemen now desperately trying to escape me. I hear their fear. I hear their pain. I consume it all. It's stronger than any drug, more intoxicating than anything I have ever known.

"Ahahaha!" Blood tastes sweet. Fear is sweeter. They tell me they're waiting. They tell me I'll join them soon.

"AHAHAHAHA!" I don't care. All I want is more death, more pain. More anger! I tear an eye from the socket and blood spatters into my face. Waves of ecstasy go through me. My rage is a white-hot flame. With it, I consume the colder flames around me.

"She died in my arms," a voice says as I punch his face over and over. I only stop when its mind stops screaming. There's no stopping me. I am Wrath.

Colors leave my sight. Morality tries to interfere. It tells me they're still partly human. I push it away. There's no room for sympathy; there's only room for hunger.

"AHAHAHAHAHAHAHAHAHAHAHAHA!" Tears stream from my face as I cackle. Blood pulses through my veins. It burns like fire. The infection is taking over. The pain and bitterness fuel me. My anger manifests itself, and I become unstoppable, immortal, and untouchable.

Enemy bones break underneath me. Ribs shatter. I use more strength than I should be capable of. I snap arms that reach at me and rip any flesh I can grab. My hand is mangled and bloody. I use it anyway. My body is cracking under the strain of my rage. Bones crack and cartilage tears. I'm being reborn. I'm awakening to my true self.

The Palemen retreat. I try to run at them. They move with me. I cannot reach. I cannot kill. I cannot feed. Crouching down, I scream out at them. The sound I hear is unimaginable. I'm no longer a human. I'm a monster and they fear me.

Hundreds of Palemen, dead and dying, lie around me. Some sanity returns as I look at all the bodies. My life is near its end, and I'm scared. The horde focuses on me. They call out to me, telling me to join them. My mind resists, but my resolve is shattered. The laughter stops as I lose control and the disease takes over. My returning sanity is ripped from me, and I'm cast from my own body.

Chris's laughter replaces my own. He isn't the survivor I thought he was, but a manifestation of chaos. He's in control now. Angry tides wash in. I'm trapped in my own mind, watching in black and white.

For the first time, I can see the people trapped in the Palemen. They're angry and they want release from their bodies. They want it to end. They want death. They, like me, are forced to watch as their bodies create tragedy.

There's no moving, no speaking, only watching. Fear rushes in on me, and I ask myself how long I'll be in this hell. Will it be days? Years? Will I have to watch as my body kills others, helpless to stop it?

Rage pulses deep from within, burning and trying to break me free. Fear engulfs me, but I'm not alone in my fear. All around me, others hold the same fears I do. If they cannot break free, what chance do I have? So many beg for death.

Their wishes fall on deaf ears. Only those trapped in hell can hear the cries for salvation.

We are the collective. We will follow the horde. My body moves, and I'm helpless to stop it. The horde's attention changes to my escaping friends. Somehow, I know Chris is the one controlling it. When I see my friends on the shore, launching a boat, I'm relieved.

My relief turns to horror when I hear Chris shout out a psychic command to the horde.

"Kill them! Kill them! Kill them!" Chris dictates commands to the horde. It moves with a grace of a horde controlled by a general. My mind lashes out, trying to stop Chris. We share a mind, so I know he plans on controlling the Palemen and having them kill my friends.

"Control is mine now. Watch me as I kill all your friends. They will be ripped apart. You will watch as I eat the heart of your child." My mind screams because my lungs cannot. My own agony joins the chorus of the others around me. The anger, agony, and regret consume me and lock me in my cage. I try to close my eyes but I can't. I'm forced to watch. Even when I try to speak to Chris, to beg him for mercy, I can't. All I can do is scream in agony.

My friends are barely in the water. With Chris acting as general, the Palemen are moving fast enough to catch up to them. We're only a few hundred yards away, and we're closing fast.

My friends look toward us, and they see that they are doomed. Their faces tell me they know I've failed them. They know that this will be the end. If I could've lasted a few more minutes, they'd be safe. Jason aims his rifle at me, and I'm glad that he does. He knows I'm a general. I don't know how, but he knows.

If he can kill me, there's a chance for them. My death might cause confusion among the masses. It might give them enough time to move into deeper water. Even in the shallows, they might be able to get far enough out to fight off the Palemen.

If I could smile, I would. I see the gun go off. My body jerks at the same instant I hear the pop of the gun. A searing pain radiates from my shoulder, and I realize that the shot missed the target.

Time slows down, and I realize in an instant that I felt the bullet strike my shoulder. As if to confirm the feeling of pain, I notice pain coming from all over my body. It's so intense it threatens to drive me mad. Instead of retreating from it, I embrace it. If I can feel that pain, I must have some control. If I can feel the pain, then the nerves are still mine.

This disease and Chris can't stop me. All my focus goes into the pain in my hands and shoulder. As I concentrate, the feeling of pain starts to spread up my arms. My flesh feels like it's burning, but I force my mind to be silent. If I scream now, Chris might figure out what I'm trying to do.

The burning spreads to my throat, and I feel burning air searing my lungs.

"Jason, don't shoot!" Words come out as a scream of agony.

If I can control my body, I can control the horde. If Jason shoots me now, though, the horde is close enough to catch them.

We're only twenty yards away, but my resistance has stopped Chris's commands.

The minds trapped inside the Palemen encourage me. They give me strength, and the pain lessens. Feeling starts to return to my body. My fellow Palemen give me the strength to keep fighting, and now I'm starting to win.

They beg me to take control and to move us into the lake. They want to end their suffering and the suffering they cause. Chris tries to silence them, to silence me.

"You fool, you think you can take this away from me…"

Chris is quiet. The horde focuses its minds on him and pushes him out. They want me. They need me, and I need them. We become one mind working toward a common goal. We desire it. We will have it. My soul is seared away as I welcome the strength of others, and my body starts to listen to me.

Our legs move. One step and water laps my ankles, or are they someone else's? Another step and I feel cold sand between open toes. Another step and I feel hard concrete. We have many bodies. We have many arms. My speed increases, and water fills my lungs. Some die. More move.

Memories of lives from before the power went out and after flash through my mind. I see primal acts. Things we regret. We use them to push us on. Instinct fights to keep us alive, to make us stop. It is strong. Our will is stronger.

Those on the boat are far away. They'll escape, and a small part of us rejoices. The job isn't done. We aren't all gone.

Time means nothing. Seconds might pass or hours. Hunger and thirst are in us. Fatigue and pain are there as well. The collective absorbs these feelings and we keep moving.

Some struggle. Some fall. We trample them, and they go silent. Most of us are in the water. We go under and breathe deep. More of us end, and fewer are under my control.

Some try to swim, try to stay afloat, but we force them down. Only when I'm the last above the water do I go under. As Palemen die around me, I gain more control of myself and remember who I am.

The voice of the many blinks out as I let the air out of my lungs and start sinking to the bottom. The water is full of corpses, some floating, some sinking.

There's no more anger in my mind—only silence. My lungs burn for air, but they're denied it. It's too late to say goodbye. A smile comes to my face. They made it. The promise I made to my father is fulfilled, and they made it.

Everyone knew what they were doing when we left. At first, we thought we would make it unscathed, but we learned. We lost a few, but we—they—made it.

My lungs can wait no longer, and they gasp for air. They only get water. A vision of a future I'll miss comes into my mind's eye as my vision starts to fade.

Evelyne runs up to Sophia and me on a beach, yelling joyfully like a little girl should. We embrace, and I smile, happy to be here. My father is behind me, and I know I have to go with him. There's no question as to why he is here. I know why.

We walk from the beach, and Evelyn waves goodbye. Sophia smiles and I wave goodbye to them. There is no sadness. Someday, I'll see them again.

Epilogue: Evelyn

March 13th

As I look at my reflection in the water, it's hard to believe that it's been so long. Even now, I can hardly believe it's been fifteen years since we first made it to Beaver Island. When I look behind me, I see what's been my home all this time, and it's fading away.

Memories of the first day we came to the island play in my head: the bittersweet of finally being safe but making it there without my father. Back then, I didn't appreciate what he did. I hated him for it. The others had to bind my wrists and feet to keep me from swimming back to him.

A part of me believed that if we went back, he would be alive. In my young mind, we could've saved him, no matter what, like he would have done for us. It took me several years to admit that I was wrong. It took even longer for me to forgive, respect, and understand what Aaron did for us all that night.

We never found the remains of my father. Sophia was sure they sunk to the bottom of the lake. All that was left of him was the Dao sword he gave us and Sophia.

The last time I was on this lake, we were making our way to Beaver Island for three days. Now, it will only take us a few hours to return to the mainland. If we had been on a salty body of water, I doubt we would have made it to Beaver Island back then. By the end of the journey, we were all weak from hunger.

We were greeted on the shore by the locals, who immediately told us to leave. If I hadn't been with them, we would never have convinced them to let us stay. They were foolish to think that because I was young, I was a child, but I'm glad for their ignorance. It's one thing to cast out adults, but sending a small child to her death is a difficult thing to do.

The patrol that stopped us on the beach agreed to let us speak with the village elder. They said we could ask his permission to stay to recover. At that point, it was Brian who saved us. He made the elder see the value of our knowledge. We were allowed to stay because we could teach them how to fight the Palemen.

It started as teaching others how to fight, but over time, things changed. After a few months, Melany started teaching other aspects of the world, and soon, Jason joined her. After a few years, the island changed.

During this time, Sophia and Brian decided they would raise me. I never stopped missing my adoptive father, Aaron, but I did grow to love Sophia and Brian. Things on the island were not perfect, especially in the beginning, but they always did their best to take care of me. After a year or so, I even came to think of them as Mom and Dad.

Melany and Jason started a school. They began teaching the children about what happened to the world and how it was before. I, of course, was not exempt from having to go to class. At first, I hated school, like all children do, but I grew to love it. Despite our age, Melany and Jason treated everyone like adults. They often said that the time of having a childhood was over.

Even after we started to live on the island, the locals were terrified of outsiders. They refused to allow anyone to join the community. That all changed when Alexis came to the island around a year after we arrived.

She came with supplies and motors, and our lives changed. I remember the day she came to us and how happy Brian was. Alexis had become a mercenary leader of sorts, and she'd saved thousands of lives.

After Brian saw her again, there was no stopping him; he started leaving the island to help others. At first, the town opposed it. When he brought back things like powered lights and water filtration systems, the opposition evaporated.

Deep down, I could still see the scars Dawn left on him, but Brian was never happier than when he was saving others. He and his sister would often collaborate on missions. The people they saved would either go to her compound or live on our island.

I remember being surprised when, on one of his return trips, Brian had Aaron's family with him—what remained of them, anyway. Back then, I didn't know them that well. Seeing a familiar face was still nice at the time. Brian's family decided to stay at the military base with Alexis, and I remember Brian being happy they chose to.

It was only about a year after Brian started going off the island that we had gone from a sparsely populated town to a city. With Brian's trips, we even had working power generators and some basic lighting, as well as working plumbing and water filtration systems.

Around that time, Sophia and Brian got married. It had been about two years since we arrived on the island, and their marriage surprised no one. It wasn't a surprise when Melany and Jason followed them.

Sophia had been focused on raising me, but after my grandmother Stephanie came, she had more time to work. Sophia set up a hospital with Stephanie's help. They put together a small compound, which was quite sophisticated considering the lack of technology.

Sophia was always kind to me, but she was never sure how to be a mother. Brian was the same. I know they both love me, but a part of me always knew they only raised me to honor Aaron's memory. That's why I understood when they sometimes focused more on other priorities. The reason I never grew to resent them was because Stephanie was there to take care of me.

Stephanie and I grew close very quickly after she made it to the island. Only a few months later, I was living with her most of the time. We learned how to grow into the new world together. What I didn't learn from Jason and Melany's school I learned from her. I'll forever be grateful to Stephanie for all that she's done for me.

When I look away from the reflection in the lake, I see Stephanie paddling next to me. Her being here warms my heart. I told her of my plans to leave the island, and she wanted to come before I could even tell her why. She's been such a great source of strength for me, and I know that without her, leaving would have been much harder.

As I look back to the island, my thoughts drift back to the past, to the first day I met an international traveler. He brought a laptop with him. The technology was so much more amazing than anything I had seen before. And technology was not all he brought.

I wasn't allowed to listen at the time, but he also brought news of the world. He told them, I found out later, that North America was the only country to lose power, but not the only place infected.

The infections didn't survive as easily in rich countries, and it was wiped out there. Poorer countries were not so lucky, and the disease stagnated. The distrust it caused started a war. When the war broke out among the richer countries of the world, things escalated and nuclear devices were used.

America might have lost all modern technology. Suffering massive population loss from the disease was getting off easy. The parts of the world that were not destroyed by the disease were destroyed by the bombs and radiation. Only a fragment of civilization remains, and most of it is in America.

As technology became more available, communication was the first thing rebuilt after lights. Cities like our own worked to connect themselves with other cities, like Alexis's military city or Stephanie's communal one. Nearby cities joined together and formed small city-states.

Without a central government, each city-state was left to erect its own form of government. As time passed, the city-states grew. More people came to the safer areas, and their areas of influence became larger. Most growth happened four years after the Palemen first emerged. By that time, they had been almost completely eradicated.

Almost all the city districts had become connected through communication. Most cites at that time also had or were working on building fences to keep any straggling Palemen out.

As Palemen became scarcer and finally died out, attention shifted. There was a desire for progress and technological advancement. The cities started pooling resources to build a technology-based center. It was the start of the new government.

Every city district sent its best electricians and computer workers, as well as their best politicians. Every city had its own way of ruling, but we all wanted some form of unity. We wanted a central government to watch over us all.

It took years to build, but a government was formed. It was a combination of the old American system and some new ideas. The leader of the country was a man who was both charismatic and a technological genius. He handles distributing technology to the states. In return, they send resources to him. It's a way to make sure we stay technologically equal.

With the equal spread of technology, Internet was recreated. This became the primary way for city-states to both fund the capital and trade with each other. As more resources moved to the capital, its power grew.

Originally, the purpose of the capital was to redistribute technology. Now it handles many other resources as well.

The cities are mostly peaceful with each other, and only a few small battles have taken place. Even so, there's talk of strengthening the capital's power of distribution. There are people who want to build a railroad stemming from the capital, which would allow it to redistribute resources.

There are cries for equality from many of the city-states, and I know they will be heard. Melany and Jason taught me about the type of government we are turning into. They fear it and try to make me fear it. I fail to see what they are so scared of.

Part of the reason I'm leaving the island is to see why the other city districts are fighting for equality. I want to see if these places are worse off than where I have grown up. I want to experience the world and see what it has to offer.

There are so many things I want to do beyond my little island that I can't even imagine them all. I think about all the fighting and convincing it took before Sophia and Brian let me leave. It's funny that they'd oppose me after all they've been through. I suppose they were trying to protect me.

What they fail to understand is that the only way I can grow is to leave. I was born into this world. I don't have any memories of the old world or anything to work toward. I'm part of this new civilization, and the only way to keep growing is to see it.

I signal to Stephanie, and we switch spots. I start paddling and get used to the repetitive motion. Soon, I'm lost in thought again. Stephanie flashes a smile at me, and I give one back.

Stephanie is almost sixty now, but if you didn't know her, you'd never be able to tell. Once again, I'm thankful that she not only came with me but also defended my right to leave. I don't think I would have made it off the island without her help. Her reason for leaving is lost on me. After a while, I become curious and decide to ask her.

"Grandma, can I ask you a question?"

"Sure, honey, go ahead."

"Why are you leaving the island? I mean, it's safe there, and it's where your family is. What possible reasons would you have for leaving?"

Stephanie looks at me and smiles. "There are several reasons I wanted to leave. I was curious to see how things have changed, especially in the capital. I've seen pictures, but I wanted to see it in person. I also wanted to visit the town we were living in when the outbreak occurred. The camp Alexis and I founded there moved into a nearby city-state, and no one lives there. The main reason I left, though, is that it's been a long time since I visited my husband's grave. We would have been married forty years in a few months, and I wanted to spend our anniversary at his grave."

I nod and smile at Stephanie. I'm glad that she has her own reasons for coming out here, and I make sure to make a list of the things she wants to do. We'll fulfill her wish to see her husband. That will be our first goal. After that, it would be fun to travel to the capital, stopping at any city-states we come near.

As I row the boat, I'm silent. I relax and let the sound of the oars pushing us calm me. After a while, Stephanie takes over, and I lie back. The first time we rowed our way to shore, it took three days. This time, it will only take a few hours.

While I wait to row again, I open my backpack and pull out a book. This book is familiar to me, and I've read it a hundred times over, but it always gives me hope. Whenever I was lonely, sad, scared, angry, or confused, I always found something in its pages to help me. I read the title for the hundredth time.

Rage: The Fall of Man, by Melany and Jason Hartman.

This book is the story of our party and its journey to Beaver Island. Beyond the journey we took, this book has pictures that Melany took, as well as an explanation of the disease and its effects. I remember the first time I read it, shortly after my fourteenth birthday. It was the first time I learned about Chris and why my father sacrificed himself.

After I read this book for the first time, I finally forgave Aaron for what he did. The book taught me so much about the others as well, and not only about what they used to do, but about how they felt through it all. I learned so much from this book, and it comforts me.

Now I know that, no matter where I end up or what crazy things might happen, I'll be okay. If I can survive everything we went through at ten years old, there's nothing to fear now.

The shore is coming closer, and I start to get nervous. This is the first time I'll set foot off the island in fifteen years. Even with the assurance I gave myself, I'm still feeling very scared. Anything could happen, and though I doubt there are any Palemen left in the world, they were never the only danger.